CHARLEY COOPER

ALSO BY LYNN ELDRIDGE

Desire In Deadwood

Hearts and Mountains

Kindred Spirits

Remember the Passion

Skyrocket to Surrender

Tame the Wild

Triple C Ranch

Chase Cooper

Chloe Cooper

Cash Cooper

CHARLEY COOPER

TRIPLE C RANCH
BOOK FOUR

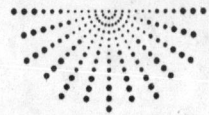

LYNN ELDRIDGE

WOLFPACK
PUBLISHING
— EST 2013 —

Wolfpack Publishing
701 S. Howard Ave. 106-324
Tampa, Florida 33609

wolfpackpublishing.com

Paperback ISBN 978-1-63977-357-2
eBook ISBN 978-1-63977-356-5
LCCN 2024933066

CHARLEY COOPER

CHAPTER ONE

Triple C Ranch-South was up for grabs.

Pikes Peak, in Colorado Springs, lay miles behind her to the west as Charley slowed down the red Mini Cooper convertible officially called Chili Red. She had bought the vehicle new a couple of years ago. She loved this practical little car and gave the steering wheel a pat.

On the north side of the road, a wooden sign posted high above a wide entrance identified the land beyond the wooden arch as Triple C Ranch-West Percheron Entrance. Her research showed this property to consist of a horse business run by former Deputy Sheriff Derek Brevard, who trained the much-in-demand Percherons for mounted police. Pressing on the gas pedal, the next sign Charley noticed read Triple C Ranch-West. Set back from the road behind split rail fencing and a gate was a beautiful country-style house with a lovely wraparound porch. Derek's wife, Chloe Cooper Brevard, ran a former bed-and-breakfast as an Airbnb now, which was built next door to their large home. They had a son and a pair of twins. Not the ranch in question.

Continuing on her quest, the next sign posted was also high above a large entryway stating Triple C Ranch-Central Cattle Entrance. If memory served, this thriving ranch, consisting of hundreds of Black Angus cattle, was owned by

Chase Cooper, eldest of the three Cooper offspring. Legitimate offspring, anyway. Leaving the stables, barn, and bunkhouse behind, on down the road apiece, the next sign read Triple C Ranch-Central. Beyond the wrought-iron gate, Chase shared this enormous wood and stone mountain-style home with his wife, Jade, and their two children. Jade was a children's therapist, and equine therapy was the focus of her busy practice. No, this property was not the one she was looking for either.

Driving a few miles farther down the scenic highway, Charley slowed the car again. Above another gated archway, a sign read Triple C Ranch-East. Boasting a rambling farmhouse, the place appeared both welcoming and imposing. Down the highway, not too far from the huge home, the next entryway gave access to Triple C-West Dude Ranch Cabins and Coopers' Lodge. The number of vehicles in the paved parking lot indicated the places were full. Running the show on the dude ranch, Cash Cooper was the youngest of the siblings. His wife, Tracy, wrote and illustrated children's books and ran the Lodge. Still not the ranch in question.

Charley assumed Triple C Ranch-South lay on the right side of the highway. Gripping the steering wheel a little tighter, gut instinct said it lay dead ahead. How did Chase Cooper, Chloe Brevard Cooper, and Cash Cooper feel about a person interested in Triple C Ranch-South after seeing it? Happy? Relieved someone wanted to take the ten thousand acres off their hands? Or furious? How dare an outsider jump into the middle of this family-owned property? Ambivalent? We're all busy and never intended to keep the property forever anyway. Perhaps each of the siblings represented a different attitude. Or were they close-knit and all on the same page? She'd met them and the Cooper patriarch so briefly, she truly had no idea.

Sure enough, on the south side of the highway, also posted high above the ground on an arched entryway, a sign read Triple C Ranch-South. A lovely log cabin faced the main road, as did the other three houses falling under the Triple C

Ranch brand. Charley veered right onto a gravel road. Traveling slowly, in order to take in her surroundings, the hitching post in front of this charming home seemed like the appropriate place to stop. Shutting off the engine but staying in the car, Charley stared at the cabin.

There were two large bay windows across the front of the place. In the center of the ten-foot-tall, covered porch was an oversized cedar door. Ponderosa pines, expertly carved into the door, embraced stained glass in the upper half. Capturing Charley's attention and heart, the stained glass displayed the Rocky Mountain Columbine. Lavender and white, the columbine was the official Colorado state flower. Gazing from the stained glass back to the porch, on either side of the front door were two hunter-green rocking chairs that matched the hunter-green shingled roof. Near the cabin was a small barn, but no garage, and there were no other vehicles in sight. The place looked deserted.

But it seemed safe enough to look around the property. The thought concerning safety would not have hit so hard until a few weeks ago. Taking a deep breath, Charley got out of the car and closed the door. Year-round, the pine trees in Colorado were green and fragrant. Ponderosa pines, reaching toward the cloudless blue sky, grew behind the cabin and framed both sides. Decorating the front of the cabin, pink seed heads of ruby muhly grass danced in the breeze. Rabbitbrush, with its yellow flowers and blue mist spirea, sprinkled the land also populated by aspen, fir, and spruce trees. A nature lover's delight.

Walking up two steps to the porch and knocking on the front door didn't bring anyone to open it. A peek through the window to the left of the door showed a great room with a vaulted ceiling boasting a fireplace, a sofa, and a matching chair. A glimpse through the window on the right side of the door displayed a dining area with four chairs around a table and beyond that a kitchen with a stove and a refrigerator. She tried the doorknob on the front door, but it was locked. Hopping off one side of the porch and veering to the back of the cabin, Charley found a second door. Also locked. To one side of the door, a window displayed a bedroom with a four-poster bed, and on the other side of the door, through a smaller window, she spied a full bath.

Wow. This place was roomy yet cozy and in mint condition.

Meandering back around the southeast corner of the cabin near the main road, an ancient, gnarly oak tree caught Charley's eye. Tall and twisted, the tree just needed a couple of leopards lying in wait on the branches to look like something out of Africa. Or if the drooping, misshapen limbs were covered in green moss and purple fog, one might suppose a mystical wizard occupied the log cabin.

"Excuse me."

Charley whirled around to find a man on horseback magically emerging from a shadowy path amid the pine trees. Sitting in a black saddle atop a huge horse, he had made the most silent of arrivals. The man wore a faded black cowboy hat which he tipped in greeting. Along with the hat, black sunglasses hid part of his face. Visible were his straight nose, a square jaw, and no smile on his lips. His hair was hidden for the most part. But what she could see touching the collar of his shirt looked dark, probably black like the stubble of beard on his face. Broad shoulders and a muscular chest strained against a pale blue shirt with long sleeves rolled up thick forearms. Snug jeans and black boots rounded out the picture of one heck of a handsome cowboy. Handsome? From what she could see so far, most definitely. Even sitting in the saddle, he looked tall.

"Hello," Charlie replied. "You aren't Cash or Chase Cooper."

"No, I'm Sullivan Custis. I own the ranch that bucks up against this one." He dismounted and sauntered toward her with the catlike grace of a wild *leopard*. Her heart thumped, but she stood her ground. He was six foot three at least. Holding the reins to the horse in his left hand, with a polite slowness he extended his right hand. "My dad is also

Sullivan Custis and goes by his middle name, Owen. So, I go by Sully. And you are?"

"Charlotte...Fleming." Giving her first and middle names, she stopped there. Her last name was why she was here, but this stranger didn't need to know that. She held out her hand in greeting. When his hand engulfed hers in a shake, her hand all but disappeared within his large grasp. Either he had a magic buzzer in his palm, or he was indeed the wizard of the cabin, because his touch sent an electric thrill through her. A magic buzzer? What a ridiculous thought. More likely a wizard due to his mesmerizing presence. Charley told herself to get a grip.

"Nice to meet you, Miss Fleming," he said. "That name rings a bell."

"Just call me Charley, Mr. Custis." She pulled her hand away from him and said, "My mother was also Charlotte, so I go by Charley."

"Okay," he said with a tilt of his head. "Just call me Sully."

"I'm meeting Cash Cooper here in a few minutes," Charley said. "I'm early."

"Are you a realtor? Are the Coopers letting this property go?"

"I'm not a realtor." Charley shaded her eyes against the setting sun and looked up at him. She wondered what color his eyes were behind the sunglasses. "Why? Would you be in the market to buy Triple C Ranch-South?"

"I've always referred to this place as Pretty Petals because of the columbine on the door."

Charley nodded. "As a native of Colorado, I'm partial to the Rocky Mountain Columbine. It was my mother's favorite flower."

"Yeah, I'm a native of Colorado too," he said. "Anyway, after my dad retired from years of serving as the El Paso County Sheriff, he deeded most of his ranch land to me. In answer to your question, I'm always open to expanding my property."

"I see." She nodded and glanced away from the man to his horse, which was just as striking. "Your horse is beautiful. What kind is he?"

"Thanks. Storm is an American quarter horse. His brown coloring with the black shading on his mane, tail, and legs makes him a bay."

Screeching tires on the highway caused Charley to whirl toward the sound. The silver Mercedes that spun out on the gravel, turning into the ranch, spit rocks as it fishtailed and skidded to a stop not far from Charley's car.

"Oh, great," Charley mumbled under her breath.

The man who bailed out of the brand-new car carelessly slammed the door. "Charley!" he shouted, stomping toward her. "Why did you leave?"

"I'd think that would be obvious," Charley said from where she stood near Sullivan Custis. "You shouldn't have followed me. I don't want you here."

"Who's he?" the shorter man asked, with a nod at Sully.

"I'm done with your rudeness, Rod Vaughn," Charley said and turned to the man at her side. "I apologize for his behavior and this embarrassing situation."

"Who are you?" Rod asked Sully directly, facing off with him.

"Who wants to know?" Sully asked.

"Her boyfriend."

"No!" Charley said firmly, "I told you that three dates do not entitle you to anything nor do they make you my boyfriend."

"But I referred to you as my girlfriend in front of Kay."

"I just witnessed her in action, so good luck with that," Charley said, referring to the woman who in fact did claim to be Rod's girlfriend. "You are *not* my boyfriend."

Rod's face reddened. "After you left, I told Kay we were done once and for all," Rod said. Ignoring Sully's presence, he grabbed Charley's arm. "You're just upset because things got nasty." He yanked on her arm and took a step. "Let's go figure this out, baby."

"Don't call me that! There's nothing to figure out." Charley pulled her arm free of his grasp. "I told you I didn't want to see you or hear from you again, Rod. I meant it. You need to leave." Turning to the stranger she'd just met she said, "It was nice to meet you too."

"Maybe we'll meet again under better circumstances," Sully replied with a frown in Rod's direction before giving Charley a tip of his hat.

"Yes," Charley said with a quick smile at Sully.

Hoping to diffuse and end the awkwardness caused by Rod, Charley decided to make her way to the porch and stepped away from the men. As she'd said, she was due to meet Cash Cooper shortly, and she certainly didn't want Rod Vaughn here for that. Maybe if she got in her car, he'd do the same and leave. She veered toward her car but before reaching it, gravel crunched behind her, and her arm was seized. When she was jerked backward on her heels, Charley's feet slipped out from under her. If she wasn't mortified enough, she lost her balance and fell to her left knee. Rod held out his hand to help her up.

"Leave me alone!" Charley snapped and smacked away his hand.

CHAPTER TWO

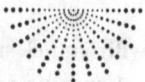

"**S**top!" Sully barked at the man named Rod Vaughn.

"Stay out of it," the guy sneered at Sully.

"I don't think so." Dropping the reins to Storm, Sully walked toward Charley.

"I said let's go, baby," Vaughn insisted agitatedly. The way in which he was leaning over Charley, blocked her from getting up unless she took his hand.

"And I said leave me alone," Charley repeated.

"Back off," Sully barked, and watched Vaughn's eyes shift from Charley to him as he reached them. Sully warned, "Do it or I'll make you do it."

Vaughn backed up a few paces and Sully was about to extend his hand to Charley, but she hopped up on her own. Sully understood why Vaughn wanted this gorgeous woman as his girlfriend. But damn, this was not the way to go about it.

Charlotte, or Charley, could run for Miss Universe and win by a landslide vote. An October breeze, known as a Chinook wind, ruffled stray tendrils of the long, loose braid down her slender back. Chocolate brown, her hair was glossy and made an attractive contrast against her daffodil yellow sweater. She quickly brushed off the left knee of her yellow and brown leopard-print pants. When she looked up, her royal-blue eyes instantly narrowed, and her dainty hands clenched into fists.

"Really Rod?" Charley asked, shaking her head. Sully followed her gaze to the pistol in Vaughn's hand. "After what happened, you should know I detest guns. How could you?"

"It's not pointed at you, Charley. It's pointed at him," Vaughn said. "We are out here in the country all alone and we don't know this stranger. We need to leave together."

"There is no *we*, Rod!" Charley spat.

"This guy could be the Cave Killer!" Rod shouted at her with a glare at Sully.

A month ago, Sully had read an account in the *Colorado Springs Gazette* about a young woman found strangled in Old Colorado City, a neighborhood within Colorado Springs. Details were sketchy, but her body had been discovered in a cave-like, underground tunnel. The local news had immediately dubbed the strangler as the Cave Killer.

As for Vaughn's story, Sully didn't know what it was, and he didn't care. He took two steps forward, and as Vaughn focused on Charley, Sully grabbed the gun out of his hand. Vaughn's mouth fell open, and he backed up several steps toward his car.

"If you ever pull a gun on me again, you're a dead man," Sully growled, holding the gun. "You got that?"

"You-you don't know what Charley's been through," Vaughn stammered, raising his hands in the air. "I'm just trying to protect her. That's all."

"Not another word, Rod," Charley told him.

"Yeah, well, he's got a gun too," Vaughn said with a dramatic nod, indicating the Ruger Redhawk .44 Magnum revolver holstered on Sully's belt.

"Yeah, well," Charley mimicked Vaughn. She was tough and sassy. Sully liked that about her. "He's not pointing it at anyone."

"Put your hands down, Vaughn," Sully said with disgust

as he looked at the older model gun he'd taken from him. "This *little* gun can kill but there's a problem, pal." Checking the magazine, Sully found it one bullet short of a full load. He aimed the gun, but not in the air, because if and when a bullet landed it could potentially do damage he didn't intend. Pulling the trigger, the .38 caliber gun did not fire. "This discontinued gun only works when it wants to. Typically needs cleaned after every firing. So, you'd better be a damn good shot or upgrade to a better gun." Putting the safety on, which it hadn't been, he tossed the weapon back to Vaughn.

"Hey!" Vaughn yelped in surprise and juggled the gun in the air like a hot potato before fumbling it to the point he dropped it on the ground.

"Hay is for horses, right Captain?" Cash Cooper, owner of Triple C Ranch-East said as he rode up on his red dun stallion named Captain. "Hi, Sully." Tipping his dark brown cowboy hat to Charley, as Sully had earlier, Cash said with a smile, "Hi there, Charley Cooper." Looking back to Sully with a frown at Vaughn, who was picking up his gun, Cash asked, "Who's the tenderfoot?"

"Don't know him," Sully muttered.

"Cash Cooper, this is Rod Vaughn. Rod was just leaving," Charley said and slashed her finger, indicating Rod should get in his car. "Goodbye, Rod."

Sully didn't care for Vaughn one bit, and gut instinct said Charley had not heard the last of the guy. What he did appreciate was Charley's stand-up-for-herself-independent attitude. Had Cash just referred to her as Charley *Cooper*? If so, that explained a lot. And at the same time, not much at all. Sully had grown up alongside the Triple C Ranches, attended most of the annual family barbecues, and thought he knew all the Coopers.

Cash dismounted his horse and jerked his thumb at Vaughn in a silent gesture for him to hit the road. Outnumbered three to one, Vaughn didn't utter another word. He yanked open the driver's side door of the Mercedes, started the engine, and slammed his car in reverse, out to the main road as discourteously as he'd entered the property. Sully caught Cash's eye and with a scowl, shook his head.

"Hi, Cash." Charley returned his greeting with a smile and then said to Sully, "I'm sorry for the terrible first impression."

"Actually, you made a really good first impression," Sully said. "I'm always impressed by a woman who stands up for herself."

"Thank you, Sully," Charley said softly with a self-conscious shrug.

"Me too," Cash agreed with Sully and chuckled. "As for first impressions, my adoring wife, Tracy, almost ran over me the first time we met."

When Charley laughed, it was a lighthearted giggle and broke the tension. "I'd enjoy hearing that story, Cash."

"Let's take a quick look around the cabin and then go meet Tracy for supper at Coopers' Lodge and she can tell you," Cash replied. "Sully, you hungry?"

"Yes. Sundown means suppertime's a comin'. At least it does this time of year when it gets dark early. I was cutting across Triple C-South to go eat at the Lodge when I met up with Charley," Sully told Cash with a nod at Charley.

"Great," Cash said, taking a key out of his pocket. After tethering Captain to the hitching post, Cash walked onto the porch and motioned to them.

"I haven't been inside this cabin in years," Sully commented and tethered Storm.

"We used to camp out here with my older brother, Chase, when we were kids," Cash told Charley. "Sometimes Uncle Clarence would sneak over here and try to scare us."

Sully chuckled at the memory. "And catch us sneaking a beer. But he never told my dad."

"He didn't tell ours either." Cash swung open the door, letting Charley enter first.

"I really regret not having the opportunity to know him," Charley said. "Clarence Cooper sounds like a great guy."

"He was the best," Cash said.

"Yes, he was," Sully agreed. "My dad always speaks well of him."

"Sully's dad is a great guy too," Cash said. "Our families always voted for Owen Custis for El Paso County Sheriff back in the day. My parents knew Sully's parents. Anyway, Owen was a busy man when we were kids. But we had the pleasure of personally working with him when he intervened a few years ago on Derek and Chloe's behalf concerning their son Cooper."

"But Cooper is okay?" Charley asked.

With a nod, Cash replied, "A story for another day." Then looking around, he said, "This cabin was a pet project of Uncle Clarence's. I always suspected he'd built it with someone special in mind." With a shrug, Cash continued, "The custom-made front door was his finishing touch."

"The Rocky Mountain Columbine was my mom's favorite flower," Charley repeated.

"Maybe my uncle knew that," Cash commented with a smile. "Last week I had one of our employees from the Lodge give the cabin a top-to-bottom cleaning." Cash stepped into the high-ceilinged combination living room and dining room after Sully and then pointed. "Charley, the kitchen appliances, countertop, and big farm sink are kind of retro, but also hardly having been used, they're like new."

"This cabin is beautiful, Cash. I looked through the windows earlier," Charley said. "It's a lot more modern and much larger than I expected. I spied a nice shower in the bathroom."

"Are you guys selling this place?" Sully asked.

"We never felt like this property belonged to us, but that's up to Charley now." Cash said and looked at her. "As property lines go, Sully is your neighbor, Charley."

"Yes, so he said." Charley squared her shoulders, raised her chin, and explained to Sully, "The man you all knew as Uncle Clarence was my father."

"Really?" Sully asked, looking from Charley to Cash. "I didn't know he had any kids."

"Uncle Clarence didn't know either. So, none of us knew," Cash said. "Until the headlines clued us in last month."

Sully thought for a minute and realized why Charley's name rang a bell. "The Charlotte Fleming murder?"

CHAPTER THREE

"Yes," Charley answered, sounding stoic even to herself. "My mother."

"Let's head on over to the Lodge and celebrate Triple C Ranch-South finding its rightful owner with supper," Cash suggested and led the way outside. Turning on the porch light, when they'd exited, he locked the door and handed Charley two keys. "It's all yours," he told her, just before his cell signaled a text. "Tracy says the special tonight is slow-cooked roast beef and mashed potatoes covered in homemade gravy with fresh-snapped green beans and strawberry shortcake."

"My kind of supper," Sully said as he untethered Storm from the hitching post.

"Sounds so much better than the fast food and frozen dinners I'm used to," Charley said, holding the key to her heart. If Cash were any indication, the Coopers must be onboard with her inheriting the cabin and land. Charley knew she would never forget this special moment.

"Come on." Cash sent a text before taking the reins to Captain. "I told Tracy we're on our way," he said and mounted his horse.

"Storm and I can give you a ride, Charley," Sully offered and saddled up on the stallion.

"I can drive my car," Charley said, but pictured riding behind Sully on his horse. Seeing the two men on horseback, she felt like a fish out of water or a city girl out of her element. How sad that she'd missed growing up out here in the country and knowing her father, the other Coopers, and...Sully.

"More fun on horseback, city slicker," Sully said with a challenging grin. When he looked over the top of his sunglasses at her, she fell into the two deep green pools of his eyes.

"Why not?" Charley said. She was long overdue for country life. "I'll grab my purse and lock my car." She did so and hurried to Sully and his stallion.

"Ever ridden a horse?" Cash asked her.

"Never," Charley admitted with a laugh.

"At least she's got on britches and doesn't have to ride sidesaddle," Cash said to Sully and then chuckled. "Another good story Tracy can tell her."

With a nod and chuckle, Sully told Charley, "Okay, slip your left foot into the stirrup and grab my hand. Give a little jump on your right foot and I'll hoist you up behind me."

Charley took a breath and missed the stirrup. On her second try, she stuck her foot into the stirrup and noticed how masculine Sully's cowboy boot was especially in comparison to her ballerina slipper-style shoe. He extended his hand, and grabbing it along with a little hop, he indeed hoisted her up and behind him on the horse. Wow! He'd made that easy. His booted foot replaced hers in the stirrup, which she couldn't reach now anyway.

"Woo hoo!" Charley exclaimed triumphantly.

"Hold on," Sully said as Cash headed Captain down the gravel road ahead of them.

"To what?"

"Me."

"Okay," Charley said. Her left hand rested lightly on his belt, and her right hand touched the holstered gun. She moved her right hand a little higher on his waist.

"You've never ridden on the back of a motorcycle either. Have you?" he asked.

"No. How did you know that?"

"You'll see," Sully said and nudged Storm into a trot behind Cash. When Charley slipped to one side of the horse's rump and then the other, she quickly wrapped her arms around Sully's tapered waist. Over his shoulder, he said, "That's how I knew."

"Do you have a motorcycle too?"

"A Harley. If you can dismount Storm without falling flat on your fanny, I'd be happy to take you for a spin."

Taking in Sully's broad back as well as the splendid countryside, Charley kept her arms around him as they trotted toward the main road. Cash was already on the other side of the highway. Traveling west in the direction of Pikes Peak, Charley soon saw Cash dismount at the combination hotel and restaurant, well-known across Colorado and beyond. Under a two-story portico, a lovely pregnant redhead and strawberry-blond little girl emerged from the building to greet him. The German shepherd with them barked a greeting at Cash who scratched his head. Then Cash scooped up the child, gave her a toss in the air, and kissed her cheek. Wrapping an arm around the woman, he tugged her to him and kissed his wife's lips.

Charley found herself smiling at the happy family of three who were about to become a family of four. She wondered what it would feel like if Sullivan Custis were to swoop her into his arms like that and kiss her. Where had that thought come from? From being wrapped around him as he sat between her spread legs atop the horse? Maybe. Sully reined in the big bay near Captain behind a split rail fence on the left side of Coopers' Lodge.

"In case I want to go for a Harley spin," Charley unexpectedly flirted with Sully and quickly added, "not saying I do, but to keep from falling flat on my fanny, how should I dismount?"

Holding out his hand, Sully said, "How you mounted in reverse."

"Okay," she said and took his hand. He let her slide her foot into the stirrup and swinging her right leg over the horse's hindquarters, she landed on her right foot and pulled her left foot out of the stirrup. With a grin, she said, "You owe me a motorcycle ride."

As Sully dismounted, Charley backed up to give him room just as a vehicle roared by on the main road. Surprised at the noise, she twisted sideways so fast she went stumbling backward. But Sully grabbed her arm and kept her upright.

Frowning past her to the road, he asked, "Wasn't that the guy we just dealt with at Triple C-South?"

Charley had glimpsed the silver Mercedes. "Yes, sorry. He must have been waiting, hoping you and Cash would leave me behind and alone."

"I pegged him as stupid." Sully shrugged with an easy smile. "I owe you a Harley spin."

"Barely," Charley said. "I almost fell down a second time today.

"Yeah, but you dismounted well, for a city girl."

"Thanks to a...country boy."

Sully's grin was both so cocky and at the same time so charming, Charley felt her cheeks grow hot with a blush. A blush? That was a first. She turned her head away from the sexy, oh yes, so very sexy man as Cash, with his family and the German shepherd, approached.

"Charley, this is Tracy Cooper, my adoring wife you've heard about," Cash said.

"Hello Tracy," Charley said.

"Hi Charley, hi Sully," Tracy, the beautiful redhead, replied.

"Hi Tracy," Sully replied.

Then, smiling at the child in his arms, Cash said, "This sweet girl is our three-year-old Carly, named after Uncle Clarence Carl Cooper."

"Tracy and Carly, it's such a pleasure to meet you," Charley said and wiggled her fingers at Carly who smiled.

With a nod at the dog, Tracy said, "This is Dude. He started out as my dog, but if he could talk, he'd tell you he belongs to Cash."

"I think Dude's favorite person is Carly," Cash said with a chuckle.

"Nice to meet you, Dude," Charley said and then smiled at Tracy. "Tracy, I've heard wonderful things about you from Cash."

"Oh, I can imagine," Tracy said with a tinkling giggle. "He usually starts off with how I almost ran him over the day we met."

"Yes." Charley laughed. "He said you'd tell me all about it."

"At least he's letting me give my side of the story," Tracy said with a grin at her husband. "Charley, you have the trademark royal-blue eyes of the Coopers." And with that, she looped her arm through Charley's as if they'd known each other forever, making Charley feel like family instead of an outsider. "Come on everybody, supper's waiting on us."

Cash locked the gate, as the horses grazed in a green pasture beside the Lodge. Sully opened the door of the Lodge, which housed not only the restaurant, but a bar and twelve guest rooms. Tracy let go of Charley and led the way through the welcoming lobby, where guests were registering at the front desk or enjoying the fireplace as they relaxed on leather furnishings.

Leaving the lobby behind, Cash directed Dude into an office, which Tracy said was hers. The dog trotted across the large room and past a desk to curl up in a comfy-looking dog bed. From there, Charley and Sully followed the Coopers into the dining room, which was Western chic with framed scenes of cowboys and cowgirls, along with wagon wheels and longhorns mounted on walls. Chandeliers with old-fashioned lanterns hung from the high ceiling above tables covered in snow white tablecloths and decorated with matching lanterns lit with candles.

"This is all so beautiful," Charley said. "The Lodge has been on my bucket list."

"Thank you. Cash had the vision for Coopers' Lodge," Tracy said as she led them to a rectangular table set for five in a semiprivate alcove. "I just help him run the place."

"She's being modest. Tracy not only runs it without my help, her and her grandmother's homestyle recipes keep business booming here in the Lodge," Cash replied. "And more than a few folks come just to collect her autograph on one or more of the children's books she writes."

Tracy glowed at his compliment and replied, "Cash fills Coopers' Lodge year-round by keeping the dude ranch hopping."

Business was obviously booming as every other table in the dining room was occupied. Sully scooted out a chair for Charley and then sat on her left. Cash had done the same for Tracy and placed Carly between them before taking a seat across from Sully. The meal indeed tasted like home cooking and Charley could see why people came from near and far to sample it. As conversation easily flowed, Charley was delighted to hear the tales as to how Tracy had nearly run over Cash the day they'd met and how Cash had scooped Tracy up and onto Captain sidesaddle that same day. Perched in a booster seat, and at only three years old, Carly was a perfect little lady at dinner with admirable table manners. After the strawberry shortcake, with scoops of vanilla ice cream, Cash, Tracy, and Carly escorted Charley and Sully to the front door. There, Carly mentioned her Cooper cousins with love and asked Charley if she knew them.

"I've not met everyone in the family yet," Charley said, taking Carly's little hand in hers. "But if they're anything like you, I'll love them."

"Oh, you'll meet all of them," Cash said with a chuckle.

"And you'll love them all just like I do," Tracy assured her with sincerity.

"Thank you for dinner," Sully said, since the Coopers wouldn't hear of them paying.

"Yes, thank you both so much for—" Charley's voice broke but she swallowed and finished firmly. "Everything."

"Ready to ride?" Sully asked her.

"Ready," Charley replied. Then, with hugs to the Coopers, she said, "See you soon."

Holding Carly, Cash asked her, "What do we say on the Triple C Ranches?"

The little girl grinned and said, "Sooner than later."

"See you sooner than later," Charley promised with a warm smile.

CHAPTER FOUR

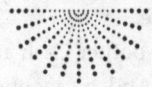

"**S**omebody flattened your back tires," Sully said to the gorgeous girl, whose slender arms circled his waist, as Storm trotted into the porch light of the Triple C Ranch-South cabin.

"Oh my gosh!" Charley gasped, leaning around Sully's left side.

"Hang on," he said and placed a hand to her knee, not wanting her to fall off the horse. Sully reined Storm in between the car and cabin and helped Charley safely slide to the ground.

"Who would do such a thing?" Charley asked, and then before he could answer she said, "Rod Vaughn."

"That'd be my guess." Dismounting his horse, Sully wondered if seeing them together on Storm had resulted in the flat tires.

"For the record, Rod has no claim on me," Charley said, walking around her car. From the front of the vehicle, she told him, "Not just the back tires. All four tires are flat! I'll call someone to come and put air in them." Charley pulled out her phone and started scrolling. With a pang in her voice, she looked up from her cell and asked, "Who do I call?"

"Nobody. I'm guessing air won't fix the problem."

She tilted her pretty head and asked him, "What do you mean?"

"My bet is that this is a slash and dash."

"He slashed my tires?" Charley's shoulders momentarily sagged, and then she lifted her chin. "I'll need a tow truck."

"It's dark outside and you don't have to do this tonight." Sully walked to where she stood at the front of her car. "I can take you to Cash's house.

"No, I don't want to bother Cash at night, especially with Tracy being pregnant. And he mentioned the Lodge being full. I'll stay here at the cabin."

"What if Vaughn comes back tonight, Charley?"

"I don't know." She grimaced. "Maybe he won't."

"Let's ride to my ranch."

"How far away is your ranch?"

"On the path through the pine trees, ten minutes."

"Do you have a car?"

"Yes." He chuckled. "I have a truck and a Jeep."

"Can you give me a ride into town?"

"Absolutely. Do you have a way back out here in the morning?"

"Well…no." She let out a frustrated hiss. "But I can call an Uber or a cab."

"We can figure it out at my ranch." Sully turned and gave her a wave. "Come on." He mounted Storm and then took his foot out of the stirrup. "Saddle up, city slicker."

"I don't see how this is *saddling* up when I don't have a saddle." But with a playful huff, Charley slipped her foot into the stirrup, caught hold of his hand, and with a hop was behind him on Storm.

"We'll have to get you one." Not only did Sully like the feel of her arms sliding around him, he liked her soft breasts pressing against his back.

"One what?"

"A saddle." Sully nudged Storm, and the stallion headed for home.

"I don't have a horse."

"You'll need one out here."

"I don't know how to take care of a horse, and where would I keep it? In the barn next to the cabin?"

"Or a stable."

"A stable like my cousin Cash has?"

"Not as big, since he has thirty-some dude ranch horses, but yes."

They rode in silence, and Sully figured she was pondering the slashed tires, the cabin, and having her own horse. Ten minutes later, light flickered across the trail and Storm had them at Sully's stables. With the floodlight shining over the top of the stable doors, Sully let Charley dismount and then slid off Storm behind her. He opened a door, flipped on the inside lights, and led Storm into the stable. Taking Storm toward his stall, he noticed Charley looking around.

"How many horses do you have?" she asked.

"Half dozen," he replied just as the backdoor opened. "Randy Custis, come meet our new neighbor, Charley Cooper."

"Hello," Randy said with a nod and a smile. He was thirty and a great friend in addition to being a cousin. Sully noted the appreciation for Charley's beauty and her figure in his eyes. Giving Storm's hindquarters a pat, Randy said, "Nice to meet you, Charley."

"Hi, Randy. It's nice to meet you too."

"My cousins, Randy and his older brother, Roy, both work for me and live in the bunkhouse beside the stables," Sully told her.

"For now." With a nod at Sully, Randy explained to Charley, "Roy just got engaged and will eventually move in with Mindy, his fiancée. But he'll still work with us." With a clap to Sully's shoulder, he said, "Roy and I wrangled good deals when Sully hired us."

"I'm the one who got a good deal," Sully said. "You guys are the best."

Randy grinned and shrugged. "Oh, I almost forgot. Trish

Potter was here looking for you earlier, Sully." With that, Randy took Storm off his hands.

"Okay," Sully replied patting the stallion's mane. He'd silenced Trish's texts but had noticed all three at the Lodge. "Thanks, Randy. See you tomorrow."

"Yup, you got it." Randy tipped his hat at them. "See you tomorrow."

Sully steered Charley out of the stables. "Let's go inside, get something to drink, and figure out what to do about your car," he suggested.

"Great, and if it wouldn't be too much trouble, I need to use your bathroom."

"Sure thing. Follow me."

Sully led the way past the corral he and his dad had built. Passing a three-car garage, to the rear of the house, took them to the side door of the home. Opening the door, he let Charley step into the softly lit mudroom ahead of him. His eyes dipped to her fanny. It was round and sexy as hell. He could still feel her legs touching his when she'd been behind him on Storm. She stopped after entering the kitchen.

"Which way?" Charley asked.

"Through the kitchen and down the hall, on the left," Sully replied and pointed. "What would you like to drink?"

"Whatcha got?"

"Beer, bottled water…beer," he said with a grin and a shrug. "I'm gonna have a beer."

"Okay. I'll have one too."

Sully didn't answer the texts from Trish asking if he was home. Between the sink and white cabinets on one side and an island with a quartz countertop and four barstools on the other, he walked through the large, rectangular kitchen to the stainless-steel refrigerator. Not a minute after Charley had closed the bathroom door, the side door to the mudroom opened.

"Sully?" came Trish Potter's voice.

Hell. Trish's dad had retired from the post office and lived on a patch of land a few miles away. After her first divorce, Trish had moved in with her father. Sully had initially met her a couple of years prior at one of the Coopers' summertime barbecues. She'd propositioned him and he'd taken her up on it. She'd disappeared for a while and was back again after divorce number two and the passing of her father. Sully had slept with her for the second and final time about six months ago. That was more than enough. He was done and had politely but firmly told Trish so. However, Trish, five years his senior, was aggressively persistent and not taking no for an answer.

"What are you doing here, Trish?" Sully asked, standing in front of the fridge.

With black hair swinging around her shoulders and wearing a dress that barely covered her backside, she slinked to him and clutched his right arm. "I'm here to invite you to Chloe Cooper Brevard's Halloween party."

"Chloe already invited me."

"Great! Let's go togeth—" She halted and stared.

"Sorry to interrupt," Charley said from the arched doorway to the hall.

Damn, Charley was beautiful. Sully was partial to long brown hair and hers was particularly eye-catching. Charley had a fresh and innocent look about her and Sully figured she was a few years younger than he was. Her royal-blue eyes blinked, and she pulled her full lower lip between straight white teeth.

"You're not interrupting," Sully said, freeing his arm from Trish. He took two beers out of the fridge, opened them, and walked toward Charley. This situation was uncomfortable, and he resented Trish's intrusion more for Charley's sake than his own. Handing Charley one of the bottles, he winked at her and said, "Here you go."

"Last time I saw you, Sully, you said it was approaching your busy time of year and you weren't dating," Trish remarked pointedly, giving Charley the onceover.

Sully didn't feel he owed Trish an explanation. "Charley Cooper, this is Trish Potter."

Charley smiled and said politely, "Nice to meet you."

"Buh-bye, Sully," Trish spat, ignoring Charley. Trish turned on her heel and headed out the door, letting it slam shut.

Charley asked, "A night for dealing with exes?"

"Yeah," Sully agreed. "Sorry about that." Then, giving Charley a smile, he said, "I have a den right down the hall. Let's go figure out your next move."

Sully led the way past his office, with photos and products of his business. *After what happened, you should know I detest guns.* Charley had stated that to Rod Vaughn. Vaughn had indicated Sully could be a strangler. Sully had an idea why she hated guns. But what else had she been through?

"What do you do for a living, Sully?"

CHAPTER FIVE

"$\mathcal{I}$ inherited a retail business from my uncle, on my mother's side. He passed away about the same time my dad retired," Sully replied, stepping aside at the doorway to a spacious den boasting a stone fireplace and leather furniture. "Randy, who you met, splits his time between my ranch and my store. Roy works for me full time at the retail store."

"I think being your own boss and working with your cousins is just too cool!"

"It is cool," Sully said with a chuckle. "Once a week, my dad drops in at the store too. But he stays busy working with Derek Brevard, Chloe's husband, training and breeding Percherons for mounted police."

"That's a great cause." Charley entered the den. Large windows on either side of the hearth offered peaceful views of the stables, a corral, and an endless green pasture. "Do your parents still live next door to your ranch?"

"My dad does in the house I grew up in." Sully smiled, and Charley's heart raced because Sullivan Custis was just that handsome. She could understand the woman named Trish wanting him. "My mom passed away three years ago."

"Oh Sully, I'm sorry to hear that," Charley said softly.

"Having lost my mother recently, I can identify with your loss."

"I'm sure you can," Sully said with compassion in his deep voice. "My mom came from a wealthy family and left me a generous inheritance. After my dad deeded thirty thousand acres of ranchland over to me, I built this house with some of my inheritance." With a shrug, he added, "Anyway, my dad lives a bachelor's life like me now."

Sully walked to an overstuffed black leather sofa and Charley followed. As he swung a hand toward it, she took a seat. He sat down a cushion away from her and held out his beer bottle. She clinked the neck of hers to his, and they both took a sip.

"I live a bachelorette life in town," Charley offered without making eye contact.

"In Colorado Springs?"

"Yes. In the Old Colorado City neighborhood of the Springs."

"Where the young woman was recently murdered," Sully commented. When she flinched, he asked, "Have you lived there all your life?"

"Yes," she replied and shifted slightly on the sofa to better face him. "You're wondering how it is that I just found out I'm a Cooper."

"Curious," he admitted, resting his arm along the back of the sofa.

"Here's what I've pieced together with help from the Coopers and a scrapbook I found that belonged to my mother." Charley took a fortifying drink, pushed a tendril of hair away from her face, and said, "Back in the day, my mother met Clarence Cooper during a week on the dude ranch that Cash inherited, and they became...involved. A few months later, when she realized she was pregnant with me, she didn't tell him. She ended things before he could figure out she was expecting."

"Clarence really was a nice man," Sully said with feeling. "He was good with children who visited the dude ranch and good with all of us kids when we were growing up. Too bad you weren't offered the chance to meet him."

"Yes," Charley said with longing. "Even though I moved into the apartment next door to my mother after I graduated high school, our relationship was strained. She was closed-off, never easy to talk to. I always felt like she was keeping a secret from me."

"Why do you think she chose not to tell you about Clarence Cooper?"

Charley shrugged and looked away. "She was a fiercely independent businesswoman, and she said that's why she never married. I'm lucky I was born because I don't think she had planned to share her life with anyone." She sighed and shook her head before looking at Sully again. "I point-blank asked her more than once who my father was, but she always said she didn't know. My birth certificate states, *Father Unknown*. I questioned her as to where my last name of Cooper came from, and she claimed she made it up out of thin air."

"I admire independence," Sully said. "But it's a shame you and Clarence missed out on each other. He would have been thrilled to have his daughter in his life."

"I would have liked to have had a father in my life." Charley felt the recent mixture of grief and fury hitting her and tapped it down. "I appreciate an independent nature too. But I'm angry that she cheated my father and me from getting to know each other." When she hung her head and stared at her lap, she felt Sully's hand on her shoulder. "Now that I know what her secret was, I can't even confront her about it."

"It was a rough secret. But don't let anger about the past ruin your future."

Charley nodded at the good advice, and Sully's hand returned to the back of the couch. "As you know, my mother was murdered, and when the newspapers said she was survived by a daughter named Charlotte Fleming Cooper, Cash Cooper reached out to me on behalf of the Cooper family. According to Cash, Clarence Cooper had mentioned my mother to the family and said if a child of his were to surface, Charlotte Fleming would most likely be the mother."

"That sounds like the Coopers. They are loyal and generous to family and friends." Sully took a drink from the bottle and asked, "Did you already have your Mini *Cooper* before you knew about your father?"

"Yes," she said with a smile. "It's the first new car I've ever owned. It just felt right."

"No doubt," Sully said with a grin. He was quiet for a moment, and Charley could almost hear other questions running through his head. "I'm sorry for your losses, Charley. First, losing your mother tragically and then finding out your father was deceased. Do the police have a suspect in your mother's murder?"

"Not yet."

"The person found strangled to death in a cave was a woman about your age. The news said your mother died from being shot. I guess from being the son of a former sheriff, I wonder if the police think the two murders are linked due to their close proximity."

"I don't know." Charley shrugged again. "I remember reading that the young woman's name was Grace Lightner and thinking that being strangled was not a graceful way for her to have to die."

"I agree."

Charley felt like a freak. She'd never known her father, and her mother was to blame. Now her mother was dead. Murdered by an unknown assailant. Her eyes went to a framed photo on the wooden mantle of the stone hearth. Sully, probably in his teens, stood between a handsome man with black hair and a beautiful blonde. No doubt his dad and mom. From what he'd told her, Sully had a normal upbringing with loving parents. What was he thinking of her and her unusual circumstances?

Unable to meet his green eyes, she said, "If you will give me your address, I'll call an Uber to come pick me up."

"Charley, I'll take you back into town." His fingers lightly tapped her shoulder. "Or you're welcome to stay here tonight. My master bedroom is on the main floor. I have three guest rooms all upstairs."

"I couldn't impose on you like that any more than I could Cash and Tracy."

"You're not imposing now any more than you were interrupting earlier."

Charley quickly ran two scenarios through her head: first, staying with Sully to be here in the country bright and early to get a tow truck for her car and second, having him take her home only to be stuck in town.

"If you're sure I'm not imposing, I'd appreciate staying," Charley said.

Sully smiled. "Great, after the tow truck comes for your car, I can run you into town."

"I'll buy you breakfast, brunch, or lunch to thank you."

"Not necessary, but you've got yourself a deal." Sully held out his beer bottle, and she clinked her bottle to his again to seal their deal. "So, how close do you live to where the murder by the so-called Cave Killer was committed?"

"Close. Just a few blocks away in an apartment on one side of a duplex where my mother lives—lived on the other side."

"Were you nearby when your mother was shot?"

"Yes. It happened in my apartment." She offered nothing more about that and glanced away from the handsome man again to say, "After her death, while cleaning out her apartment, I found the scrapbook and a photo of her with a man. On the back of the photo, in her handwriting, it read *Charley's daddy and me*."

"That must have come as a shock."

"It did. But I didn't know who *Daddy* was until I met Cash, Chase, and Chloe in an attorney's office. I showed them the photo, and they identified Clarence Cooper immediately. I liked them on the spot, and I felt a kinship with the three of them. But at my insistence, we had DNA testing done."

"And?"

"The results showed enough hits in a row and chunks of DNA that matched over twenty-three pairs of chromosomes to convince us we are first cousins."

"So, you lost your parents, but found a fantastic extended family," Sully said. "I don't know any better people than the Coopers."

"Yes," Charley agreed with a nod. "They could have resented me, but they seem to be welcoming me with love and kindness." She placed a hand over her heart. "I am beyond blessed to have them in my life."

"Have you met your grandfather, Crawford Cooper, who goes by Coop?"

"Oh, yes. In the attorney's office," Charley said with a smile. "Coop just turned ninety, and he is a hoot. I fell in love with him."

"Yes, he's the best. Coop lives in a log cabin on Chase's ranch with his longtime girlfriend, Tammy, who is Tracy's grandmother. There's another story for you." Sully shook his head and said, "I don't know what else is going on in your city life, but you're in good hands out here in the country." The grin Sully gave her sent a thrill through Charley. What would it be like to put herself in Sully's large hands? "Would you like to see your choice of bedrooms?"

"Yes, please."

Sully scooted to the edge of the sofa. "Come on."

"Okay," Charley said and stood as he did. She followed him out of the den and down the wide hallway to a two-story foyer. High above the double front doors was a stained glass window. It depicted a big bay stallion in a green pasture with Pikes Peak in the distance and lavender columbines in the foreground. She stared in wonder. "How magnificent, Sully."

Sully grinned with a shrug. "I got the idea from the

stained glass front door that Clarence Cooper had made for your log cabin." He went up the staircase first and stopped on the second-floor landing. Pointing, he indicated the main guest bathroom and then flipped on the lights of the bedrooms. "Take your pick."

"I like all three. You pick for me."

"The bedroom we're in now has its own private bath." Sully crossed the floor and turned on the bathroom light. "Take it."

"Sully," Charley began, walking to the queen-size bed, where she stopped and looked at the handsome man, "I want you to know that I don't stay the night with random men."

"I didn't figure you did. But you met me through my friendship with the Coopers and knowing I was raised by the former El Paso County Sheriff, you feel safe."

"Exactly," Charley said. "I do feel safe here with you."

Giving her an appreciative nod, Sully said, "There are towels and soap in the bathroom. Please make yourself at home."

"Thank you, Sully. See you bright and early in the morning?"

"Yup."

CHAPTER SIX

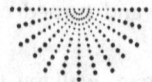

$\mathcal{S}$ully heard a bloodcurdling scream.

"What the hell?" He sat up on the side of his bed and glanced at the clock: 3:30 a.m.

Acutely aware he had an overnight guest, Sully hurried across the room and climbed the stairs two at a time. It had taken him forever to fall asleep, knowing a stunning stranger was in bed on the floor above him. He came to a stop at her closed door and hearing a whimper, he gently tapped his knuckles against the wood.

"Sully?"

"Yeah. Are you okay?"

"Yes," Charley said. "Come in."

Sully opened the door. Moonlight, streaming through the window, haloed her pretty head as she sat in the middle of the bed. Her long brown hair was loose and cascaded around her shoulders. Under the sheet her knees were pulled up to her chest. She looked vulnerable, delicate, and frightened.

"What's wrong?" he asked, entering the room.

"I'm so sorry I woke you. I thought I only screamed in the nightmares I've been prone to lately. I didn't know I was screaming out loud."

Sully walked a few steps closer to the bed. "What can I do to help?"

"Keep me company?"

"Sure," he said, and when she patted the mattress, he took a seat on it facing her. She had the sheet pulled over her breasts, but he saw bra straps on her shoulders. Realizing he was sitting on something, he tugged her leopard-print pants out from under him and knew she was sleeping in her underwear. He should have offered her one of his tee shirts. "What's causing your nightmares?" When Charley didn't reply, he asked, "The death of your mother? Or the strangler? Both? Or something else?"

Charley only nodded and then rested her forehead on her knees. Feeling protective of the beautiful young woman, Sully clenched his jaw. Reaching for Charley, he pulled his hand back before he made contact. A strange man touching her was probably the last thing she wanted. But when a sob escaped her, he threw caution to the wind and tugged her into his arms. Resting her head on his shoulder, she used the corner of the sheet to dry her eyes and sniffled.

"He didn't succeed with me," Charley whispered.

"Who didn't succeed?"

"The man who killed my mother. My presence during her murder has not been disclosed by the police to the press."

"What do you mean he didn't succeed?" Sully asked and then instinctively knew. "You mean raping you?"

"Yes, he only got as far as tearing open the top of my robe. I screamed and fought. A moment later, my mother called my name from the living room. The guy stopped and ran. He shot her on his way out of my apartment."

"Damn." Sully tightened his hold on her. Relief that a murderer had not been able to rape Charley hit him faster and harder than he would have expected. "I'm thinking I might find this guy and kill him."

"No, Sully," Charley said with alarm in her voice as she leaned away from him. Her eyes glittered with tears.

"Whether or not he's the Cave Killer, he's out there and he's dangerous."

"Yeah," Sully gritted through his teeth. Charley was quiet, and he didn't want to push her. "How did he get into your apartment?"

"I had left my door unlocked because I was expecting my mom. I came out of the shower and there was a man in my bedroom wearing a ski mask." Charley gently pushed out of his arms. "He grabbed me and shoved me onto my bed and I —I don't want to talk about it."

"I understand. You've been through a lot in a short span of time. But I'm a good listener if you change your mind." He paused and added, "Or if you need help, Charley."

"I'm basically a stranger to you, Sully," Charley said with a shake of her head. "Why would you help me?"

"I liked you on the spot, Charley Cooper," he told her, just as she'd said to him about the Coopers.

Charley smiled and then a soft laugh escaped her. "I like you, too, Sullivan Custis."

"Back to sleep?" he asked.

"Back to sleep," she agreed, but when he stood, she grasped his hand. "Stay with me?"

Wearing only his boxer shorts, Sully hesitated for the span of one breath taken and then said, "Sure."

"I'll try not to scream," Charley whispered.

With that, Charley moved over in the bed and laid down. Sully stretched out on his back beside her. She rolled away from him to her right side. He heard her take a deep, shuddering breath. He stared at the ceiling. Lying in bed with a woman and not touching her was a first. Charley Cooper was a first too. In every way imaginable.

When Sully woke, it was morning and he was alone. He sat up and saw that Charley's leopard pants were no longer at the end of the bed. Had she left without telling him? He rolled out of bed and went downstairs. In his master bedroom, he was pulling on a pair of jeans when he heard her call out to him from the kitchen. He smiled, liking the sound of her voice. He answered her, and then grabbing a shirt, he padded barefoot to the kitchen where he found Charley dressed and standing near the coffeemaker.

"Morning," he said.

"Good morning," the gorgeous girl replied with a blush staining her ivory cheeks. "May I interest you in a cup of coffee before the tow truck arrives?"

"When is the truck due?"

"They said between an hour and a half to two hours."

"Yes, I'd like to have coffee."

"You sit and I'll pour," she said and began opening cabinet doors.

"To the right, above the coffeemaker," he said about the coffee mugs she was obviously looking for. She'd braided her hair again and it swung down her slender back. Her waist was small and her hips saucy. When she turned to him, he brought his eyes up her body to meet her gaze.

"How do you take your coffee?"

"Black." He knew she'd caught him eyeing her, but she didn't call him on it. "How do you take yours?"

"A dollop of milk and no sugar."

"Milk's in the fridge." Sully watched her walk to the refrigerator and take out a jug of milk. He liked the way she looked in his kitchen. Like she belonged.

For the next hour, they shared light, sometimes flirty, conversation as they sat on the barstools pulled up to the quartz-topped island in his kitchen.

"Oh no," Charley said after looking at her phone. "The battery is dead." Glancing at him she asked, "What time is it, Sully?"

Glancing at his watch, he said, "Ten."

"I'd better get going. Are you sure you don't mind giving me a ride to my car?"

"No, of course not. I'll put on my boots and be right with you."

Sully went back to his bedroom, brushed his teeth, ran a comb through his hair, and returned to her wearing his cowboy boots. Grabbing his keys, he led the way to his garage. He saw Randy in the distance, heading into the stables and gave him a wave. Randy acknowledged him with a thumbs-up. Heading into the garage alone, Sully backed his truck out, stopped, and went to the passenger's side. After opening the door for Charley, she climbed into the double-cab truck. Sully slid in behind the steering wheel as she fastened her seat belt. Charley looked around at the land and his country-style, two-story house with a wistful smile on her full lips.

"Your house, surrounded with the green pastures and ponderosa pines, is so serene," Charley said. As he drove down the driveway leading from the backyard to the main road, she pointed. "Blooming season is mostly over for columbines, but I see the remains of some along the front of your porch. What colors are they?"

"You have a good eye for perennials. Along with the lavender ones, there are yellow, purple, and red."

"Lavender columbines symbolize the blending of differences and finding harmony."

"Really?" he asked. "Like the differences and harmony between the city and country?"

Charley gave him an appreciative smile and nod. "Yellow columbines bring friendship, positive energy, and happiness," she said softly. "Purple ones are often used to indicate a resolve to win. And red columbines symbolize love and passion."

"I didn't know any of that." Sully tilted his head in surprise. "The hummingbirds help keep the red ones pollinated."

Charley nodded as if she knew that, too, and changed the subject. "You did a great job building your house, Sully," she said with one last look. "It's spectacular."

"Five thousand square feet of peace and quiet. Thank you," he replied and held out a phone charging cord to her.

"You're welcome." She plugged in her cell phone and told him, "I've never ridden in a truck before."

"Is that right?" he asked, heading the Dodge Ram north.

"That's right," she replied, taking in the countryside. Looking back at him, she added, "I'd never ridden a horse until yesterday either. And never have I been in bed with—"

Nearing the crossroad where they would head west toward the Triple C Ranches and Colorado Springs, he cocked a brow at her and waited. "With—?"

"With, umm…such crazy circumstances."

"Okay." Sully chuckled. He drove to Triple C Ranch-South and turned left onto the gravel road leading to the log cabin.

"Sully, thank you again for your help last night and this morning," Charley said, without getting specific about sharing a bed. "I really appreciate it."

"My pleasure." That was an understatement.

They saw her car and stared.

CHAPTER SEVEN

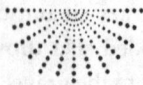

"*T*he convertible top has been dented," Charley whispered. "Was it like that last night?"

"It could have been. It was dark when we were here, so we could have missed it. Man, somebody's got a bad temper." Sully brought the truck to a stop alongside her car. "We should call the cops."

Charley put her doubt into words. "What good would it do?"

"You'll need to make a report for insurance purposes," he said. "Vaughn obviously has a bad temper. Maybe the police can get fingerprints and figure out if he did this."

"I don't know." Charley unbuckled her seat belt and said, "I respect and support all police, but I've dealt with them a lot lately. They're probably tired of me." She opened her door and got out of the truck. Walking around her beloved Mini Cooper, she fought back anger and tears as she mumbled, "Darn it."

"Four tires and a repaired convertible top and you'll be back in business," Sully said, walking toward her.

"Yes," Charley agreed and pasted a smile on her face.

"Does your duplex have a garage?"

"No, just a two-car parking pad," she said, shaking her head as Sully frowned.

"Here comes the tow truck."

The tow truck driver was adept at his job and soon had her car loaded up. After asking the man to take it to a body shop Sully had recommended, the tow truck driver hauled her car onto the highway and disappeared down the road.

"So, how about the breakfast, brunch, or lunch I promised you?" she asked.

"I'll take all three."

"Okay," she said with a laugh. Sully opened the truck door for her, and she climbed into her seat. "It's almost lunchtime, what sounds good?"

"Mexican?"

"Perfect. I love Mexican food."

Sliding in behind the wheel, Sully started the engine. "I know a great little place in Old Colorado City," he said, referring to her neighborhood. Built along Colorado Avenue, the nineteenth-century red brick buildings housed a variety of art galleries, jewelry stores, quaint shops, and cozy cafés. "It's called the Canyon Cantina."

"Yes, the Canyon Cantina is one of my favorite places to eat," Charley told him and was rewarded with a grin on his handsome face. "My place is walking distance from the Canyon Cantina. Since parking can be tough to find, if you'd like to go to my apartment we can park there and walk."

"Sounds good to me," Sully said.

They chatted as Sully drove to Colorado Springs and eventually headed across town into the Old Colorado Springs neighborhood. There, Charley directed him to her duplex. Perched on the backside of a hill, the two apartments were set up above a corner shop that opened onto a wide sidewalk of Colorado Avenue. Sully turned left onto a side street, drove up the hill, and parked his truck on one-half of a double-sized parking pad.

As Charley unplugged her cell phone, she asked, "Would you mind if we make a quick stop inside my apartment so I can brush my teeth?"

"Let's go."

Hopping out of her side of his truck, before he could open the door for her, Charley led the way down the short cobblestone path to her one-bedroom apartment on the left side of the duplex. She typically kept her place in good shape, so she wasn't concerned about inviting Sully into her home. But today, as soon as she neared the door, she realized it was slightly ajar. The doorknob was askew and the lock was scratched. Pushing the door open, she stepped into the living room and Sully followed her.

"Dear Lord," Charley whispered.

Both of her white orchids had been swept off the Formica countertop separating her living room from the kitchen. The pots had broken, scattering dirt and petals across the hard-wood floor of the living room. Sofa pillows had been tossed and a wingback chair had been turned on its side. To the right of the living room, in the breakfast nook area, her peace lily plant had been pulled out of its pot by the roots and dumped onto the kitchen table. Her sweet little peacock plants lay in broken pieces on the floor and her African violet had been emptied out onto the kitchen windowsill. Without another word, she walked down a closet-length hallway and turned left into her bedroom. There, her parlor palm lay on its side in the middle of her queen-size bed. Her spider plants sat askew in their hanging, macramé baskets in front of the bedroom window.

"Who has it in for you, Charley?" Sully asked, coming up behind her and taking off his sunglasses.

She turned to him, flushed with anger and embarrass-ment. "I don't know."

"Rod Vaughn is a loose cannon, and I could see him damaging your car. Would he do this too?"

"Yes. Maybe." Moving past Sully, Charley flipped on the bathroom light. Her shower curtains had been slashed into ribbons. "I don't know what to think."

"You have to call the cops."

"No," she said, leading the way back down the hall and into the living room.

Sully caught her arm and turned her to him. "Yes, you're in danger, Charley."

"I'll be okay."

"How?" he asked, his hands on his hips. "When you're raped, dead, or both?"

"Sully!"

"I'm serious, Charley. My dad would say to call the cops right now." Standing in the living room, he pulled his phone out of his pocket and made the 9-1-1 call. "What's your address?" he asked and when she gave it to him, he relayed it to the dispatcher. Hanging up, he told her, "They'll be here shortly."

"Okay," she said and nodded.

"They don't want us to touch anything, so let's go wait for them in my truck. Come on." Closing her front door, they first checked the unoccupied apartment next door. It was undamaged. In the truck, Sully rolled the windows down and they waited for the police to arrive.

"This all started right after I met Rod Vaughn," Charley admitted without prompting while staring at the duplex.

"What started? Vaughn pressuring you?"

"Yes. I met Rod at work when he came in to buy flowers. He said he needed to make up with his girlfriend, Kay."

"You work as a florist?"

"Yes, at Fleming Flowers, the flower and plant shop directly underneath this duplex. I'm a nature lover and have a degree in horticulture."

"That makes sense," he said, having seen the variety of plants in her apartment. "No wonder you knew so much about columbines."

"My mother owned and worked in the flower shop all my life." Charley felt her eyes grow wide with dawning. "I'll bet the shop looks worse than my apartment."

"Might as well go take a look," Sully said.

They left the truck where it was parked. Walking down the hill and around the side of the building, they passed a plate-glass window boasting *Fleming's Flowers*, before reaching the all-glass front door. Since it was Sunday, the shop was closed, with a sign stating such on the door. Like her duplex door, the knob and lock were damaged. Charley knew before she looked, that didn't bode well for her shop. Indeed, as she pushed open the door, she found the cute little place in shambles. Plants and flowers lay in broken disarray from one end of the shop to the other.

"No transportation and no business all within twenty-four hours," Charley said. "Great."

"Do you scare easily?" Sully asked.

"I never thought so. Why?"

"I think somebody is trying to scare you or is really angry with you."

"Rod Vaughn is definitely angry with me, but if he thinks he can scare me into being with him, he's dead wrong."

Two police cars pulled to a stop in front of the flower shop. Charley and Sully met the officers on the sidewalk and ushered them inside. After they looked around the shop, Charley told them, with input from Sully, about the vandalism to her car. Then she left one of the officers with Sully and escorted the second one up to her apartment. The officers took reports on the apartment, shop, and car, promising to get back to her.

"I'm starving," Sully said as Charley locked the door to the shop. "How about lunch?"

"Yes," she replied. In addition to the shop, she had locked the door to her apartment, for whatever good it would do.

"Do you own this property or just rent it?"

"We...I own it. Why?"

"Because of the location, it's a valuable piece of real estate. Would your mother have promised this property to someone besides you?"

"No, we only had each other. But even if she did, who would want to tear things up?"

"I don't know. Could someone be mad at her but taking it out on you?"

"I don't think so. Like I said, she kept to herself."

Since the shop was on the corner of the block, they only had to walk a few steps to the stoplight. It turned red and they crossed the street. A little farther up Colorado Avenue put them at the Cantina Café. Taken by the hostess to a booth, they slid into seats on opposite sides of the table from each other. Given water with lemon along with chips, salsa, and menus, Charley looked up and sighed.

"As if things couldn't get any worse," she said under her breath.

"What now?" Sully asked and then saw Vaughn entering the restaurant.

"Rod lives in Manitou Springs," Charley said regarding the small town three miles away that lay at the foot of Pikes Peak. "Kay lives here in the Old Colorado City neighborhood."

CHAPTER EIGHT

"They both have convenient access to your property," Sully said. Over the top of the menu, he saw Rod Vaughn staring at Charley. When Vaughn's eyes switched to Sully, Sully glared at him.

"Are they sitting down?" Charley asked, purposely not looking.

"Yes, about three tables behind you." Sully took another glance and said, "Nope. I take that back. He sat down. She's coming this way."

"Charley," a woman with short, platinum blond and hot pink hair said.

"Hello, Kay."

"Rod and I are back together. I hope there're no hard feelings."

"Of course not. I'm happy for you," Charley said as her cell signaled a text.

"Who's this handsome man with you?" the woman asked.

"My new business manager," Charley improvised.

"Really?" Kay asked, looking at Sully.

"I'm advising her to sell her place here in the city and move her shop to the country," Sully said, off-the-cuff.

"Wow," Kay said and glanced over her shoulder at

Vaughn, who was frantically motioning to her. "Good luck, Charley. Nice to meet you—"

"Yeah," Sully said without giving his name. And with that, he dismissed her by looking at his menu.

After the woman, whose hair at the back of her head was maroon, walked away from their table, with a soft laugh, Charley asked, "Where did all that come from?"

"I don't know, but you started it," Sully replied with a smothered chuckle. "Maybe we can write this lunch off as a business expense now that we're partners."

"Yes, definitely," Charley agreed with a giggle. "By the way, that text I got was from Rod saying he and Kay are definitely not back together."

"Something tells me they deserve each other," Sully muttered with a shake of his head.

When the waitress returned, they ordered burritos and quesadillas with rice and beans, along with margaritas on the rocks. They enjoyed their meal without further interruption. Sully wouldn't let Charley pick up the check, and upon leaving the cantina, they both ignored the table where Rod and Kay sat. Out on the sidewalk, they headed back to Charley's place. They paused at the door to her shop.

"I need to start the cleanup process," she said.

"Nah," Sully said. "Leave it for today. It'll be there tomorrow. Come back out to the country with me. We'll go for a ride on horseback or the Harley, and I'll show you around your new ranch. Then I'll make smash burgers for supper."

"That sounds too good to pass up but—"

"Then don't pass it up. Come on."

"Since I don't have usable shower curtains, may I take a shower at your house?"

"Absolutely."

Sully held out his hand, and she slipped her dainty one into his. They walked up the hill to his truck, and Charley ducked into her apartment long enough to put a few things into a leopard print duffel bag. Back out in his truck, Sully headed for home. He couldn't help but wonder who was plaguing the beautiful young woman sitting in the passenger seat of his truck. He could tell with a quick glance at her pretty profile she was perplexed as well.

"In the last month, I've experienced an attempted rape, two murders in my neighborhood, my car damaged from top to bottom, and my apartment and shop vandalized," Charley said softly with a note of wonder in her voice. Looking at Sully, she said, "I don't understand it, but I'll figure it out if it's the last thing I ever do."

"In the last month you've gotten a whole new family and made friends with your new neighbor-slash-business manager."

"Yes." When Charley smiled at him, her blue eyes sparkled with what Sully was fairly certain represented a mixture of tears and joy. "Thank God for family and friends."

Sully reached across the console and took her hand. He gave it a squeeze and winked at her. She sighed and looked out the window. He let go of her hand and drove out of the Springs into the country. Entering the driveway of his ranch, he stopped the truck outside of his oversized three-car garage.

"Horseback or Harley?" he asked, and with a click of a remote, the garage door opened.

"Hmm...Harley today, country boy."

"You're on, city slicker."

He pulled the truck into the garage, and they hopped out. His Harley was parked in an empty space next to the truck. Two spots over was his Jeep. Leaving Charley's bag and purse in the truck for now, he fitted her with a helmet. She was a mixture of innocence and sex appeal wearing a black helmet. He put his own black helmet on and backed his Harley out of the garage.

"First time on a motorcycle, right?" he asked and strad-dled the Harley.

"Right," she said.

"Step onto the foot peg and thread your leg between me and the sissy bar," he told her, and when she'd done so, he gave her left knee a pat. "Hold onto me like you did when we rode Storm."

Never had a ride on his bike been so much fun as it was with Charley Cooper wrapped around him. He toured her through her ten-thousand-acre ranch and then took her across some of his thirty-thousand acres. Sully drove her over hills, around curves, into valleys, and across the countryside, all the while seeing it fresh through her eyes. They made stops here and there as she asked questions. The afternoon hours passed quickly, and by the time they pulled into his driveway again and parked the Harley, Sully felt like he'd known Charley forever.

"Hard to believe we only met twenty-four hours ago," she said, taking off her helmet.

"My thoughts exactly." Sully placed his helmet and hers on a shelf in the garage near the motorcycle. "Twenty-four hours ago it was suppertime. Hungry?"

"I am, but I'd love to take a shower if it wouldn't be too much trouble."

"Absolutely no trouble."

Sully grabbed her bag out of the truck, and Charley carried her purse. They headed into his house and as they passed Sully's bedroom on the main floor, he wished she'd ask him to share a bed with her again. He escorted her upstairs to the guest bedroom, where she'd spent the previous night, and set her bag down on the bed she'd made.

"Thank you, Sully," Charley said.

"No problem, come back downstairs whenever you feel like it. I'll rustle up supper."

"Okay, I will."

Sully left her, and by the time he was in the downstairs foyer, he heard the shower running in her bathroom. He paused and looked up at the stained glass window. Lavender columbines would always remind him of Charley.

The yellow ones outside might indicate their friendship. To him, the purple ones represented her resolve to figure out who had killed her mother and who was plaguing her. And red columbines symbolizing love and passion? Oh yeah. Every time Charley looked at him, her sparkling blue eyes captured him. Each time he touched her, energy crackled.

Leaving the foyer and walking down the hall to the kitchen, Sully wondered what it would be like to kiss her. Man, he sure wanted to find out. Entering his bedroom, he pulled off his shirt and flung it on his bed. What would it be like to toss Charley into his bed? Instinct told him it would be so good.

He pulled off his boots, and when her shower stopped, he stepped into his bathroom. A quick, cold shower did little to cool the heat Charley had ignited in him. She was a sexy temptress, from her pretty brunette head to her dainty feet. Pulling on a tee shirt and pair of sweatpants, he padded barefoot out to the kitchen. He turned on a flatscreen at one end of a countertop and opened the fridge. Placing a package of hamburger on the quartz island in the center of the kitchen, he heated the oven and layered a baking sheet with French fries. Placing the fries in the oven to bake, he was making smash burgers as the evening news came on.

Sully stopped and turned to the flatscreen as the news-caster's first story caught his attention. The body of a second young woman who had been missing from the Old Colorado City neighborhood, close to where Charley lived, had been discovered in yet another underground cave-like tunnel. The El Paso County coroner had taken possession of the body, and the cause of death was not available at this time.

"Damn," Sully muttered under his breath.

Hearing movement behind him, he turned. Charley stood fixated on the flatscreen. Her long hair fell in glossy waves around her beautiful face. Her blue eyes were wide, and her full lips a soft pink. She wore a purple sweatshirt with a Fleming Flowers logo imprinted above a bouquet of the Colorado state flower. As Charley walked closer to the

TV, Sully saw the writing on the back of her sweatshirt. *Discovered in 1820 on Pikes Peak, the Rocky Mountain Columbine, with its rich aroma attracts bees, hummingbirds, and butterflies. The lavender petals are a symbol of the sky, the white cup represents the snow-capped mountains, and the gold center symbolizes Colorado's gold mining history.* With the sweatshirt, Charley wore a pair of snug purple gym shorts. Her legs were long and shapely, and her small feet were bare, with shiny lavender toenails.

CHAPTER NINE

"*I* knew her," Charley said, coming to a stop near the island. "We had a couple of college classes together." Turning from the flatscreen to Sully, she said, "Her name was Heather Mason."

"They found her earlier today," Sully said, placing hamburger patties into a cast-iron pan on the stove. "They think she's been dead for at least three weeks. Toadflax was in her hand."

"Toadflax is a noxious weed. It's typically found in degraded areas like untended lots, gravel pits, or along forgotten roadsides," Charley said, turning to him.

"Right, I keep toadflax out of my pastures," Sully said as she turned to him.

"Toadflax was in Grace Lightner's hand too." Looking back at the TV, Charley said, "Heather was a nice girl. She was studying agriculture. We had lunch together a few times on the UCCS campus," she said, referring to the University of Colorado at Colorado Springs.

"I'm sorry for the loss of your friend," Sully said. "An on-the-scene reporter said some cave explorers found her body. One of them said she had marks around her neck."

"Just like Grace Lightner." Charley shivered at the recent and terrifying memory. "I wonder if the Cave Killer has a tattoo of a scorpion. I tried to pull off the ski mask of the man who attacked me, but I only got it as far as his chin. In the process of fighting against him, I tore the neck of his hoodie. He had a scorpion tattoo on his collarbone." She touched the left side of her collarbone to show Sully where it was.

"Scorpions are predators," Sully said as she grimaced. "You told the police about the tattoo, right?"

"Yes," Charley said softly and nodded.

"Good." Sully clicked off the flatscreen and said, "Have a seat at the island because smash burgers and fries are coming your way."

Charley smiled at the handsome man who was cooking for her. No man had ever cooked for her until today. Sully gave her a sexy, green-eyed wink, and when he smiled, it showed his straight white teeth. A white tee shirt hugged his broad shoulders and chest and a pair of black sweatpants clung to his muscular legs. From the thick black hair on his head to the sprinkle of black hair on his toes, Sully was the most attractive man she'd ever laid eyes on. Just looking at him made her heart race and skin pop out in goose bumps. When she had wrapped her arms around him on the horse and on his motorcycle, she could almost forget her new fear of men.

"What have you got to drink?" she asked. Then, before he could answer, she remembered. "Bottled water and beer."

"Right," he replied with a chuckle. "Both are chilling in the fridge."

"I'll get us two beers," Charley said.

"Sounds good to me."

Shortly after she brought the beer to the island, he placed burgers on plates. She'd spied ketchup and mustard in the fridge, retrieved the condiments, and then took a seat on one of the barstools. Sully scooped up fries and piled some on both their plates. Setting the plates down, he sat on the barstool beside her. Taking a bite of her burger, her eyes widened. It was delicious.

Swallowing, Charley said, "This is the best burger I've ever eaten."

"I can't take much credit," Sully said. "It's Triple C Ranch-Central beef."

"It's absolutely scrumptious."

"Stick around a while and I'll barbecue you a steak," Sully said.

"I'd like that."

They talked and ate and had another beer. Before Charley knew it, her phone said it was almost eight o'clock. Making Sully stay put, she insisted on being the one to clean up and stacked their plates in the dishwasher. Then they moseyed into the den, sunk into the comfortable leather sofa, and Sully found a movie that made them both laugh. Afterward, they watched a news update. Heather's parents were asking for anyone with information about the murder of their daughter to please come forward. The newscaster pointed out that the killer of the other recent murder victim, Grace Lightner, was still at large. Then he reminded viewers of the murder of the Fleming Flowers shop owner in a nearby neighborhood. He signed off with a question to viewers: *What was happening in Old Colorado City*?

"Wanna sleep with me tonight?" Sully asked. Charley turned her head to look at him and slowly nodded. "C'mere, Charley," he whispered and stretched out an arm to her.

Charley scooted across the sofa cushion to him, and his strong arms closed around her. She tilted her chin up to look at him, and his head lowered. When his mouth touched hers for the very first time, it was as electrifying as when her hand had touched his for the first time. He wrapped both arms around her and pulled her closer. When his lips parted, hers did too. His strong hand gently cupped her cheek and then he broke the kiss. His green eyes smoldered, and Charley wondered what she'd gotten herself into with this man. Instinct told her he was as experienced as she was naïve. She trembled and clutched the front of his tee shirt.

"I barely know you, Sully."

"And nothing is going to happen tonight," he told her. "Okay?"

"Okay."

With a confusing mixture of regret and relief, she relaxed, and they finished watching the news. When Charley yawned, Sully clicked off the flatscreen and grasped her hand. Standing, he tugged her off the sofa and led her down the hall to his bedroom. Flipping back a thick comforter on the king-size bed, he left her standing near a nightstand and walked around to the other side of his bed.

"That's your side and this is my side," he said, crawling into bed.

"I'll try to stay on my side." Charley crawled in after him and drew the comforter and the sheet up to her chin. "And I'll try not to scream."

"I don't know about staying on my side, but I won't scream."

When Sully chuckled, a giggle escaped Charley. She rolled onto her side, facing him. He had stretched out on his back with his hands stacked under his head. He winked at her and closed his eyes. She lay with her eyes open for several minutes until she heard his even breathing. When she closed her eyes, her mind plagued her with the murder of her mother. Then she saw the destruction to her car and her vandalized apartment and the flower shop. The body of her college classmate, under a tarp at the entrance to a cave, flashed like it had on the news. It grew darker, and from behind a copse of trees, a faceless killer stepped into the open, shocking Charley. As he stalked toward her, she tried to run but her feet wouldn't move. When his hands snatched her throat, she jerked backward and cried out.

"Help!"

"Charley," came the deep masculine voice beside her. "Wake up."

It took her a few seconds. "Sully?"

"Yeah. You're safe."

Charley rolled into his arms and clung to him. Her heart

pounded frantically, and she could hardly breathe. She'd had variations of this nightmare every night since the assault and murder. But only these last two nights had someone been there to catch her when she fell out of the terror and into reality. She took a deep, staccato breath trying to calm herself.

"Sorry," she whispered against his shoulder, her arm around him.

"It's okay," he said, his hand flattening to her back as he held her to his muscular chest.

"What time is it?"

"About one, I think."

"I should go and let you sleep."

"Where would you go in the middle of the night with no vehicle?"

"I don't know." She detested bothering him and feeling scared. "Back to sleep?"

"Good answer." With a gentle kiss to her forehead, Sully loosened his grip and patted her hip. "Roll over."

When Charley rolled over, she felt Sully's hard body come up solidly against her back. His strong arm looped around her waist, pulling her closer. This felt good. Safe and secure. It felt so good in fact, she closed her eyes. She'd never slept with a man. But now that she'd slept with this man, she could imagine doing so every night. Where would something like that lead?

"G'night," she whispered.

"Night."

CHAPTER TEN

*W*hen Sully woke, he reached for the woman who had spent most of the night in his arms.

"Charley?"

No answer. No sign of her either. Never had he spent the night with a woman with whom he'd not had sex. But with Charley it was worth it just to hold her soft, feminine body to his. She smelled sweet and fresh like flowers. When he'd kissed her mouth, her supple lips had parted, and when he'd wrapped his arm around her, she'd snuggled closer. He wanted that and more. But only from Charley. Only from Charley? Really? Where was she?

As Sully sat up on the side of the bed, he smelled bacon. He smiled. After pulling on a sweatshirt and jeans, he made his way to the kitchen and feasted his eyes. Facing away from him at the sink, she'd pulled her hair up into a pony-tail. Her sweatshirt lay over the back of a barstool, leaving her in a white crop top. There were several inches of skin showing between the hem of the snug top and the waist of her gym shorts, giving him a full view of her sexy fanny. How great would it be to have this woman here with him every morning? She whirled around as he strode into the kitchen.

"Hi," she said with a pearly white smile. "Have a seat at

the island because bacon and eggs are coming your way," she said similarly to him as he had to her the previous evening. "Coffee too. Black, as I recall."

Grinning, Sully took a seat at the island. Charley brought him a cup of coffee and set her own mug down beside his. Then she went to the stove and returned with two plates of crisp bacon and scrambled eggs. After she'd placed the plates on the island, Sully caught her hand and tugged her between his knees.

"Thank you," he said and gave her a quick kiss.

"The least I could do," she whispered.

He placed his hands on her hips and his eyes dipped from her blue ones. At the touch of his gaze, her breasts beaded underneath her tight top. Lower still, her indented belly button peeked at him over the top of her gym shorts. With a groan and a pat to her hip, he reluctantly let her go and she sat down beside him.

Sully took a bite of the eggs and said, "So you're not only beautiful, you also can cook."

"Thank you." A blush had heightened the color on Charley's ivory cheeks, and she said, "You're not only handsome, you can cook too."

Sully smiled his acknowledgment. As they ate, he made a point of not turning on the flatscreen. In his opinion, they'd had enough news for now. Still, he couldn't help but wonder if the murders of the young women in Old Colorado City had any ties to the attack on Charley. Had those women been raped? Was the assault on Charley related in any way to the vandalism to her car, her apartment, or her shop? On that score, he knew Charley was facing daunting cleaning tasks in Old Colorado City.

"How are you going to tackle your apartment and flower shop?" he asked.

"With a bucket, a mop, and a vacuum cleaner." When Charley swallowed her last bite of breakfast, she took her plate to the sink. Coming back for Sully's plate, she rinsed both and put them into the dishwasher. Turning to him, she said, "I don't want to keep you from the retail business you mentioned, so I can call an Uber to take me into town."

"Nope, I'll take you. My business is closed on Sundays and Mondays."

"My shop is always closed on Sunday and Monday too," she told him with a look of surprise on her pretty face. "I'll get my stuff together."

Charley excused herself and retrieved her bag of belongings. She used the guest powder room on the main level to get ready to go back into town. Sully stepped into his boots and grabbed a button-down shirt to take with him. When he met up with her in the kitchen again, she was wearing blue jeans and white tennis shoes with her sweatshirt. As simple an outfit as that was, she made it look stunning. And with a flick of her long braid, she oozed sexy and sassy. She swung her purse over her shoulder, Sully grabbed her overnight bag, and they set off for his truck. They drove onto the main road, and when they neared Triple C Ranch-South, Sully slowed his truck to have a look. Ponderosa pines swayed in a gentle breeze, the stained glass door was tightly shut, and the rocking chairs on the covered porch were as welcoming as always.

"Everything appears calm and quiet," Sully said.

Charley agreed, and forty minutes later, in Old Colorado City, Sully turned onto Colorado Avenue. Reaching Charley's corner, he drove them up the hill to her duplex. Parking the truck, he grabbed her bag. She fished her keys out of her purse, and he followed her to the small porch of the duplex.

"The doorknob is bent and the lock scratched, but at least the door is still shut." Relief sounded in Charley's voice.

"Even so, it would be a good idea to get the locks changed on your duplex and shop," Sully said. "I'd be happy to replace them for you."

"I can't ask you to do that," she said. Stepping into the foyer of her apartment, the mess of the plants assailed them.

Charley sighed, and walking forward, she shook her head, making her ponytail dance. "I can call a locksmith."

"How about this," Sully began, "you tell me how many new locks you need, and I'll go get them. I can work on the doors and keep you company while you clean."

In the living room, Charley turned to him, her big blue eyes filled with concern. "Sully, you don't have to do that."

"I wouldn't offer if I didn't want to do it." He set her bag on the sofa and picked up the wingback chair. Setting the chair upright, he asked, "How many locks do you need?"

"There's only one door to this apartment." Charley scratched her head and said, "Downstairs there are two locks. On the front door and on a side door into the shop."

"I'll be back in less than an hour with three sturdy new lock and doorknob combinations," Sully said as Charley picked up her purse and pulled out her wallet. He placed one hand over hers, and with his other hand, tilted up her chin to look up at him. "I'll take dinner with you sometime instead of your money."

"Deal," Charley said softly. She looked vulnerable and a little scared standing in the middle of her plant-strewn living room.

"You wanna come with me?"

"No, no." She shook her head. "I should start cleaning up."

"Do you need anything else?"

"A shower curtain?"

"No problem. Will you be okay until I get back?"

"Sure," she said, taking a nervous step toward him.

Sully pulled her into his arms. "Do you have a gun, Charley?"

"No, I detest guns," she reminded him, her slender arms wrapping around his waist. "I'll never own a gun. A gun killed my mother."

"Come with me to get the locks."

"No, really I'll be fine." She stepped back and said, "I'll

put the chain across the door and stay right here until you get back."

Sully reluctantly agreed. But he made sure she slid the chain lock across the door before leaving her. What would she say when he told her about his retail business? He put that out of his mind and drove to the nearest big box store to get the new doorknobs with locks and keys. When he returned, she looked through the peephole before letting him in.

She'd been busy. Her apartment's countertops and floors were clean. She said she'd stripped her bed and put the dirty linens into an apartment-sized washer. A fresh comforter and sheets were already on the bed. A black garbage bag held the plants she couldn't save, and she was repotting a lone white orchid she hoped to salvage.

Charley washed her hands and stopped to look at what he'd bought. She agreed the locks he'd bought were perfect and so was the shower curtain. As he installed the new front door lock, she made ham and cheese sandwiches for the two of them. After pouring iced tea into glasses, they took their plates into the living room. Charley turned on the noon news and Sully wished she hadn't. Another body of a young woman had been found in a cave-like tunnel. This time, the grisly discovery was made by police dogs and police searching for clues to the two previous murders. The coroner's guess was this third victim, by the name of Yolonda Garcia, had been dead for a couple of weeks. In her hand was toadflax.

"Most folks, even locals, aren't familiar with the history of Old Colorado City," the male television reporter, standing on Colorado Avenue not far from Charley's flower shop, was saying. *"Established in 1859, now part of Colorado Springs, Old Colorado City used to be the wild side of town. Once home to saloons, gambling halls, brothels, and prostitutes, the law didn't exist. But what labeled this frontier town as peculiar were the countless cave-like tunnels. Those cave tunnels do still exist."* The reporter waved a hand, indicating the underground

passageways were everywhere in the vicinity. *"These caves and tunnels were originally dug in a time of conflict between Anglo-American pioneers and Native Americans. During raids by the Arapaho and Cheyenne, the pioneers used the tunnels as escape routes between houses and businesses. Over the years, many of the houses were converted into storefronts. But the caves and tunnels were left intact and, running rampant, some of them eventually connected legitimate businesses to secret, sleazy dealings underneath the streets. Until recently, it was thought that this seedy underworld was long gone. The Cave Killer has proven otherwise."*

"I didn't know about those cave tunnels, did you?" Sully asked.

"No. I had no idea at all," Charley said in obvious shock. "Yolanda, the latest murder victim, was in a class with Heather and me," she told him while shaking her head. "Grace Lightner was strangled a month ago. They think Heather was killed three weeks ago, and now Yolanda was killed two weeks ago. Somebody is killing girls a week apart."

A knock sounded at the front door, and Charley jumped.

"I'll get it," Sully said and got off the couch. He crossed the room and opened the door to a middle-aged man in a white shirt and dark suit. "May I help you?"

"Sorry to disturb you. I'm Detective Burt Groves from the Colorado Springs Police Department," the officer said and showed him a badge. "Is Charlotte Cooper here?"

"Yes," Sully replied and allowed him into the apartment.

"I'm Charlotte Cooper," Charley said, coming forward.

"Miss Cooper, I'm in charge of the cases involving three females, all in their twenties, who have been recently murdered here in Old Colorado City." Groves, probably in his early fifties, had a kind face and a crease of concern across his forehead. "I am also aware of your mother's murder and an assault on you. I'm here in hopes you can tell me about those incidents to help us ascertain if there is a possible link between the crimes."

"Of course," Charley said and turned to Sully. "Detective Groves, this is my friend, Sullivan Custis."

Detective Groves paused to look at Sully and asked, "Is your father, Sullivan Owen Custis, the former sheriff of El Paso County?"

"Yes, sir," Sully said. "That's him."

"Please tell Owen that his ol' buddy Burt Groves said hello."

Sully nodded as the connection clicked. "I've heard my dad mention your name," he said, shaking hands with his father's friend. "I'll be sure to tell him."

"Please, sit down, Detective Groves," Charley said and swung her hand toward the wingback chair. He took a seat, and Charley sat down on the sofa. When she looked at Sully and smiled, he sat on the sofa too.

"First of all, I'm sorry for your loss," Detective Groves said to Charley. Then he asked several questions and took some notes. "I know you said the suspect wore a ski mask and hoodie, but is there anything specific that could help us identify him?"

"Yes, as I told the police officers who showed up here that day, he had a tattoo of a scorpion on his collarbone." Charley once again indicated on herself the approximate location.

"Right, I have that in my report." Detective Groves nodded and listened intently as they told him about the vandalism to Charley's car, duplex, and shop. "Whether we have one murderer or multiple murderers, you fit the profile of the young women strangled. Be careful."

"I know." Charley flinched. "I'll be careful."

"Do you have any suspects in the death of Charlotte Fleming?" Sully asked.

Before the detective could answer, a second knock came at the duplex door. Once again, Sully got up to answer it. A man with freckles and bright red hair, not nearly as tall nor as muscular as Sully, stood on the small porch. His brown eyes were small, and crescent-shaped lines dented his sallow cheeks framing a thin-lipped mouth. Sully guessed the guy to be about fifteen years his senior.

"Is Charley here?" the wiry man asked.

"Leon?" Charley called from the living room, evidently having recognized the voice.

"Yes," the man said, and as Sully stepped back, he entered the apartment. "Hi." He raised his freckled right hand and stood somewhat gawkily in the living room. "I just stopped by the shop. What happened to it?"

"Someone vandalized it," Charley said as she and the detective both stood.

At that point, Detective Groves thanked them for their time, gave Charley his card, and said he'd be in touch. Sully walked him out to his car. When Sully asked again, the detective shared with him that they had no viable suspects in the shooting. As they spoke, he confided that not only had the three young women in the cave tunnel deaths been strangled, but what had not been released to the press was the fact the victims had stab wounds to the heart.

"Thank you for the information," Sully said.

"You're welcome." Detective Groves handed Sully his card and asked him to call if anything else should happen. "In the meantime, remind Miss Cooper to be careful. As I told her a few minutes ago, she fits the profile of the strangler's victims."

"Right," Sully said, shaking hands with the detective. "Thanks again." Then heading back to the apartment, he heard the guy named Leon speaking.

"Yeah," he said to Charley as she stood a few feet away from him in her living room. "Your shop is so messed up, you gotta rename it *Little Shop of Horrors*."

With a strained glance at Sully over the somewhat insensitive joke, Charley said quietly, "I'll consult my business manager about that."

Seeing Sully, he asked Charley, "You have a business manager?"

"Yes, I do. Leon Lefeld, this is Sullivan Custis, a friend of mine." Then with a smile at Sully, she added, "Leon works part-time for me."

Sully gave Lerfeld a dismissive nod and said to Charley, "Let's go see about putting the new locks and knobs on the doors downstairs."

"Is that how the bad guy got in?" Lerfeld asked, seemingly becoming more attuned to the seriousness of the situation. "He broke the locks?"

"Yes," Charley replied. Then turning to Sully, she said, "Leon took a horticulture class with Heather, Yolanda, and me."

"I can't believe Heather and Yolanda are gone," Lerfeld said and bowed his head.

"Neither can I," Charley agreed softly. "Leon, Sully owns the ranch next to mine out in the country."

"Oh," Lerfeld said. "Did you get to look around your ranch the other day?"

"Yes, it's wonderful, and I met my new neighbor," she said and smiled at Sully.

Sully smiled back at her and grabbed up the plastic bag holding two new locks with the drill and screwdriver set he'd had in the back of his truck. He headed out of the apartment, with Charley locking the door and Lerfeld following them down the sidewalk. In the shop, Charley and Lerfeld got to work cleaning up while Sully tackled the front door. Sully wondered how it was that Leon Lerfeld *just stopped by the shop* when it was closed.

"You live around here, Leon?" Sully asked after he'd installed the lock on the front door.

"Yes, I moved back here after spending twelve years near Pueblo, Colorado. I inherited the house of my uncle who raised me," Lerfeld replied, a broom and dustpan in hand. "He left me a monthly income as well, so I've been taking some long-overdue college classes." Then, as if he knew what Sully was getting at, he said, "My house is only a few blocks from here. I was heading to lunch and planned on asking Charley to join me."

"My mother was slowing down and hired Leon a few months ago. After she passed, Leon stopped by a few times when the shop was closed to see if I'd like to go to lunch."

"Did you two meet at the university or in the flower shop?" Sully asked.

"The university. That's how Charley knew I'd be qualified to work here, and she recommended me to her mother," Lerfeld said. "I attended Charlotte Fleming's funeral to pay my respects to her, of course."

Sully frowned. "Of course." Sully suspected Lerfeld had become interested in Charley at the university and hoped that in addition to the job, the lunches and funeral attendance would be a way to ingratiate himself to her.

"I'm happy to help Charley anyway I can," Lerfeld added.

Sully clearly saw lust in the red-haired man's dull eyes as he ogled the gorgeous girl, but Charley seemed oblivious. Lerfeld was too old for Charley in Sully's opinion. But Sully said no more and headed to the side door to remove the old lock and doorknob. With Lerfeld helping Charley, by the time Sully was finished his work, they had the shop returned to order.

"I've lost some inventory, but at least things are somewhat back to normal," Charley said with a look around. "Thank you, Leon. You're a lifesaver."

"My pleasure," he said. "It'll be dark soon, I should get going."

"Do you need a ride?" Charley asked.

"No, thanks. I rode the scooter my uncle bought for me before he died," Lerfeld said. With a glance at Sully, he added, "I can't get Charley to take a ride with me. She said she's afraid of motorcycles."

"Is that right?" Sully asked and cocked a brow at Charley. They'd ridden for miles and miles out in the country on his Harley.

"That's right," Lerfeld said with a somewhat defeated

shrug. "Well, it's Monday, so I guess I'll see you tomorrow, Charley."

"See you tomorrow, Leon," Charley said and walked him out of the shop. Then returning to the open doorway, she gave him a goodbye wave.

"So, you're afraid of motorcycles?" Sully teased her as she twirled around to him.

"Thanks for not blowing my cover," Charley said with a grin and shut the door. "I don't want to encourage Leon. I think he has a little crush on me."

"Ya think?"

"I think so. Therefore, I keep distance between us because—" With a flirtatious grin and lifting her left shoulder, she added, "I'm not interested in Leon."

"Is there somebody else you're interested in?"

Charley boldly let her blue eyes zip down his body and back up, raised her chin, and started past him. "Maybe."

Sully caught her arm and pulled her to him. "Who?"

Charley giggled. "None of your business, country boy."

"Tell me, city slicker."

"Maybe the guy I slept with the past couple of nights."

When Sully lowered his head, Charley's arms slid around his neck. She stood on tiptoes, between his booted feet, as his mouth came down on hers. A loud rap on the window of the front door was jarring. Charley whirled out of Sully's arms, and they both saw Lerfeld staring at them from the other side of the glass.

"Forgot my cell phone," Lerfeld said through the door.

"Okay," Charley said, and letting go of Sully, she spotted the phone on a counter. She got it and walked to the front of the shop. Sully was ahead of her and opened the door.

"Thanks," Lerfeld said to Charley.

"You're welcome," she replied. "Have a nice evening, Leon."

"Right," he mumbled, and when Sully closed the door, he caught the envious glare Lerfeld directed at him.

"Yeah, make that a *big* crush on you," Sully said.

"Maybe now he knows his interest isn't returned."

"Maybe."

They locked the shop doors and walked back up the hill to the duplex. Sully asked if the police had taken stock of the other apartment once occupied by her mother on the right side of the duplex. Charley said they had done so. They had dusted for prints in both apartments to no avail. She had since packed up her mother's belongings. Except for a few sentimental effects, her mother's clothing and other personal belongings had been donated to charity. Back in her apartment, Charley gave Sully a bottle of water and the remote to the flatscreen.

"After cleaning up my shop, I need a shower," she said. "Thank goodness I have a new shower curtain. If you'll wait for me, I'll treat you to dinner."

I'd be happy to wait for you as long as it takes, Sully thought. "Sure."

CHAPTER ELEVEN

*W*ith her thoughts on the devastatingly attractive man in her living room, Charley hurried through her shower and blow-dried her hair. Dabbing on mascara and lipstick, she put on a short black dress and black stilettos. When she joined him, Sully stood. He'd traded his sweatshirt for a button-down shirt, and it was his turn to look her up and down. She felt her cheeks heat, and when he grinned, she did a little curtsy.

"Damn," Sully said in a husky voice, hands splaying on his hips.

"What do you feel like eating?" she asked him.

His grin grew cocky, and he said, "You."

"Sully!" She wasn't a hundred percent sure what he meant, but a blast-fire of bashfulness heated her cheeks. She swallowed and asked, "How about a steak?"

"Sounds good." Sully held out the extra keys to her that had come with the new doorknobs and locks.

"I don't have anyone to give the extra keys to. Why don't you keep them for now? You know, in case I lock myself out."

Sully took her hand and locked the door behind them. In the parking area just outside of her apartment, he opened the passenger's door of the truck. But before Charley got in, he pulled her to him for a kiss. Charley's heart raced as his muscular arms circled her and molded her to his hard body. She rose on tiptoes, and when his tongue touched her lips, she opened her mouth. His hand slipped under her long, loose hair to the nape of her neck, and her tongue met his. His lips melted hers, and when he gently broke the kiss, she turned and slid into his truck. Ten minutes down Colorado Avenue put them in the heartbeat of Colorado Springs.

"What's your favorite steakhouse?" she asked.

"Ever been to Southside Suzy's?"

"Once for lunch on my twenty-first birthday."

"How long ago was that?"

She arched a brow. "Four years."

"So, you're twenty-five."

"Yes. And you're—"

"Thirty-two," he said, pulling into a parking space. "Ever married?"

"Never," she said. "You?"

"Never. Engaged?"

"No, and I've never lived with anyone."

"Same here," Sully said with a smile. "Yeehaw."

"Yeehaw." Charley giggled.

Sully turned off the engine and hopped out of his truck. He came around to her side and helped her out. He looped her arm through his, and they went into the busy restaurant. Folks from all walks of life from Colorado Springs and beyond dined at this well-known eatery.

"Hi Vince," Sully said to the semi-retired, older gentleman behind the bar.

"Hey, Sully boy, how're you?" Vincent South asked.

"Great. Think you have room for us somewhere for dinner?"

"I bet we do," he replied as his daughter, Suzy, walked toward them.

"Hi, Sully, good to see you," Suzy said. She had short,

spiked hair, a sprinkling of freckles across her nose, and a big smile.

On the way here, Sully had told Charley that Suzy co-owned the establishment with her father. Her boyfriend, Richard, was the undisputed leader of the Sons of Steel motorcycle club and a longtime friend of Sully's and the Cooper family as well.

"Suzy, good to see you too," Sully replied. "This is my friend, Charley. She owns the ranch across the highway and down the road from Triple C Ranch-East."

"Any friend of the Coopers is a friend of ours," Richard, tall and slim with coal black hair and beard and wearing his motorcycle colors, said. Charley instinctively figured Richard was a good friend to have. But if you were a foe, he and his club were probably a force to be reckoned with. "Welcome, Charley."

"Thank you, and nice to meet you all," Charley replied to Richard with a smile that included Suzy and Vince.

"Not just a friend of the Coopers, she's their first cousin," Sully told them.

"A double welcome, Charley," Suzy said. She picked up menus and led them to a quiet table in the corner of the busy restaurant. "Enjoy."

They ordered salads, steaks, and baked potatoes. Just before their entrees were served, Sully told Charley the beef came from Chase Cooper's ranch. Then their salad plates were cleared away and they enjoyed every bite of their delicious meals. Deciding they were too full for dessert, Sully grabbed the check before Charley could. When she protested, he said maybe she could pay sometime in the future.

"Promise?" Charley asked, hoping that meant he was counting on seeing her again.

"Sure," he said with a chuckle and a wink.

Sully tipped the waitress and promised Suzy and Richard they'd be back again. Charley didn't miss the envious stares of other women at the bar as Sully gave Vince a wave as they exited the popular establishment. Sully held Charley's hand on the way to his truck and opened her door. Heading back to her place, when he drove up the hill to her duplex, she regretted having to say good night to him. Turning off the truck engine, he came around to her side and walked her to her front door.

"Do you feel safe staying here tonight?" he asked.

"I think so," she said as he unlocked her door. She stepped into her apartment, and when she turned to him in the small foyer, she asked, "I don't have any beer, but would you like to have a glass of wine?"

"Sure."

Sully locked the front door and made his way into the living room. On the Formica countertop of the half-wall separating the living room from the kitchen, the white orchid looked like it might survive. From a kitchen cabinet, Charley brought out a bottle of red wine and placed it on the counter. She set a corkscrew next to the bottle, and carrying two wineglasses, walked around the corner of the kitchen to where Sully stood. He picked up the wine bottle and corkscrew, and they settled themselves on the sofa. Sully opened the wine, and Charley clicked on the flatscreen. Chatting, they had finished their glasses of wine when the late news came on.

The leading story was grim.

"Yes," Burt Groves stated to a news reporter. "Another body was found in a cave late today here in Old Colorado City."

"This victim brings the strangling deaths of young females to four. Correct?" the reporter asked and held a microphone toward the detective.

"I didn't say it was strangulation," Groves clarified.

"This young woman's name is—" The reporter glanced down at a note in his hand and said, "Amy Ramirez. Is that right?"

"No comment," the detective said with a fierce frown.

Turning to the camera, he said, "We are urging the public to lock their doors and not go out alone at night. Please be careful."

"But because of the toadflax in the victim's hand, we can assume the Cave Killer has struck again," the reporter prodded.

"No comment," Detective Groves repeated and walked away from him.

"What did I tell you?" Charley said and looked at Sully. "The Cave Killer is murdering a girl once a week!"

"Why don't you come home with me?" Sully said. "You won't have to think about being safe in the country. You'll know you're safe with me."

Charley shook her head. "I need to open my shop tomorrow morning, and you said your business is open Tuesday through Saturday as well."

"So don't open tomorrow," Sully said and clicked off the flatscreen. "Stay closed until they catch this guy."

"But I was planning to call the shop about my Mini Cooper tomorrow."

"I guarantee you your car won't be ready yet."

"Then I'll need a rental car."

"Make your calls from my house. I'll get you wherever you need to go, Charley."

"What about Leon?" she asked and nervously ran the fingers of both hands along her scalp, brushing her hair away from her face. "He'll be back first thing in the morning."

"Text him. Let him know you're not going to open right away."

"I haven't made that decision yet."

"Okay." Sully paused, looked her square in the eye, and added, "In any case, don't give Lerfeld a new key to your duplex or shop."

"He's never had a key to either one. But why do you say that?"

"Just being careful like Detective Groves suggested."

"What about your store?"

"I'll let Roy know I won't be in," Sully said. "Randy is taking a small group out to ride tomorrow. But Roy can handle things in the store without us."

"Will you stay here with me tonight, Sully?"

CHAPTER TWELVE

*S*ully smiled at the beautiful woman with the wild brown hair and glittering blue eyes. On the sofa beside him with her bare legs curled under her short black dress, she smiled. He knew how soft her lips were, and he wanted to do so much more than just sleep beside her.

"I could be persuaded," he said.

"What would it take to persuade you?"

He crooked a finger, and she scooted closer. Sully pulled her soft, feminine, sweet-smelling body into his arms. He kissed her, and she melted into him. Lying back lengthwise on the sofa, he tugged her on top of him. Her elbows braced her on the outsides of his shoulders as her legs slipped between his. He cupped the nape of her neck with one hand and flattened his other hand to her back. With a slight pressure to her neck, she lowered her mouth to his. Their lips touched, and he groaned when her tongue met his. Sully moved his hands down her slender back and massaged the cheeks of her sexy derrière. She wiggled and softly moaned. As their kiss deepened, he tugged up the hem of her dress. When his hand touched the silk of her bikini panties, a groan of desire escaped him.

"Charley," he whispered. "Tell me no."

"Mmm, Sully," Charley murmured in his ear. "Yes."

Gently, Sully rolled her off him toward the back cushion of the overstuffed sofa. When he leaned forward, with some of his weight shifting onto her, she gasped.

"Are you okay?" he asked.

"I don't know."

"What's wrong?"

"Nothing."

"Okay." But when Sully leaned down to kiss her, she stiffened again. "Come on," he said and rolled off the sofa. Standing over her in admiration, he thought she was surely a goddess come to life. Her long hair was fanned out on a sofa cushion, and her royal-blue eyes held him captive. Her snug black dress was hiked up to the edge of her panties, and her long legs lay gracefully exposed. He held out his hand. "You go to bed. Alone."

"I'm sorry." Charley sat up, took his hand, and stood. "I don't know why I pulled back."

"Might be a little too soon for you to have sex again after the attempted assault."

"I've never had—" She stopped and stared at the floor.

"Never had—" Placing a finger under her chin, he tilted her head up. "Sex?"

"No. Never." Innocently, she asked, "Have you?"

"Well, hell yes," Sully replied. He chuckled and wrapped her in his arms. He rested his chin against the top of her head and smiled. Damn. As if he didn't like this gorgeous girl enough already, she was a virgin. Charley could be all his. He would happily teach her everything. "We just met. We don't have to rush anything, Charley. If you promise to lock your door, I'll leave."

"No!" She instantly leaned back and looked up at him. "Please don't go." When Sully hesitated, she whispered timidly, "Can't you stay and sleep with me like you did last night?"

"Yes, I can," he replied. Charley's smile stole Sully's breath away. How many guys would gladly take his place with this woman? Countless. One had recently tried. He'd met two face-to-face who wanted to. He'd noticed several guys admiring her at Southside Suzy's. Those thoughts put a crease between his brows until he saw the uncertainty in Charley's eyes. Wiping the frown off his face, he said, "Let's go fall asleep."

Charley slipped into her bathroom as he walked into her bedroom. He switched on an overhead light and stripped off his long-sleeved shirt. Taking off his boots, he hesitated in removing his jeans. But he had slept beside her twice now, once in sweatpants and once in his boxer shorts, so he stripped off his jeans too. Tossing back the comforter, he stretched out on her bed, stacked his hands behind his head, and closed his eyes. All he saw was Charley.

She had twirled around to face him at her ranch. She'd been angry as she told Rod Vaughn to leave her alone. She had sat shaking and terrified in his upstairs bedroom. She'd felt so good wrapped around him on the Harley. She was sad upon seeing her apartment and shop vandalized. She'd been patient with Leon Lerfeld who had a crush on her. She was smiling and laughing as they ate dinner at Southside Suzy's. Charley exuded a thrilling combination of naïve innocent vulnerability and sensuous sex appeal when asking Sully to stay the night.

"Are you asleep?" Charley whispered.

"No," Sully said. When he opened his eyes, she brought her gaze up his chest from where it had been below the waist of his boxers. Standing beside the bed, she wore a pale pink, thigh-length shift. The nipples of her full breasts were visible against the ivory lace across the top of the gown, and he glimpsed the outline of bikini panties under the thin fabric. He groaned and flung his forearm over his eyes. "Please douse the light, city slicker."

"Okay, country boy." She did as he asked and crawled into bed.

Sully turned onto his side, facing her, and she rolled into his arms. Careful not to put any of his weight on her, he kissed her sweet mouth. She wrapped an arm around his back, and he settled his left hand on her hip. She wiggled closer, and he moved his hand up her ribcage. His fingers met with the side of her breast, and when his thumb caressed her nipple, Charley moaned.

Damn, she was a red-hot fire in his blood, and his body quickly hardened in response. She rolled onto her back, filling Sully's hand with her right breast. He eased her gown up and slid his hand over the naked skin of her flat stomach. What happened to falling asleep? She tightened her arms around him, and his fingers found her breast again. He caressed her right breast and then her left before trailing his hand down her ribcage. His brain warned him to stop as he hooked his thumb into her panties. Then Charley opened her mouth, and her tongue touched his lips. Sliding two fingers into the front of her panties brought forth an urgent moan from her. But when he moved his leg over the top of hers, her entire body stiffened.

Sully stopped and said, "Roll over." Charley did so, and he hugged her sweet body protectively to his chest. "G'night."

She swallowed a gulp and whispered, "Good night."

CHAPTER THIRTEEN

harley woke to the sun spilling in around the edges
of the shade in her bedroom window.

"Sully?" she said, not finding the handsome rancher in
bed with her.

"Out here," came his deep voice from the living room.

Charley rolled out of bed and looked at the clock, which
read eight a.m. She heard Sully's voice in the living room as
he spoke to someone. She made a quick call. Still in her
nightgown, she rounded the corner of her bedroom and
walked down the short hall. She saw Sully standing barefoot
at the plate glass window of her living room. With his cell
phone to his ear, he wore only his jeans. Turning to her, he
smiled and she nearly swooned. There was a day's growth of
beard on his handsome face. His chest was broad like his
shoulders, with a smattering of masculine black hair. He had
a six-pack of muscles spread across his torso. Below his
indented navel, a trail of black hair disappeared into his
snug jeans.

"Morning," she whispered and detoured into her kitchen.
As Sully finished his call, she brewed two cups of coffee for
them.

"Got my store and horses covered for today," he said,
sliding his cell into his back pocket and walking toward her.

Placing his forearms on the countertop, he looked her up and down. Charley's heart raced as she set a mug of steaming black coffee in front of him. "How about you? What did you decide about your flower shop?"

"I decided to play it safe as you suggested and close my shop for a while. I called Leon to let him know, but he didn't answer, so I left a message." They took seats across from each other at her kitchen table, and as they talked, Charley imagined enjoying this routine with Sully every morning. "How about we go down the street for breakfast? I know a cute little place."

"Are you coming to the country with me after breakfast?"

"Yes, if your offer still stands. I'll need to water the plants in the shop before we go."

"You know my offer stands," he said. "Is it okay if I take a quick shower?"

"Of course," Charley said. Although she'd taken her shower the night before, she suddenly pictured herself wet and naked in the shower with Sully and trembled. Handing him a clean towel, she said over her shoulder, "I'll get dressed while you do that."

Twenty minutes later, they were both dressed, Sully in his long-sleeved shirt and jeans, and Charley in a silvery blue sweater and leggings. They left the duplex and walked two stores down from her shop to a breakfast and brunch café open from six a.m. to three p.m. She knew the waitress and asked for the check before they had even ordered. Sully cocked a scolding black brow at Charley, and she gave him a sharp snap of her head. He chuckled.

They dined on waffles and bacon, and when they were done, moseyed back to her shop. They entered through the front door, and Charley began watering her plants. She was in the front half of the shop when the bell over the door tinkled, announcing someone had arrived.

"Good morning," Leon said with a slight smile that faded

when he spotted Sully sitting behind the private counter, where the cash register was, toward the back of the shop.

Charley made a mental note of Leon's displeasure at seeing Sully but said cheerfully, "Good morning, Leon. I guess you didn't get my message."

"I noticed the closed sign hanging on the door," he said, his freckled brow slightly wrinkling as he ignored Sully and her comment. "Are we not opening for business as usual?"

"Actually, no," Charley said, a watering can in hand as she paused to explain. "With everything that has happened to my property along with a fourth Cave Killer murder, I've decided not to open for a while." The bell over the doorway tinkled again, and this time, Rod Vaughn burst into the shop. Charley glanced over her shoulder at Sully who merely cocked a brow. Leon backed up a few paces from Rod, but Charley stood her ground and faced him. "Rod, what are you doing here?"

Scowling from Leon to Sully, Rod said, "I'd like to talk to you in private, Charley."

"This is as private as it's going to get," Charley replied.

When she'd gone out with Rod, it was because he'd said he was down after things hadn't worked out with Kay, the woman for whom he'd bought the flowers. She'd felt sorry for Rod, but she'd not been interested in more than friendship. He didn't make her heart flutter like Sully did. Never had he stirred her cravings like Sully. She had taken Rod's first kiss on her cheek and certainly not allowed him any liberties. She'd never once entertained the idea of crawling into bed with Rod as she had Sully. At the end of their third outing, Rod had walked her to her door, and she'd declined to invite him into her apartment. Rod had informed her it was customary to have sex on the third date. When he'd grabbed her, she had quickly turned her head and he'd planted a sloppy kiss on her neck. She had twisted away and shoved him backward with both hands. Bidding him a firm farewell, she'd darted inside her apartment and locked her door. He'd smacked her door and shouted goodbye. Charley had breathed a sigh of relief.

But a couple of days later Rod had shown up in her shop profusely apologizing and begging for a fourth date. She'd escorted him to the café down the street. Once they were in a public place, she took the opportunity over a cup of late afternoon decaf to confirm there would be no more dates. Zero. Kay must have followed him, because she had shown up and made a scene by throwing a glass of water in Rod's face. Charley had quietly exited the café and driven to Triple C Ranch-South. There, she faced Rod once again. But that time, Sully and Cash had been there to back her up in getting rid of him.

"I am not back together with Kay," Rod told her.

"Rod, that doesn't matter to me," Charley said, not to be unkind but to get through to him. "I told you I was done."

"Look, what happened on your porch won't happen again," Rod said, ignoring Leon but shooting a sheepish sideways glance at Sully.

"What happened?" Leon asked.

"None of your business, carrot top," Rod said.

"Your rudeness never fails, Rod," Charley said. Out of the corner of her eye, she saw Sully stand up and saunter around the counter. "Either you leave, or I will call the cops and they'll make you leave, Rod."

"Which one of these guys is taking my place with you?" Rod asked her and pointed first to Leon. "Not the guy with the broom." Pointing to Sully, he said, "So, the guy with the gun?"

"She asked you to leave today, like she did the last time I saw you, pal," Sully said, walking toward them. "Take off and don't come back."

"Or what? You'll pull your gun on me?" Rod asked.

"If that's what it comes to," Sully replied, stopping beside Charley.

"A gun?" Leon asked no one in particular.

"This dude has a whole store full of guns. I Googled

him," Rod stated, looking from Leon to Sully. That was news to Charley, and her brows raised in question. "Oh, yeah, Sullivan Custis here owns the Ranchers Gun Club and Shooting Range just outside of Colorado Springs." Looking at Charley, Rod said, "That's how he knew about the misfiring of my *little* gun. He's an expert gunsmith. Just thought you should know that, Charley, since you *detest* guns."

"Rod, you need to leave," Charley said. "Now."

"You're going to be real sorry," Rod told her.

"Is that a threat?" Charley asked. When Rod didn't reply, she said, "I do not want to see you again, Rod. If necessary, I will take out a restraining order against you."

Leon opened the front door as an invitation for Rod to leave. Rod whirled on his heel and shoved Leon. Leon pushed him back. Rod threw a punch and Leon ducked, but in doing so, stumbled backward against a display. Potted plants and silk flowers went flying.

"Stop!" Charley shouted as clay, dirt, and Leon hit the newly scrubbed floor.

Sully waded in between the two men. He grabbed Rod by the back of his shirt and flung him out of the front door. Charley helped Leon to his feet. Rod staggered and fell onto one knee in the middle of the sidewalk. Tearing his pant leg, Rod jumped up and came at Sully but stopped short when Sully placed his hand on the Ruger in his holster.

"Get the hell out of here and do not come back, Vaughn," Sully growled, striding out of the shop and onto the sidewalk. "Or *you* will be sorry."

Rod swiped a bead of sweat off his forehead and backed away. With a glare at Charley and pointing at Sully, he said, "You're making a mistake with him, Charley."

"Mine to make," Charley told him, arriving at Sully's side.

Mouthing curses under his breath, Rod hurried to his Mercedes and jerked it away from the curb into traffic.

Horns blared at him as Charley and Sully reentered the shop.

"Thank you both," she said to Sully and Leon. "Maybe Rod finally got the message."

"Maybe," Sully gritted through his clenched jaw, hands on his hips.

Shoulders slumped, Leon stood as if totally defeated near the broken pots of plants and flowers. Sully's cell phone rang, and Charley shut the front door.

"Are you okay, Leon?" she asked as he grabbed a broom.

"Yes."

"I'm sorry Rod lost his temper with you," Charley said.

Leon looked past her to Sully and mumbled, "It's okay."

Sully slid his phone into his pocket and said, "I need to run out to my ranch, Charley. You want to come with me?"

"No, I'll stay here and clean up this latest mess. You go ahead." Charley started for the back counter where she had left her phone. "Then I'll check on the status of my car."

"I'll take you to get it whenever it's ready," Sully offered.

"I can take her," Leon piped up, and looking at Charley, he smiled. "That is, if you'll ride with me on my scooter, Charley."

Charley saw Sully tilt his head. She could read a lot into his simple move. Was he wondering if there was more to the story with Rod, which there wasn't, or perhaps he was pondering if she would ride with Leon on his scooter after all? Maybe he was trying to second-guess what she thought of the gun on his hip or the ones in his retail store. Could her opinion on guns change? Sully hadn't been without one since she'd met him. Funny, that hadn't bothered her in the least. But seeing Rod with a gun had scared and angered her. So maybe it was the man holding the gun and not the gun itself that mattered.

"There's no hurry," Charley said to both men. "Like Sully told me, my car probably isn't ready yet."

"Let's get back to work then," Leon said and began sweeping.

"All right, Charley. See ya," Sully said without being specific as to when.

"Okay." Charley hoped Sully would be back later. But maybe he'd had enough of her and her problems, so she didn't press him. "See ya, Sully."

"Yeah." With a lift of his chin, Sully disappeared out the side door.

Charley missed him even before the door had closed.

WHO DID THAT GUY THINK HE WAS? HE HADN'T COUNTED ON… what was his name…Sullivan Custis coming into the picture. Didn't he have enough on his plate with one man, much less two seeking Charley's attention? He paced and cursed while chewing his thumbnail. His brain worked feverishly. His body tensed with frustration. The voices told him to keep it together. He knew exactly how he could best do that. He walked into the cool night air. So what if Custis carried a gun? Who cared if he was bigger, more muscular, and far better-looking? What about that other man in her shop today? He was a threat to their relationship too. Charley was his. All his. She just didn't know it yet. He opened his mouth to scream. Then he saw her, alone and unaware. He'd throw off the police with the disposal of this one. He wasn't stupid. Longing for the blissful numbness he so badly needed, he pulled the ski mask over his head.

CHAPTER FOURTEEN

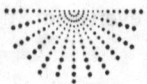

"Thanks for your help, Randy," Sully said inside the stables on his ranch.

"Of course," Randy replied. "None of us saw the damn thing when we came back from the skeet shoot. I hate snakes, especially prairie rattlers."

"In October, they're looking for a place to hibernate for the winter," Doc Henderson, the veterinarian, said standing next to the mare that had been bitten, named Rain.

"I've got the Springs Snake Control and Removal experts on the way. If there are any more rattlesnakes trying to hibernate, we'll find 'em," Sully replied with a pat to the mare's mane. Rain was a little sister to Storm. He'd had both horses for a couple of years, and Doc Henderson had always taken good care of them and his other four horses.

"The snake was a small one." The veterinarian nodded to the dead rattler a few feet away that was missing its head thanks to Randy's sure aim with a gun. "So, Rain's bite isn't nearly as bad as it could have been."

"Right. Still, I appreciate you getting here first thing this morning, Jill," Sully said to the vet. "And for coming back to check on Rain this afternoon."

"Any time, Sully. And even though the snake was small, I administered steroids and an anti-inflammatory to minimize tissue damage and to help with potential shock. Along with the tetanus shot I gave Rain, the antibiotic will take care of any bacteria the snake may have transferred into the wound when it bit her." The vet closed her bag and stepped out of the horse stall. "Swelling and infection are the main concerns. So, watch for both and call me if need be."

"We will," Sully said. He walked the vet out of the stables and back to her car as the exterminator truck came to a stop near the barn. "Thanks again, Doc," he said as she got into her car. He gave her a wave, thinking this was not the way he'd planned to spend the day. But he greeted the two men from the snake control company and escorted them to the stables. "After you've inspected the stables, please take a look around the exterior of the house, garage, and barn." He left the snake experts to take over the rattler hunt from there. Sully checked his phone to see if he had a missed call or a text from Charley. Then it dawned on him, he hadn't given her his number. "Damn."

Sully called Cash Cooper and asked for Charley's number. He punched her number into his cell. It rang. No answer. He hung up. His number would have come up as unknown, so she might not have answered for that reason. Or maybe she hated guns so much she no longer wanted to see or speak to him. Whatever the case, she was a beautiful, independent woman, and he wasn't the only man who wanted her. Maybe she'd made other plans for the evening. He called again. No answer. This time he left a message.

An hour later, Sully was checking on Rain when the men from the snake company tracked him down. In a far pasture, they'd found the den from where the prairie rattler had slith-ered. Maybe it was looking for one last mouse meal before the long winter. In any event, they had captured half a dozen venomous snakes. Then they had spread a commercial-grade snake repellent to create a barrier around the house, garage, barn, and stables, deterring other rattlers from looking for a home in which to hibernate during the cold months approaching. Since the snakes' food source needed to be eliminated, rat poison had been strategically spread as well. Sully thanked the exterminators, paid them, and returned to his house.

It was around four when Sully checked his cell to make sure he hadn't missed a call or text. None. Why hadn't Charley invited him to come back? Why hadn't he offered to treat her to dinner? Dammit. He turned on the flatscreen in his bedroom. Blue lights from police cars and red lights from a fire truck were on the scene in Old Colorado City.

"Hell," Sully muttered. He punched in Charley's number. No answer.

He sprinted outside to his truck, cursing himself for leaving her. On the main road, he stepped on the gas. Please don't let her be hurt. Or worse.

The trip into town seemed to take twice as long as usual. Leaving the highway and heading toward Colorado Avenue, Sully finally neared Charley's shop and duplex. He saw lights on in the windows of her apartment. He also saw the lights of police cars just up the street from her place. Making a quick decision, he veered up the short hill beside the shop and turned into the driveway of her duplex. He hopped out of the truck and knocked on her door.

"Charley!"

No answer. Sully called her phone. It rang from inside her apartment. He pulled the extra key to the new door lock out of his pocket and opened the door. Her phone lay on the kitchen counter. The place was quiet and just the way they'd left it earlier in the day. Locking the door, he sprinted back out to his truck and took off along Colorado Avenue. Nearing the blue lights of the police cars, Sully saw an ambulance parked near the firetruck now as well. He strained in the late afternoon duskiness to see beyond the police, paramedics, and onlookers. Glimpsing Rod Vaughn and Leon Lerfeld, it appeared the two of them were getting into it again as they had been earlier that day.

"Charley," Sully whispered in relief as he finally caught sight of her.

Standing under a lamppost, she was caught between the two men, who were obviously vying for her attention. Sully parked his truck as close to the scene as he could and jogged across the street. As a body on a gurney was rolled toward the ambulance, he heard the raised voices of Vaughn and Lerfeld. Sully stepped onto the sidewalk halfway down the block behind the trio. Charley whirled away from the two men, and the frown on her beautiful face disappeared the instant she saw him.

"Sully!" Charley called and raced toward him.

Vaughn and Lerfeld turned as well. Shock registered on their faces. Whether it was from seeing him or watching Charley running away from them to him, Sully didn't know. Maybe both. In any case, Sully walked toward Charley, and as she neared him, he opened his arms. She flung herself against him, and he wrapped her in his embrace. Her arms clasped around his neck and her feet left the ground.

"What the hell's going on?" Sully asked and set her feet back on the sidewalk.

"Another girl has been murdered!" she said, looking up at him. "Detective Groves just got here, and he told me it happened within the last couple of hours. But this time, the body was dumped into a big trash bin, and there was no toadflax. She was found by a restaurant employee."

"Where?" Sully asked as Vaughn approached with Lerfeld trailing behind him.

"Behind the café where we had breakfast."

"Really," Sully muttered, remembering that's the place where they'd seen Vaughn and his on-again, off-again girlfriend. Dumped in a trash bin didn't fit the pattern of the so-called Cave Killer, but Sully bet it was the same guy. He took Charley's hand and said, "Let's go." She held on tightly as they stepped off the curb and walked between two parked cars.

"Charley!" one of the men, maybe Vaughn, shouted.

"Charley," the other one, Lerfeld, Sully guessed, echoed.

Sully ignored them, and Charley did too. They crossed

the street, went straight to his truck, and he opened the door on her side. She hopped in and he closed the door. As he made his way around the front of the truck, he saw Vaughn and Lerfeld across the street scowling at him. With a victorious tip of his cowboy hat, Sully climbed into his truck and started the engine.

"What made you come back to town?" Charley asked as he pulled away from the curb.

"You," he said, driving along Colorado Avenue. "I got your cell number from Cash and called you earlier to tell you why I got hung up. Then I saw the report on the news and tried to call you again. When I couldn't reach you, I headed to your apartment."

"I heard the sirens and went to see what happened," Charley said. "I grabbed the new key to my apartment but forgot my phone on the counter."

"Yeah, I found your phone." Sully made a U-turn and headed back toward her shop and duplex. The ambulance was gone, and the police cars were pulling away from the scene of the murder. There was no sign of Vaughn or Lerfeld. "What were Frick and Frack doing there?"

Charley hesitated for a split second and then laughed. "You mean Rod and Leon?"

"Yes," Sully grumbled and turned up the hill to her duplex.

"They both claimed they were in the vicinity." Charley smiled and said, "Thank you for rescuing me from them and for the ride home."

Sully drove up her hill, stopped on the parking pad in front of her apartment, and gripped the steering wheel. He looked at her and said, "Charley, come home with me tonight." She glanced away from him to her apartment. "And stay until women stop dropping dead all around you. I think it's concerning that the dead include your mother and two women you knew."

"I didn't know the first victim or the last two," she reminded him. "The café owner, Denny, said the girl murdered today was new in town and he'd just hired her. He feels terrible." Charley thought for a moment and said, "My mother didn't fit the profiles of the other victims."

"Yeah, but we know you do," Sully said. "Your mother just got in your attacker's way. Please close your shop indefinitely and come out to the country until they catch the killer."

"Come inside, Sully," Charley said and grasped the door handle of the truck.

Sully caught her arm and asked, "So you can pack?"

To his immense relief, she nodded. "Yes. Leaving the Closed sign on the shop door after you left, I figured I wouldn't open again until the killer is caught."

"Good." Sully let go of her arm.

"But I hate being so intimidated that I'm closing my shop."

"You've already been attacked once. You're being smart, not intimidated, Charley."

Sully got out of the truck and came around to her side. As she alighted, he pulled her into his arms and lowered his head. She tilted up her chin, and his mouth came down on her soft, supple lips. Her arms wrapped around him, and her hands flattened to his back as she stood on tiptoes to kiss him. Letting go of her, he gave her fanny a familiar pat and took her keys out of his pocket. This time, he put them on his keychain after unlocking her apartment door. Going inside, she went to the counter and checked her cell.

"I see your missed calls." As Charley said that, her phone rang, and she rolled her eyes. "It's Frick, I mean Rod. I'm going to block him." No sooner had she started to do so than her cell rang again. "Frack, now. I'm going to text Leon that I'll advise him when I decide to reopen the shop."

Sully nodded. "What do you need me to do to help you?"

"Nothing. Just keep me company." She brought him a glass of wine, and pouring one for herself, she motioned for him to follow her into her bedroom. He sat down on the bed and watched as she took a carry-on-size suitcase out of a closet and began filling it.

"Do you have a costume for a Halloween party?" he asked. "Your cousin, Chloe, invited me, as usual, to her annual party."

"I do. I love Halloween. I usually dress up that day and pass out candy in the shop."

"Great. What will you be?"

"You'll have to wait and see. What will you be?"

"Your date."

Charley laughed and asked, "What was going on at your ranch today?" Gathering items from her bathroom, she put them, along with a hairdryer, into her suitcase.

"A mare, named Rain, was bitten by a prairie rattler on the way to a skeet shoot."

"Oh no." Charley turned to face him. "Is she okay?"

"Yes, I think so. But I wanted to make sure, so that's why I didn't come back to town sooner. The vet treated her and checked on her twice."

"Thank goodness. I hate snakes."

"Like you hate guns?"

"I decided it's not the gun but the person holding the gun that matters."

Sully dipped his head once and smiled. "I agree."

"Okay." With a look around a few minutes later, Charley put a laptop into her bag and then grabbed the charger for her cell phone. "I'm ready to go."

"Let's hit the road," Sully said and picked up her suitcase.

THE BLISSFUL NUMBNESS HAD HIT WITH THE WOMAN'S DEATH. But he'd almost been caught by that stupid café employee. Hiding had interfered with his showing up at Charley's apartment. He'd planned to be the hero, protecting her from the Cave Killer. Not only that, but she could have provided him with an alibi as to his whereabouts at the time of the murder. He'd been barely half a block away when he heard yelling at the restaurant. He'd kept walking in the opposite direction. When the voices said enough time had passed, he walked back down Colorado Avenue, planning to see the action and go tell Charley about it. But Charley had already heard and was there. Then the other two guys showed up. First the one he'd encountered that morning at her shop, and then the one named Sully. Picturing how Charley had run to that big, brawny gun-toting rancher, he screamed and battered his head with his fists.

CHAPTER FIFTEEN

"*I* know it's too late to see my log cabin tonight, but maybe we could check on it tomorrow. I was planning to stay there a night or two before the vandalism happened to my car," Charley said as they passed the entrance to Triple C Ranch-South.

"Sure. If that's what you want," Sully said.

"Yes, Cash said they had put fresh linens on the bed and towels in the linen closet for the bathroom. I can pick up some groceries tomorrow and stay there tomorrow night."

"Okay," he said, turning right onto the road leading to his ranch. "Does that include me?"

Charley's heart skipped a beat as she smiled at the handsome man. "Yes, it does."

"I need to stop in at my gun club, but you can take my Jeep to the grocery store."

"I remember seeing your Jeep in your garage."

"Yeah, I got it a couple of years ago. Being white with black trim it reminds me of a stormtrooper from *Star Wars*."

"Me too. I love Jeeps. Does the top come off?"

"It does, and so do the doors. It's a fun vehicle. Especially out here in the country."

"You're fun, Sully," Charley said softly.

Sully pulled into the driveway of his ranch, drove around

the side of the house, and stopped in front of the garage. With a click of the remote, the door went up, and an overhead light came on as he parked the truck inside the building.

"Stay where you are," Sully said. "The garage light goes off quickly and I don't want you to trip over anything in the dark."

"Okay." Charley's excitement and nerves at spending another night with this man were bubbling inside of her. But she stayed put as he had asked, and a moment later, he was at her side of the truck. As the overhead light went out, the truck light came on as he opened her door. With a smile, she swung her body to face him.

"Listen to me," Sully said, keeping her in place by flattening his large hands on her knees. "You're fun, too, and I really do like you."

"I like you too."

He smiled and her heart raced. "I meant it when I said you can stay with me as long as you like. You can sleep with me or in any of the guest rooms. You can use the Jeep to come and go as you please. All I ask is that you don't go to your duplex or flower shop alone. For now, I don't want you ducking bullets, knives, or killers."

"I'm a lucky *ducky*," she said playfully but spread her knees and pulled him into her embrace. She wrapped her arms around his neck and whispered in his ear, "I don't know why you care about me, but thank you, Sully."

"I expect nothing from you in return," he said. "Whatever happens or doesn't happen between us, I want you to be safe."

Charley loosened her grip around his neck enough to lean back and kiss him. His strong arms slid around her and scooted her forward on the seat. As he molded her to him, he pulled her out of the truck. When her feet touched the floor of the garage, her lips left his. He took her hand, closed the garage door, and they walked across the backyard in the moonlight. Sully unlocked the side door to his house, and they were in the kitchen when her cell phone rang. She stopped, fished her phone out of her purse, and looked at the caller.

"Chase Cooper," she told Sully. She answered her phone as Sully set her bag down. "Hi, Chase." He had heard about her vandalized vehicle, through Sully from Cash, and was concerned after seeing on the news that another murder had been committed in her Old Colorado City neighborhood. He and Jade wanted to know if she'd like to stay with them as they had plenty of room. "Thank you so much, Chase. But I'm in good hands. Sully drove into town and picked me up since my car is still in the shop and I haven't gotten around to getting a rental car." She listened and smiled at Sully. "Yes, I agree. Sully is a good guy." Chase then asked about her flower shop. "I'm keeping it closed for a while." Lastly, she said, "Yes, Sully and I will see you all at Chloe's Halloween party. Thank you for checking on me, cousin."

"Chase is a good guy too," Sully said after Charley clicked off her cell. "So is Cash."

"Yes, I'm truly lucky to have found them, Chloe, and Coop." She swallowed the lump in her throat and finished. "Better late than never."

"They're lucky too."

Charley gazed up at him and said, "I want to sleep with you tonight, Sully."

"Good deal," he said. The slow, cocky grin that formed on his lips heated her cheeks. "In that case, I need another shower."

"So do I."

"C'mon," he said and grabbed her bag. When he held out his hand, she took it, and he trailed her behind him to his big bedroom. Flipping on a soft light, he swung his hand toward the master bathroom. "Ladies first." He set her bag down on the bed, strode to a walk-in closet, and used a bootjack to pull off his boots.

Charley opened her bag and pulled out panties. Next, she took her shampoo and makeup out of the bag and walked into the master bath. It was large, with his and her sinks along with a glass shower and a Jacuzzi, both big enough for two. In the far corner, through an ajar door, she saw a toilet. Quietly shutting the main door to the master bath, she disrobed and turned on the shower. Stepping under the hot spray of water, she closed her eyes and enjoyed the sensation. Using her shampoo, she soaped her hair and then washed her body. Ready to get out, she realized she had two problems.

"Sully?" she called, turning off the water.

"Yeah?"

"I don't have a towel or a nightshirt."

She watched him nonchalantly saunter into the master bath. He placed a white tee shirt on the counter and opened a closet at the far end of the room. He turned toward her but didn't investigate the shower. Instead, he put a towel on the counter, shut the door, and left her alone. Charley stepped onto the thick rug outside the shower door and grasped the towel. She dried her body and wrapped the towel around her wet head. Pulling on his soft cotton tee shirt and her panties, she left the bathroom and entered the bedroom in search of her comb and hair dryer.

"My turn?" Sully asked from where he was stretched out in an overstuffed chair with his sock feet resting on a matching ottoman.

"Yes," she said. He drained what was left in what appeared to be a glass of red wine. He got up and swaggered across the room to her. From the dresser, he handed her a glass of wine. After the day and evening she'd had, a glass of wine sounded wonderful. How did Sully always know exactly what she needed? She took the wine and said, "Thank you."

With a nod, he headed into the shower. He didn't bother to close the door, and as curious as she was, Charley didn't steal a peek. Standing in front of the dresser with an attached mirror, she drank her wine and blow-dried her hair. She shivered with excitement and anticipation at the thought of doing more than just sleeping next to Sully. But then she recalled her terror when the intruder, potentially the Cave Killer, had grabbed her in her bedroom and thrown her onto her bed. Like scenes from a scary movie that couldn't be stopped, she heard her mother scream her name before being shot. She turned off the dryer, ran her fingers through her hair, and picked up her wine. With a sigh, she sat down on the far side of Sully's bed and hung her head.

"Hey, city slicker." Sully turned off the bathroom light, leaving the bedroom bathed in the soft glow of moonlight. He rolled into bed behind her, and when she turned sideways to look at him, he smiled. Stretched out on top of the comforter, he wore a pair of boxer shorts and nothing else. "What's wrong?"

"Murders, assault, vandalism, no car, and no shop worth opening. Two guys in town who have embarrassed me on several occasions."

"You're handling it all really well, Charley," he said, and she shrugged. "It's up to the cops to catch the criminals. There's nothing more you can do now except keep yourself safe. You're doing that by vacating your property and staying out of sight, right?"

"Right." She nodded and looked away. "I want to feel something besides fear, defeat, and loneliness," she told him. But not with just anybody. With Sully. Never had she been attracted to a man until she'd met Sullivan Custis. Never had she considered spending the night with a man until Sully came along. She gazed at him, and his forest-green eyes mesmerized her. His lips had kissed her like she'd never been kissed before, sending hot chills racing up and down her entire body. His shoulders were broad and his arms were strong, and when he held her to his muscular body, she floated into a world where she was safe and protected. She wanted all of that and so much more, but only from Sully. "I need you to—"

He waited, and when she silently shook her head, he asked, "You need me to what?"

She whispered, "Take charge of me tonight. Do you know what I mean?"

Charley lowered her gaze and stared at her lap. Sully got off the bed and walked around it, coming to stop in front of her. She looked up at him and he smiled. He reached down and took hold of her upper arms, bringing her to her feet. As soon as he embraced her, the familiar feelings of security and serenity enveloped her. Along with a whopping dose of craving this man's touch, she liked the fact that he thought she was fun. And he liked her too.

"I always use a condom," he said.

"It's not the right time of the month for me to get pregnant."

With a sexy grin, Sully cupped his large hands to her face, lowered his head, and kissed her. Then letting go, he grasped the comforter and sheet and tossed them toward the end of his king-size bed. With a grin, he scooped her up and she giggled. Bracing a knee on the side of the mattress, he leaned over and placed her lengthwise toward the middle of the bed. He stretched out beside her and pulled her into his arms. She rolled to her side and wrapped an arm around him. His body was firm and warm. His mouth closed over hers, and she tingled.

"Let's start by taking off the tee shirt," he whispered. She nodded, sat up, and also sitting up, Sully helped her tug his tee shirt over her head. His eyes lowered to her naked breasts. He gently cupped her breasts in his hands and then released her. Lying down, he said, "C'mere."

Charley molded her breasts to his hard chest. She closed her eyes and lost herself to his kisses. He trailed kisses down her neck to her breasts, and she sucked in a breath as his mouth closed over a nipple. She moaned as his lips and tongue teased her other breast.

"Mmm, Sully," she whispered. His mouth closed over hers again, and his hand ran over the front of her panties, slipping down to the vee between her legs. Yes, how thrilling! Then his fingers dipped into her panties, touching her bare skin. Her most secret spot jittered and jolted with fiery flames. "Sully," she moaned softly, arching her hips to his touch. "Yes."

Sully pulled her panties down and off. Charley opened her eyes and lay naked to his gaze, hoping she measured up to this experienced man's expectations.

"You *are* one pretty girl." His voice was husky.

Charley bit her lower lip and tucked her fingers into his boxers. With a tug on the waistband, she was letting him know she wanted them off him. Sully obliged and dropped them over the side of the bed. When he rolled back to her, his lower body covered hers.

"Sully," she gasped nervously and stiffened.

CHAPTER SIXTEEN

"*Y*ou're okay," Sully whispered. "I'm in charge, and I'm making sure you're safe. Right?"

"Right." She shivered and took a breath.

"Wanna stop?"

"No. Please don't stop."

With the fingers of his left hand, Sully touched the feminine folds between her legs. Petal soft and velvety smooth, this woman was electrocuting every cell in his body without even trying. He kissed her again as he dipped a finger just inside her. Exploring, he found her wet and tight. He groaned and rolled all the way on top of her. Charley's body grew rigid underneath him, but she clasped her arms around his back.

"You're doing fine, Charley," he whispered.

"Tell me what to do, Sully."

"Spread your legs for me."

He felt her take a deep breath, and then she spread her legs apart. His hips nestled between her thighs, and he gently parted her silky feminine flesh. Pressing his hardened manhood to her femininity, he paused.

"Sully?" she moaned with questioning naiveté.

"Push against me, and we'll do this together."

Her royal-blue eyes opened, full of trust and hope. She closed them again, and when he pressed himself into her, she pushed herself onto him. He sensed a slight barrier, and then he was erotically squeezed as he slid into the hilt. Pulling almost out, he slipped back in. He'd had his share of women, but never had sex felt so fantastic. Immediately, Sully mentally corrected himself—this wasn't just sex. Being with Charley was making love.

"Mmm, yes, Sully," she whispered breathlessly near his ear.

"Yeah," he groaned. "This is so good."

Sully took his time. He let Charley's body stretch and adjust to him being inside her. He allowed himself the enjoyment of her soft breasts against his chest while she enveloped him within her body. Slowly, he picked up speed. In and out, faster and deeper he plunged, riding the high of making love to the sensuous, sweetest, most sensational woman he'd ever met. Inside and outside, Charley was a beauty the likes of which he'd never known. His desire built hot and fast, and he knew in the next couple of thrusts he would lose himself. Then Charley moaned, her fingers spreading wide as she clutched his back. When she bucked under him, it was his undoing. She squeezed him internally, and the orgasm sweeping her into ecstasy spiraled his pleasure to a pulsing climax of pumping his hot seed deep inside her gripping body.

Their hearts pounded against each other. She gasped for breath, and his breathing was shallow as he throbbed within her. They stayed as one until their heartbeats slowed and their breathing returned to normal. Sully kissed her, and only then did he pull out and roll off her to his back. He tugged her to him, and she rested her head on his shoulder. Flattening her delicate hand over his heart, she slipped a leg between the two of his. This felt so right. Charley felt so right.

She whispered, "I'm glad you were the man who taught me to make love, Sully."

"Me too." It flashed across his mind to say that he wanted to be the one and only man to whom she made love. "I'm honored."

"I wouldn't have wanted it— forced on me like what almost happened in my apartment."

"Hell, no." Sully clenched his jaw. He reached down, grasping the sheet and comforter. Feeling protective, he brought the bed covers over the two of them and held her close.

"I'm exhausted because of you," she said with a satiated giggle.

"I'll let you sleep...for a while." He kissed her and said, "Roll over, city girl."

Charley rolled to her side and snuggled her rounded fanny perfectly into the crook of his body. He groaned at how good that felt and wrapping an arm around her waist, cupped his hand to her breast.

"Wake me when you're ready to flirt with me again, country boy," she said around a yawn and placed her hand over his.

"Flirt with you?" He chuckled. "Count on it."

Damn, this was too right to be wrong. How was he ever going to let this girl go? Maybe he wouldn't have to. Sully closed his eyes with a smile on his lips. When he woke again, it was not to the screams he'd heard from Charley in past nights. Tonight it was to her soft voice.

"Are you awake, country boy?"

"Yeah," he said.

"Me too." Charley rolled over within his embrace, and when he rolled to his back, her dainty hand came to rest over his belly button. "Wanna flirt?"

"With you, city slicker?" he teased and thought *only with you.* "Always."

Charley boldly moved her hand lower. Sully groaned when her fingers did a sexy slide down the length of his manhood. He was already hard by the time her hand closed around him in a gently massaging caress. Enjoying every stroke, when he could take no more, he rolled on top of her. Without stiffening, she spread her legs and they flirted.

CHAPTER SEVENTEEN

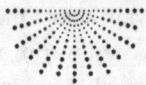

"*I*'m not sure I can walk," Charley told the magnificent male who had taken charge of her and spiraled her into the stars during the moonlight hours. His chuckle was husky with a hint of masculine pride. She hugged herself to him as they lingered in his bed. "I'm serious, Sully."

"Want me to get you some ibuprofen?" Sully's arm was around her as she lay with her head on his shoulder after they'd made love again that morning.

"Maybe." She giggled playfully. "No."

"Stay in bed and sleep. Pretend you're on an extended vacation," he suggested and stretched. We don't have any horseback riding or skeet shooting scheduled at the ranch today, so it will be quiet. Randy will have fed the horses by now, and Roy will have opened the store. I'm going to check on Rain and head to the gun club for a while. But I'll come back and take you to lunch. Sound good?"

That sounded way too good to pass up. "Then may I drive your Jeep to my cabin and take a closer look at it?"

"Yes, you can follow me in the Jeep, and I can show you the gun club on the way."

"Great." Charley lifted her head, and with a kiss to his

cheek, she rolled out of his embrace and onto her stomach. "Maybe I'll be able to walk by then."

Sully sat up and gave her naked fanny a pat before getting out of bed. "There's a spot of your blood on my sheet, city slicker."

"I told you I was a virgin, country boy. Now go."

He chuckled. "See you sooner than later."

Charley heard him walk across the room and turn on the shower. Sully's bed was cozy, warm, and safe. She closed her eyes, and when she opened them again, a couple of hours had passed. She rolled to her side and her first thought was that she was already missing Sully. How could that be? She'd just met him. Whatever the case, it was true. She missed him. She liked him. She'd made love to him. Three times! What would it be like if she stayed here in the country close to him as he'd mentioned? She had that cabin. She smiled and got out of bed.

She'd showered, dressed in a red sweater and blue jeans, and was in the kitchen with a cup of coffee by the time he returned from his stables and gun club. Black hair, green eyes, a stubble of black beard, and a cocky grin filled her senses, making her weak at the knees. Masculinity and muscles were wrapped up in a black suede jacket, snug blue jeans, and black cowboy boots. She pictured grabbing this irresistible man and taking him back to bed.

"The sheets have been washed and are in the dryer," she said as casually as possible. Taking off his jacket, he wore a white button-down shirt with a logo for his gun club over his heart. With the shirt, he wore his black cowboy hat. With a smile, she added, "Hi."

"Hi," he said with a grin, strode straight to her and wrapped his arms around her. "I see you were able to *walk* to the kitchen."

"Barely." She giggled and blushed. "I'll remake your bed when the sheets are dry."

"I'll help." His mouth came down on hers, and she stood on tiptoes as she kissed him. When he leaned back, he asked,

"How about a tour of my gun club before we have lunch at Coopers' Lodge?"

"Sounds wonderful. It will be my first visit to a gun club. I can't wait to see it."

"Good. I like a girl with an open mind." Letting go of her, Sully sauntered across the kitchen and picked up a set of keys from a small wicker basket on the counter. "Keys to the Jeep," he said and dropped them into her hand. "Yours as long as you like."

"Thank you, Sully." Charley gave him a hug. Then she fixed him a cup of coffee, and coming to stand beside him, she asked about Rain.

"She's good. Randy thinks so too," Sully replied, taking a seat on a barstool at the counter. He tugged Charley between his knees and kissed her. "I missed you."

She wrapped her arms around his neck and admitted, "I missed you too."

"Good." He grinned as she slid onto a barstool next to him.

They drank their coffee, and as they talked, he told her there was a nip in the October air. So, when they'd finished their coffee, she donned a red leather jacket over her sweater. Placing their coffee cups in the sink, she followed the handsome man out of his house to the garage. With his own key to the Jeep, Sully unlocked the driver's door, and opened it for her. She climbed into the Jeep, moved the seat forward, and adjusted the mirror.

"I'm all set," she said.

"Follow me."

Sully shut her door and got into his truck. Like his truck, the Jeep was a late model, automatic, and easy to drive. Charley eagerly followed him away from the house and onto the highway. A few miles down the road, Sully made a right turn and a sign reading Ranchers Gun Club and Shooting Range came into view. A bit farther was the gun club building and the outdoor shooting range beyond it. Charley knew from their Harley ride that this was all on Sully's land.

He pulled into one of thirty parking spaces, and she stopped the Jeep beside him. Hopping out of the Jeep as Sully walked to her, they entered his gun club. It was a large, open area with several big windows and a two-story ceiling.

"How nice," Charley said. "It's welcoming."

"Upstairs," he nodded at the staircase straight ahead, "we present classes on gun safety, and we can sign off on concealed weapon training. My dad donates his one day a week here to teach a class or two. Over to the right is the soundproof indoor shooting range." He indicated a heavy, closed door. "Beyond the outdoor range, we also have skeet shooting."

"Hey, boss man," a man said in greeting to Sully as soon as they walked closer to several glass counters displaying a large variety of weapons to be sold.

"Roy Custis, this is Charley Cooper," Sully said in introduction. "She's a cousin to Chase, Chloe, and Cash Cooper."

"Nice to meet you, Roy."

"Same here, Charley. All the Coopers are members here, and so are Derek and Chloe Brevard," Roy said politely and then looked back at Sully. "Some guy was just in here wanting to know where the owner was."

"Who was it?"

"He didn't give his name. He was medium-height and stocky."

"What did he want?"

"He wanted to know if the gun he showed me was known for not always shooting. I said yes, and then he asked if I'd take his gun in on a trade."

"Vaughn," Sully said with a glance at Charley.

"Sounds like it," she said, resenting Rod Vaughn more than ever. Intruding into her work world was bad enough. Intruding into Sully's was unforgivable as far as she was concerned. "I'm so sorry he's making such a pest of himself."

"Don't worry about it," Sully replied. "What did you tell him about a trade, Roy?"

"Hell no," Roy said with a shake of his head and then corrected himself. "Well, just no."

"That's exactly what I would have said."

"When I also told him we only do trades with club members, he got an instant bad attitude," Roy told them. "He said as a gun shop, we should take his gun in on trade no matter what. I told him to take it back to the place he bought it and ask them to trade or for a refund."

"Good answer. What did he say?" Sully asked.

"Nothing I could understand," Roy replied with a shrug. "Then he grabbed up his gun and cussed me all the way out of the shop."

"Sounds like the run-ins Charley and I have had with him," Sully said.

"His name is Rod Vaughn," Charley added. "Rude is always Rod's go-to behavior when he doesn't get his way. Again, I'm sorry he's causing trouble."

"I handled it," Roy assured them. "I just wanted you to know, Sully."

"Thanks," Sully said. "Don't do any business with him if he comes back when I'm not here. In case he asks, tell him we aren't accepting new club members right now. Tell him there's a hold on sales and send him to Whispering Pines or one of the other gun clubs in the Springs."

"Will do."

"Come on, Charley, I'll show you where we practice shooting," Sully said.

Walking behind the counter, Sully grabbed two sets of ear protection. He led the way to the heavy door, but before opening it, they put on their ear protection. Inside the shooting gallery, she noted that she could hear voices but not the shooting. Charley saw ten glass-sided booths. Sully waved to a couple of customers and chose a booth nearest the door. At the far end of their booth was a target of a man shaped like a burglar, or a bad guy of some sort, on the run.

"Can you hit the bull's eye? Whatever that might be on such a target?" Charley asked.

"Where would you like the bullet to hit him?"

"I don't know." Charley looked away from Sully and studied the target. Turning back to him, she asked, "The chest or the head?"

"Yeah." Sully pulled his gun out of his holster, aimed, and fired four times in quick succession. He punched a button in the booth and, hooked to an overhead chain, the target flew toward them.

"Wow!" Charley stepped forward and stared, astonished. The bad guy's heart, both eyes, and the middle of his forehead had bullet holes smack-dab in the middle of them. "Remind me never to make you mad."

"My dad first brought me here on my sixteenth birthday. He had just been elected sheriff of El Paso County for the first time. At that point I had been shooting a shotgun and a revolver for about four years on our ranch. But since the owner was my mother's brother, and with my dad signing a waiver and a consent form, my uncle let me start shooting here."

"So, you've been practicing for half your life."

"Yes. I told my dad after we left that first day that I was going to buy this place when I grew up. As it turned out, when my uncle died, he had left it to me." Sully sent the target sliding backward on the overhead chain. "This is a Ruger Redhawk .44 Magnum," he said in regard to his gun. "There are two bullets left. Give it a try." When Charley nodded, he said, "This is how you hold it." He demonstrated using both hands to hold it while keeping the index finger along the barrel and off the trigger.

"Okay, I can do that," Charley said. The second Sully gave her the gun, her hand dropped about four inches. "Wow! It's heavy."

"Yes." He gave her instructions on how to stand, then moved behind her. "Aim for the middle of the target, put your finger on the trigger, and squeeze."

Charley did so, squeezed hard, and nothing happened. Not to be defeated, she squeezed harder. BOOM! The powerful gun sent her stumbling backward, straight into a wall of muscle. Sully caught her, kept her upright, and steadied her. He helped her regain the proper stance and indicated she should shoot a second time.

"I don't want to use up your last bullet," she said over her shoulder.

"I might know where I can get some more ammunition."

Charley repositioned her grip on the gun, like he'd taught her, and aimed dead center. She squeezed the trigger, and when it boomed the second time, she took only a single step back. She placed the gun on a small shelf, and Sully brought the target forward. There were no new holes in the paper.

She teased, "I must have shot the target through the holes you made."

"Yeah, let's go with that." Sully chuckled and winked. He was so good-looking, so strong, and so masculine that Charley felt the familiar swooning sensation. Then he said, "You weren't afraid to give it a try and that's what matters. We'll practice and use a smaller, more manageable gun next time. For now, let's head to the Lodge."

"Yes, let's. I've worked up an appetite," Charley said.

"I worked one up last night and this morning," Sully replied. Her cheeks heated as he gave her a cocky grin. When they were back out in the main part of the store, they removed their ear protection. He grabbed her hand, and they walked across the room. Letting go of her, he went behind a glass case and set their ear protection on a counter where he said it would be disinfected for the next user. Then he unlocked one of the gun cases and removed a pistol. Turning to Roy, who was waiting on two cowboys, Sully said, "Roy, I'm taking this new SIG Sauer P365 9mm."

"Okay, boss," Roy said as Sully locked the case.

Sully also gathered up a couple of boxes of ammunition and loaded the new gun as well as his revolver. He demonstrated for Charley how to put the safety on and take it off before they returned outside to his truck and Jeep.

"I don't want you to be without a gun, with a serial killer on the loose," Sully said as they paused beside the Jeep door. "This SIG Sauer is an excellent concealed weapon for a woman because it can kill as easily as it will fit in your purse."

"How much does it cost?" Charley said as he handed the gun to her. "I'll pay you for it."

"I don't think so," he replied with a shake of his head. "I put my 20-gauge Remington youth model shotgun, which I used as a kid when I was about your height and weight, in the back seat of the truck. I'm going to hide it for you at your cabin. All you have to do with a shotgun is aim it in the general direction of the target and at least some of the shot will hit them."

Charley tucked her fingers over his belt buckle and pulled herself closer to him. "Maybe you could just stay with me in my cabin until the killer is caught."

"Maybe." Sully cocked a brow. "You learn to shoot, and I'll buy some plants from your shop for my gun club."

"I was thinking your gun club could use a plant or two," Charley said as a plan formed in her mind. "What kind of plants would you like?"

Before he could answer, the horn of a truck, similar to Sully's, honked. Since they were headed to lunch, for now Charley placed her gun inside the console.

"There's my dad," Sully said with a smile. "You can meet him."

CHAPTER EIGHTEEN

"**D**ad, this is Charlotte Fleming Cooper," Sully said, never having felt so proud to introduce a female friend to his father. "She is the Coopers' first cousin and goes by Charley."

"I've heard great things about her from Chloe, saw the two of you, and stopped to introduce myself," Owen Custis said and looked at Charley. "Chloe's husband, Derek, used to work with me as a deputy sheriff. Now I work with him and his Percherons. Anyway, today Chloe stopped in the stables while I was there and told me all about you," Sully's father said and smiled at Charley. With gray hair and a mustache, his dad was only about an inch shorter than Sully and somewhat stouter. "Charley, they are so happy to have you as part of their family. It's my pleasure to meet you."

"Thank you, Sheriff Custis," Charley said and extended her hand. "It's nice to meet you."

"I'm just plain ol' Owen, now," he said humbly as they shook.

"I've heard great things about you too," Charley said. "From my cousins and your son."

"Sully's a good son," his dad said with a beaming smile at him. Sully was proud of his father and glad for the chance to introduce him to Charley. Owen said, "If you two haven't had lunch, let me treat you. I was on my way to Coopers' Lodge."

"That's where we're headed," Sully said.

"I'd love that," Charley said and smiled at Owen.

As they were going three separate ways after lunch, they each drove their own vehicle and met up at Triple C Ranch-East. Once they were inside the Lodge and seated at a window table, they were given water and menus. Tracy Cooper spotted them, and when she made her way over to them, Charley stood and gave her a hug. Tracy told them the specials of the day and left them to visit among themselves.

"Chloe said you live in Old Colorado City," Owen said with a slight frown of concern.

"Yes, I own a duplex and flower shop on Colorado Avenue," Charley replied.

"There's a serial killer on the loose in your neighborhood," Owen said without hesitation. "The pressure to catch him is immense. The Colorado Springs Police Department has their best detective in charge."

"Yes, Burt Groves," Sully said. "We met him, and he said to tell you hello."

"Burt's the best," Owen said with a nod. "I'm sorry about your mother, Charley."

"Thank you," Charley said.

"Your mother's death doesn't fit the Cave Killer's method of operation. Derek and I agree that there are two killers on the loose," Owen said, like the former sheriff he was. "We also agree that you fit the profile of the Cave Killer's victims, Charley."

"Yes, Sully has pointed out that same fact."

"The difference, of course, being you were attacked in your home and the other young women were found down in the caves except for the last victim," Owen said. "If the killer thinks he threw the police off by dumping that woman in the trash, he didn't. DNA is being collected, and I believe it will tie him to the other stranglings. In any event, Groves and the CSPD are doing everything they can to catch the killer, including uniformed and plain-clothed cops patrolling the area."

"Charley is staying with me for a while," Sully said just as Tracy came back to them with a basket of buttery rolls. "To be on the safe side."

"Good!" Tracy said, having heard and standing next to Charley. "That makes me feel better. Cash and the others will be happy to hear that too. Will y'all be at Chloe and Derek's Halloween party?"

"I will be," Owen said. "Sully and Charley?"

"Charley packed a costume. I have my usual costume, so we'll be there."

"Excellent," Tracy said. "See you then, if not before."

Tracy squeezed Charley's shoulder and left them to their conversation. The subject of murder transitioned into more pleasant topics, and lunch was served by one of the wait-staff. Charley and his dad had hit it off, and a good deal of the talking was between the two of them as they got to know each other. Sully smiled. Man, if this, too, didn't feel right. After consuming their three specials, his dad grabbed the check before Sully could, and they walked out to their vehicles. Owen gave Charley a hug and Sully a pat on the back. After getting into his truck, with a wave, Owen was gone.

"Remind me where you're heading from here," Sully said as he and Charley stood in the open door of the Jeep.

"To the grocery store," the gorgeous girl said with a heart-stopping smile as her blue eyes sparkled up at him. "I'm going to cook dinner at the cabin."

"Am I invited?"

"You're the guest of honor."

Sully grinned. "You're going to King Soopers or Walmart in Black Forest, right? Not into Old Colorado City?"

"Right. Probably Walmart, I need a few things besides groceries."

"Meet you at the cabin later?"

"Sooner than later."

"Keep your gun in your purse when I'm not with you, Charley."

"Okay."

"All right," Sully said with a nod. "Be on the alert."

"I will be."

Sully pulled her into his arms, and when her lips met his, she kissed him. Letting him know she cared, she gently leaned into him during the kiss. Where had this woman been all his life? "Do you want me to go with you, Charley?"

"No," she said, splaying both hands to his chest. "I'm a big girl. I'll be fine."

"You're a little girl," he said, towering over her. She slid into the Jeep and rolled down the window. Sully shut her door and said, "After I close the shop, I'll come to your cabin."

"Here's an extra key in case you happen to get there before me." Charley handed him a key and he caught her hand. Bringing it to his lips, he kissed the back of her fingers. He let go and as he walked away, she called out, "Want to flirt with me at the cabin tonight?"

Sully made a half-turn, and with a wink said, "You'll need a wheelchair."

"Sully!" Charley squealed and laughed.

Chuckling, he climbed into his truck and followed her from the parking lot to the highway. There, she turned west toward Pikes Peak, and he watched her fade into the distance. She wouldn't go to Old Colorado City, would she? No reason to, right? No, she wouldn't, Sully decided and turned east. Who the hell was the maniac killing women in their twenties? All of Colorado was acutely aware of the murders. Hell, the reports were on the national news. The whole country was watching. No sooner did he turn on the radio than the mayor was talking about the closure of businesses and dip in tourism blamed on the Cave Killer's murder spree.

A spree? Yeah, it was. Sully gripped the wheel and turned into the Ranchers Gun Club and Shooting Range. He recalled Roy telling them about Rod Vaughn's visit and suddenly wondered what caliber bullet had killed Charley's mother. The gun he'd taken off Vaughn used a .38. The cops wouldn't give him the information he was looking for, but they might share it with the former El Paso County Sheriff. Pulling into his usual parking spot behind the store, he pulled out his phone and called his dad. He knew Owen Custis would do his damnedest to find out.

That afternoon, a steady stream of customers kept Sully and Roy busy. Almost every one of them mentioned the murders in Old Colorado City. So, the killing spree that was bad for most businesses was good for his. Sully well understood the need to feel safe. He'd given Charley a gun merely hours earlier. When Sully glanced at the clock, he and Roy started winding down the shooting booths and finishing sales in preparation of closing up shop. It was a record-breaking day at the cash register. Twenty minutes later, Sully was locking the door behind him and Roy. They spoke for a couple of minutes in the parking lot, and then Sully got into his truck. He read a text from Randy. The horses were in their stalls, brushed, watered, and fed for the night. He mentioned Rain in particular. She was fine. Sully headed to the cabin on Triple C Ranch-South.

When he turned onto the gravel drive and steered toward the log home, a sense of peace fell over him. The Jeep was parked at the hitching post, and warm lights spilled out of the cabin windows. Plush green cushions, matching the rockers and shingles on the roof, now adorned the rocking chairs. Two big clay pots bursting with yellow mums, surrounded by bright orange pumpkins, ornamented either side of the stained glass door. The cedar door was wide open, and when he got out of his truck, a gentle breeze brought a whiff of delicious smells his way. He walked onto the porch and looked into the cabin. On the left, a crackling fire burned in the hearth in front of a sofa newly decorated with pillows and a matching throw. To the right, the table was set with a white tablecloth, pretty dishes, silverware, and two wineglasses. A bottle of red wine along with a colorful bouquet of pink tiger lilies, red roses, and lavender columbines were the centerpieces.

CHAPTER NINETEEN

"*B*oo!" Charley said to the handsome rancher on her porch. Coming from around the back of the cabin, she smiled at him.

"Boo," he said back to her. With a nod toward the decorative additions to the cabin, he said, "You've been busy."

"It's called motivation," she subtly complimented him. Holding up what was in her hand as she climbed the porch steps, she said, "I remembered seeing these wild cattails in back of the cabin." She wrapped her empty hand around Sully's biceps muscle and pulled herself close. With a grin, he lowered his head and kissed her. She bent over then and stuck the cattails in strategic spots among the yellow mums. "Did you know that in Victorian times cattails were a symbol of peace and prosperity?"

"I did not know that," Sully said. "But I thought when I pulled up how peaceful the cabin looked with your touches. All it needs is a hound dog asleep on the porch."

"I miss having a dog," she said, stepping into the cabin. "I had the sweetest little beagle, named Bingo, all through high school and college. Bingo would go to the flower shop with me and stay all day. But she's gone now."

"I love dogs and have had a couple over the years," Sully

said as he followed her into the cabin and shut the door. "A large dog could provide some protection."

"Have a seat," Charley said and pulled out a chair at the table for Sully in the cozy dining area of the great room. When he sat down, she handed him a corkscrew and the bottle of wine. Walking to the stove in the nearby kitchen, she asked, "What kind of large dog?"

"My favorite was the black Labrador retriever I had during and after college," he replied as he twisted the corkscrew. "Labs are a friendly, loyal, and energetic breed. In middle school and high school, I had a German shepherd, like Cash and Tracy have now. You met Dude, their dog," he reminded her as she nodded. "Derek and Chloe also have a German shepherd named Spike." He popped out the cork and poured two glasses of wine. When she came to him, he handed her a glass. "What shall we drink to?"

"A large dog?"

"A large dog."

Sully pulled her onto his lap, and they clinked their glasses. After a sip of wine, when Sully kissed her, Charley tingled. She'd made love to him three times within the last twenty-four hours, and yet she'd thought of little else all day. She couldn't get enough of this man. That was a first and she couldn't explain it. It was just…Sully. And only Sully. Charley told herself not to question it, but just to enjoy it.

"Do you like salad, salmon, and scalloped potatoes?"

"I do," he replied.

She smiled. "Well, that's not what we're having."

Sully laughed. "What?"

"I'm teasing." Charley giggled. "That's exactly what we're having. Sit tight." When she tried to scoot off his lap, he set his wine and then hers on the table. Holding her to him, as he kissed her, his tongue touched hers. She pictured letting dinner burn as she burned right along with it. When he loosened his hold, she kissed him again and then stood up between his legs. "We'll have the salmon first."

"First?"

"I mean we'll have the salad first," she said and laughed. "See what you do to me?"

"Tell me about it, city slicker," he said and cocked a brow.

Walking away from him to gather her senses, she opened the refrigerator and asked, "Are you ready for a tasty wild rocket salad with halved cherry tomatoes and cubed goat cheese with a splash of apple cider vinegar and virgin olive oil?"

Sully tilted his head and said seriously, "I had a tasty wild virgin last night."

Taking the bowl of salad out of the refrigerator, she turned to him and arched her brow. "Did you, now?"

"Yeah, we have yet to put the sheets back on my bed."

Walking to him, Charley said, "Today I bought a comforter for the cabin bed."

"Sounds like you might be planning to stay here instead of with me."

"My cabin tonight and your house tomorrow night?"

Sully's smile was slow and sexy. "Yeah."

Charley had enjoyed cooking for him and heaped a serving of salad on his plate. When they had finished their glasses of wine and the salads, she brought plates of salmon and scalloped potatoes to the table. Along with the entrée, she had purchased fresh bread from the bakery. It all melted into their mouths. When their plates were empty, Sully carried them to the kitchen and placed them in the deep, farm-style sink. As she rinsed the plates and put them into the dishwasher, he added logs to the fire. With a glance over her shoulder, Charley saw him sit down sideways at one end of the sofa, rest an arm along the back of it and crook a finger at her. Thrilling zaps of excitement jig-jagged their way throughout her entire body.

Leaving the kitchen, Charley shut the dining room drapes. Stopping at the front door, she locked it. In the living room, she drew those drapes as well and walked to Sully. He stretched out on the sofa and held out his hand. When she took it, he pulled her down on top of him. She had purchased a soft, dark orange sweater that reached her hips and black leggings when she'd been shopping. He ran his hand down her back and over her fanny. With a moan of longing, she closed her eyes and nibbled his ears between kisses.

The fire crackled, but it wasn't the cause of her red-hot skin. Wherever Sully touched her, she was on fire as surely as the logs in the hearth. He patted her fanny with both hands and suggested she pour two more glasses of wine. She scooted off him and headed to the dining room. He rolled off the sofa, followed her, and held the glasses as she poured. Pausing near the table, they kissed and sipped their wine.

"Time to flirt?" she whispered shyly.

"No," he said and set his glass on the dining room table. "I'm going home."

"What?" she asked in surprise and set her glass down as well. "You're leaving?"

"Hell no," he said around a smothered grin and then laughed. "But you're not the only one who can tease."

"Sully!" She laughed. "You're so ornery, I might not give you dessert."

Sully scooped her up in his arms and carried her through the cabin to the bedroom. He stood her beside the bed and pulled her sweater over her head. She tugged up his sweatshirt, emblazoned with his gun club logo over his heart, and he shed it. Both items landed on the polished hardwood floor. He pulled off his undershirt as she unbuckled his belt. She popped open his fly, shoved at his jeans, and he dropped them. Then he pulled her leggings down and she stepped out of them. She pushed his boxers down until they were stopped by his hardened manhood. Molding her against him, he unfastened her bra and tugged down her panties. When she stood back, her underwear fell to her feet. She pulled the front of his boxers out and let them drop to the floor. Sully kissed her and tossed back the new comforter along with the sheet. Charley lay down and held her arms out to him.

Sully stretched out on top of her. On previous occasions, she had stiffened. But no longer. Not now. Not tonight. Not with this man. Instead, similarly as he had done to her when she was fully clothed, Charley ran her hands down his naked back and over his slightly rounded male buttocks. He groaned, and she liked the power that it gave her at making this experienced man want more. He kissed his way down her throat, and her nipples beaded as his lips closed over her right one and then her left. She eagerly spread her legs, and his kisses found her most secret feminine spot. She thought she might lose her mind as a rolling orgasm engulfed her. Sully worked his kisses back up her body and his fingers opened her slippery folds.

"Wrap your legs around me." His deep voice was husky. "And we'll flirt."

Charley wrapped her legs around his hips. And with Sully's push, they became one. He was in to the hilt. Gloriously, blissfully they were one. She met his every thrilling thrust. Each plunge into paradise was a ride to remember. Charley felt the heat building within her again and clung to him. How could she ever let go of this man? Mentally or physically? The rapture hit, and she squeezed his long, hard inches with gripping, bursting pleasure.

"Sully," she moaned, floating in sweet ecstasy.

He answered with rhythmic throbs over and over deep inside her. She closed her eyes and savored every rock-hard, pulsing sensation. Only when their breathing had slowed did she unwind her legs from around him. He separated his body from hers, rolled off her, and pulled her into his arms. With her head on his chest, she listened to the beating of his heart.

"You've gotten flirting down," he praised.

"I've had a sensational teacher. I might give him dessert after all."

Chuckling, he gave her a squeeze. "Besides what you just gave me, what's for dessert?"

Charley giggled and rolled out of bed. She stepped into her panties and pulled her sweater over her head. "Come on," she said and grabbed his hand. "It's being served in the living room."

Sully rolled out of bed and tugged on his undershirt and boxers. He followed her and headed into the living room as she went into the kitchen. He added logs to the fire and stirred them to life. She returned to him with two plates, each holding a brownie with a scoop of vanilla ice cream on top. They sipped more of their wine as they ate, and then Sully's cell phone rang.

"Hey, Dad. What's up?" he asked and listened. "The shell casing recovered by the cops at the Fleming crime scene is a .38? Damn. I wish we could run a ballistics test on Vaughn's gun to see if it's a match." Sully paused, nodded, and then said, "Yeah, I realize there's no legal reason to seize his gun. Too bad we didn't buy it when given the chance." Again, he listened and then said, "Thanks for keeping me updated." They spoke for another minute before Sully hung up. He looked at Charley as if deciding whether or not to share the conversation.

"What is it, Sully?"

"Maybe nothing." Sully paused, and when she tilted her head, he said, "Vaughn's caliber of bullet from the gun he's been waving around is the same caliber used to kill your mother."

～

HE PACED THE FLOOR. WHERE WAS SHE? NO DOUBT WITH THAT rancher in the big truck. He had decided the other guy he'd run into in her shop was of little to no consequence. It was the one named Sully ruining everything. This morning he'd stopped by her shop. Still no sign of her. He had walked up the hill to her apartment. Not there. Gnawing on his thumbnail, the voices said that Charley had to come home sometime. Maybe not. Maybe the cowboy planned on keeping her all to himself. He shrieked at that thought. What were they up to? Had she had sex with the guy? Picturing that, he screamed again. He had to get Charley's attention.

CHAPTER TWENTY

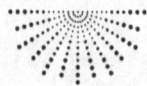

"*D*o you think Rod wanted rid of his gun because he killed my mom with it?" Charley asked.

"He'd be an idiot to try to unload it at my shop," Sully replied. "But he might be that stupid. Or maybe he was there hoping to confront me and find out if what I told him about the malfunctioning was accurate." Sitting on the sofa beside him, Charley hugged herself as he said, "Or maybe he wanted to gauge if I suspected something about him."

"I don't know what to think," Charley said. "But I do know one thing, Rod was really angry when I refused to—to—"

"To what?" Sully asked when she looked away from him.

"*Flirt* with him." With a sigh, she asked, "When will I ever be able to go home?"

"I don't know." Sully pulled the beautiful, vulnerable woman into his arms. "But you have options. You have this cabin, and you can stay with me at my house."

"But my flower shop is in Old Colorado City," she said, her pretty brow furrowing. "My duplex is there. My livelihood is on Colorado Avenue."

"Livelihood in the midst of death."

"In the midst of death," she echoed softly. "How sad."

"Business has dropped off there anyway. Let's take things one day at a time."

"You're right." Charley eased her way out of his embrace and sat up straighter on the sofa. "I don't mean to sound sorry for myself."

"You don't, and I understand." He swept a long lock of hair away from her face to her back. "If I thought I was unsafe in my own home and business, I'd feel as discouraged and unsure of what to do next as you do."

Charley nodded. "I have you and the Coopers. Barely more than a month ago I was all alone."

"Come with me to work tomorrow," Sully suggested. "Randy and I have a group of three coming in who want to ride and do some skeet shooting. I checked on Rain, and you can ride her tomorrow. It will be a gentle exercise for her. You'll be doing us a favor."

Charley stared at him. The fire in the hearth crackled and glistened in her royal-blue eyes. The softest of smiles touched her full lips, and her head tilted. She was so beautiful, and she had such a spectacular body. He was honored to have been her first. He smiled and then inwardly balked at the probability of not being her only or her last. Hell. As gracious as she was funny and as compassionate as she was brave, a realization crossed Sully's mind.

He was falling in love with Charley Cooper.

Sully reared back a little at that jarring thought. Where did the idea of love come from? He'd never been in love. Never thought he would be. Never thought he needed to be. He watched a single tear roll down her soft, ivory cheek and gently thumbed it away.

"I'll be forever grateful to you for how you stepped in from the day I met you and took charge. You're handsome, smart, and generous. You could be anywhere with anyone you chose," Charley whispered. "But you're here with me tonight." She twined her arms around his neck and holding him to her heart, she said with conviction, "You're my hero, Sullivan Custis."

Yeah, he loved her. Not just tonight. Forever.

~

"ALL RIGHT, CITY SLICKER," SULLY BEGAN OUTSIDE THE STABLES
the next day after handing the reins to the mare to her and
placing her hand on the pommel of the saddle. "Slide your
left foot into the stirrup like you did when you rode behind
me on Storm. Give a little hop on your right foot and swing
yourself onto Rain."

"I will." Charley didn't miss the stirrup on her first try
this time, but her tennis shoe slid all the way through the
stirrup. Her eyes widened, and her cheeks turned red. "Or
not."

"Randy, take our customers and head out to the skeet
range," Sully said. "We're going to ride to Triple C-East and
get Charley a pair of boots."

"Okay, boss," Randy called, and with a nudge to his
horse, led three well-paying gentlemen away from the
stables.

Charley said, "I've never seen Cash's store or stables."

"He's got everything a city slicker needs to turn her into
a country girl."

"Well, hang on," Charley said, and with a pat to Rain's
neck, she started toward his truck. "Can you open your
truck for me?"

"Sure. Why?" he said and unlocked the truck with his
key fob.

"My purse is under the seat of your truck. I need my
credit card."

Sully clicked the remote a second time, locking the truck
just before Charley yanked on the door handle. Her head
snapped backward, her braid danced, and she turned to him
with her hands on her hips. She was so cute and sexy. He'd
held those saucy hips this morning when she'd straddled
him in bed, and, totally naked, she'd fed him strawberries

before they'd flirted. He hadn't taught her how to make love cowgirl style yet. But he intended to.

"Let's saddle up," he said. "You can pay me back later."

"Okay," she said agreeably. "I *will* saddle up this time."

Sully stood by to make sure she was safe, and this time, her foot didn't slip through the stirrup. When she was settled on Rain, Sully gave her knee a pat and saddled up on Storm. They took the shortcut between his ranch and Triple C Ranch-South. Ten minutes later, they passed in front of her cabin. Everything was calm and quiet, so they ventured along the main highway. Crossing it took them to Triple C Ranch-East. Riding down the main drive of the ranch would take them to the house. Heading along the right side of the drive wrapped around to the dude ranch. Sully veered to the left, which took them to Cash's store. Sully dismounted, and Charley did so all on her own. After tethering the horses so they could drink from the water trough, Sully grabbed her hand. Opening the door and letting two customers, carrying bags, leave first he and Charley then entered her cousin's shop.

"Howdy folks," Cash called from behind the counter. "Come on in. What's up?"

"Hi, Cash," Sully said, lifting his hand in a wave.

"Hi, Cash," Charley echoed. "Apparently, I need some cowboy boots."

"Sully brought you to the right place," Cash said. Coming around the counter, he gave Charley a hug and then shook hands with Sully. "What size do you wear, Charley?"

"Seven."

"Over here," Cash said, and with a wave over his shoulder led them through the roomy shop full of saddles and every kind of riding accessory, past the Western wear for men and women, to the displays of men's, women's, and children's boots. "Let me know what strikes your fancy, Charley."

"My gosh," Charley said, taking in the wide variety of

styles and colors as she began to look. "I love all the choices."

"I didn't know if this would be your day in the store or out on the trails," Sully said, knowing Cash and his employees took turns running the store.

"I'm sticking close to home these last few weeks of Tracy's pregnancy to be on the safe side," Cash said. "Speaking of being safe, what's the latest on the Old Colorado City murders?"

"In addition to Charley's mother being shot, there have been five women in Charley's age range strangled to death," Sully said.

"What's your dad have to say about the killings?" Cash asked.

"We've considered that guy, named Vaughn, who you met the other day as the killer."

"I can see that," Cash replied with a frown. "I didn't like him."

"Me, neither. Turns out Vaughn has a gun that takes the same caliber bullet as the one that killed Charlotte Fleming." Sully paused and said, "That's off the record."

"Got it," Cash said with a nod. "Absolutely."

"But Vaughn's killing doesn't fit the other murders," Sully added.

"Right," Cash agreed. "That's what I was thinking."

"What about these boots, Cash?" Charley asked, holding up a red leather boot.

"Excellent choice," Cash said and walked toward her. "A very well-made boot with the perfect heel to keep your foot from sliding through the stirrup."

"Yup, she needs that," Sully said with a chuckle.

"True," Charley said and laughed. Cash had her size in stock, and Charley, smiling happily, said they fit perfectly. "What do you think, Sully?"

Bringing his eyes from her feet up her legs, to her flat stomach, and over her full breasts to her feminine shoulders, and stopping when her blue eyes captured his, Sully said, "Beautiful."

"Perfect," Cash said. "Wrap 'em up or are you gonna wear 'em?"

"I'll wear them. We're going skeet shooting," Charley said. As Sully pulled a money clip out of his pocket, she quickly asked, "How much are they, Cash?"

Cash didn't answer but had noticed Sully take out his money. He nodded for Sully to follow him to the back counter to the cash register. Sully knew when Cash told him the price, it was one hell of a deal and was about to argue.

Cash held up a hand and said, "First-time family purchase sells for cost."

"Cash, no, you don't have to do that," Charley protested, walking toward them.

"Already done," Cash said as he gave Sully back the change due to him. "We can't have you falling off—" He looked at Sully and asked, "Who's she riding? Rain?"

"Yup, Rain," Sully said as Cash placed Charley's tennis shoes into the boot box and then into a bag. "Rain was bitten by a small prairie rattler the other day, but she didn't have much reaction and is doing well."

"Time of the year when snakes are looking for one last meal before they hibernate," Cash commented, rounding the counter. Handing the bag to Sully, Cash looked at Charley's boots and said, "You're gonna be a cowgirl before you know it."

"I hope so," Charley said and hugged Cash. "Thank you, cousin." Turning to Sully, she slipped her dainty hand into his and said, "Thank you, Sully."

They spoke for a few minutes and then more customers bustled through the door. Sully also thanked Cash and they shook hands before he and Charley walked across the store to leave.

"See you at Chloe and Derek's on Halloween," Cash called as they reached the door.

"We'll be there," Sully replied. "Got my costume."

"What are you going to be?" Charley asked him again outside the store.

"Your date."

"So you've said." She laughed as they walked to the horses. "How can that be your costume?"

"Because," he said with a laugh, and using the handle of her bag, draped it over the pommel of Storm's saddle. "You're a full-time job."

"You take that back!" she snapped with a grin as she untethered Rain.

Leading Storm and walking toward her, Sully said, "You're a handful."

"So are you," Charley said. Sully stopped in front of her, and when he bent his head to kiss her, with a quick glance left and right, Charley covertly cupped her hands to the soft bulge in the crotch of his jeans. "Mmm."

Teasing her, he said, "Charley!" And then, with a groan, he pushed against her hands.

"Wanna flirt at my house before we catch up with the skeet shooters?"

"Hell, yes. Forget the skeet shooters. Randy has them under control." With a grin, he took hold of her and turned her toward Rain. "Saddle up, cowgirl." He gave her a boost, and she was up on Rain. He mounted Storm, and with a wink at Charley, he said, "Let's go flirt."

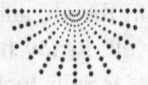

CHAPTER TWENTY-ONE

"*H*appy Halloween," Charley whispered into the mirror in the master bath at Sully's house.

Charley had been with Sully at her cabin or his house for three and a half weeks. He wouldn't hear of her paying him back for the gun or boots. In turn, she made good on her plan to surprise him with a delivery of Rocky Mountain Columbines and a few of her favorite plants for his store. She'd cooked for him, and he'd grilled steaks as promised. They played in his jacuzzi, made love at her cabin as well as his house, had ridden in his Jeep with the top and doors off, and become inseparable. Every time they were at his gun club, he'd given her target practice lessons and she had helped with his customers. Sully claimed that not only was she a naturally great salesperson, but the male customers were all charmed by her and therefore bought his most expensive weapons and doubled their needed ammunition.

This morning, she and Sully had ridden out with Randy, who, like Roy, owned his own horse, and a group of four skeet shooters. She had marveled at how professional Sully was with the two men and two women in explaining the technique of skeet shooting. Randy had launched several clay targets from a target thrower, and using a 12-gauge shotgun, Sully demonstrated his skill by hitting every single target. He was friendly, encouraging, and patient as he gave final instructions to the foursome before they tried to follow in his footsteps. Once again, Randy had sent clay targets flying into the sky, and over the next hour, a few targets were hit.

With Sully and Randy and the guests urging her on, Charley had given it a try. After missing three clay targets, the last one exploded in the air, and everyone clapped. A good time was had by all. Randy had escorted the guests back to the Custis stables as Sully took Charley on a side trip to a stream that ran across Triple C Ranch-South and floated lazily through his ranch. She'd packed their lunches, and they'd eaten deli sandwiches and potato chips while sitting on a boulder near the water.

Always enjoying the sound of Sully's mellow baritone voice as he talked about his love of ranch life, his horses, and running his gun club, a recurring tune that had been playing softly in the back of Charley's mind once again rushed to the forefront in full melody.

She was head-over-heels in love with Sullivan Custis.

Refocusing on the bathroom mirror now, being in love with Sully crescendoed so loudly in her head, Charley glanced at the closed bathroom door as though he might have heard her thoughts. She was crazy in love with her protector. Her defender. Her hero.

"I love you, Sully," Charley whispered into the mirror.

"Hey, you," Sully said from the other side of the door, making Charley jump.

"Hay is for horses!" she squealed and heard Sully laugh.

"Time to show me your costume."

"Have you got yours on?" she asked through the door.

"Yes."

Charley gave herself a last look in the mirror. A light brown cap with chin-length ears covered most of her head. She'd sliced a hole in the middle back of the cap and pulled her braid through it. She'd drawn black eyeliner around her eyes, dabbed on extra mascara, and colored the end of her nose coal black. She was zipped into a form-fitting, softly furred light brown, white, and black one-piece costume. She fastened the bejeweled red collar, with the name *Bingo* on it, around her neck. It delighted her that the collar matched her shiny red lipstick and red leather cowboy boots.

Placing her hand on the doorknob, she said, "Promise not to laugh."

"I promise."

Charley opened the door. Sully stood before her, with his large hands on his tapered hips. He wore his black cowboy hat over his thick black hair. A couple days of growth of black beard gave him that rough and rowdy look that was so sexy. A black leather vest fit over a long-sleeved white button-down shirt tucked into a pair of snug blue jeans. A black leather belt, fastened by a big silver buckle boasting his gun store logo, matched his black cowboy boots.

"You look gorgeous, cowboy," Charley said. "Where's your costume?"

Sully pulled back the left side of his leather vest to display a silver star. "Wyatt Earp, Deputy US Marshal here to protect the—" he paused to overtly look her up and down, "sexiest beagle puppy west of the Mississippi River."

Charley did a little curtsy. "Thank you."

"Gotta tail?" he asked. Charley turned around and wiggled her fanny, making the brown and white tail dance along with her braid. "Hell. Do we have to go to the party? Can't we stay here, and I'll strip you outta that costume instead?"

"No." Charley giggled, twirling to face him. "We told everybody we'd be there."

"Damn." Sully groaned. "We'll say we forgot." Pulling her to him, his strong arms closed around her as his lips touched hers. His mouth opened, and their tongues played.

Then leaning back, she said, "Don't try to sidetrack me, Wyatt. We have to go." Sully grumbled, but let her tug him out of the bedroom. Charley grabbed her purse and the keys to her little red convertible that they'd picked up earlier that day. "Want to take my car?"

"Yes, since you drove it here, I'd like to drive it to Triple C-West and see how it handles," he said.

"Please do the honors, Marshal Earp," Charley said and dropped the keys into his hand.

"Okay, but we're coming back to my house as soon as we can."

Sully drove them to Triple C Ranch-West, where orange lanterns hung from the pine trees along the driveway. Several cars were already parked near the house. More orange lanterns lit up the pretty, wraparound porch decorated with hanging ferns, white rockers, and carved pumpkins.

As Sully stopped the car, Charley said, "We have to stay for at least an hour."

"We'll see," Sully said with a cocky grin and got out of the car. She did as well and met him as he came around to her side and returned her car keys. She put the keys in her purse and her phone in her pocket, as he said, "Your Mini Cooper handles nicely."

"Glad you think so," she said. The insurance company had only been willing to repair, not replace the slashed tires. "Thank you for the new tires, Sully."

"You're welcome. I want you to be safe on the highway," Sully said. "If it rains, snows, or is icy, these country roads can get treacherous. So be safe and don't speed." As they paused in the lights of the porch and driveway, he said, "I think the convertible top looks like new."

"It looks just like the day I bought it. Thank you for recommending that body shop."

"My pleasure." He nodded toward the main road as a hay wagon full of people, pulled by two big horses, turned onto the long drive. "Here come Cash and this week's dude ranchers."

Charley and Sully waited for them beside the porch steps. As the hay wagon neared, Cash and little Carly waved to them. Cash hopped down from the driver's seat and turned to Carly, who'd been beside him. A middle-aged man who Sully identified for Charley as Sam Reynolds, Cash's ranch foreman, handed Carly to her father.

"Happy Halloween," Cash called to them as Derek strode onto the porch.

"Happy Halloween," Derek called to everyone. His costume consisted of a buckskin vest over his shirt, jeans, boots, and a buckskin cowboy hat. "Welcome. Where's Tracy?"

"Coming in the car with Kellie," Cash said.

"Who's Kellie?" Charley asked Sully.

"Sam's wife. She manages the restaurant at the Lodge."

No sooner had Sully spoken than a car carrying the two women just mentioned turned onto the ranch. Kellie parked the car, and Cash helped Tracy out. Cash introduced Sam and Kellie to Charley, and then the two senior employees of Triple C Ranch-East assisted Derek in ushering the dude ranchers inside to the party.

"I love the hayrides," Tracy said to Charley and Sully. "But we decided with me being just over eight months pregnant, I should travel by car this Halloween."

"You and Carly look absolutely adorable, Tracy," Charley said.

"Thank you. So do you," Tracy said. She and Carly wore matching pumpkin costumes. "This costume was conducive to my pregnant belly."

"It's perfect," Charley agreed.

Cash was dressed similarly to Sully and Derek, but with a white mask across his eyes. A truck pulled into the driveway next. Chase and Jade were in the front seats, along with nine-year-old Colton and seven-year-old Courtney in the back seat. Two weeks prior, Chase and Jade had taken Charley and Sully to dinner at the Lodge so that Charley could meet Jade and the kids.

Charley found Jade as kind and gracious as she was beautiful. In past years, Chloe said Jade had come to the

Halloween party as Marilyn Monroe, and that would certainly fit the woman whom Chase called his blonde bombshell. As for Chase, he was handsome and formidable as always, a man clearly devoted to his wife and children. This evening, Chase wore a black mask over his eyes. Jade, with her blond hair, was a perfect Glenda the Good Witch from *The Wizard of Oz*. Courtney as Dorothy, her hair in pigtails, wore a blue and white dress and sparkly red shoes. Colton, doing his own thing, was a ninja.

"Happy Halloween!" Chloe Cooper Brevard said in greeting.

Dressed like a lady from the wild and wooly old West, Chloe stood in the doorway of the big country house. Earlier that week, the Brevards had treated Charley and Sully to a backyard barbecue. Like she had with Colton and Courtney, Charley had fallen in love with the Brevard children: Cooper, who was ten, and the eight-year-old twins, Austin and Abilene. Entering the house, for the next few minutes it was a veritable free-for-all as everyone, including the dude ranchers, greeted everyone. The children had put together special treats for each other, and those were busily exchanged, too, along with hugs.

"I'm Miss Kitty tonight and you remember my husband, Marshal Matt Dillon," Chloe Brevard said to Charley, referring to Derek as they stood near a unique indoor fishpond in the foyer. "Your costume is adorable, Charley. As you know, we are big fans of dogs and cats here."

"Yes, thanks. It's nice to see you both again, Chloe," Charley said. "Marshal Dillion, I believe you have something in common with my date, Marshal Earp."

"Glad you could make it, Sully," Derek said with a grin as they shook hands.

At that point, the kids made note of Charley's puppy dog costume and wanted pictures taken with *Bingo*. Sully grinned and winked at her as she posed with her little cousins. The Coopers' Aunt Rachel and her husband, Martyman, as everyone called him, introduced themselves and said they had reprised their recent roles as Bonnie and Clyde. Owen Custis arrived and threatened to take the bank robbers to jail. But instead, Bonnie and Clyde showed him, along with Sully and Charley, to their speakeasy, otherwise known as the wet bar in the den. Charley took a glass of wine as Sully and Owen accepted beers. They mingled as they moseyed from room to room, talking to folks and sampling appetizers.

The party snacks were as festive as they were tasty. In the dining room, a variety of crackers surrounded a cheese ball in the shape of a scarecrow wearing a noodle hat above his olive eyes and pecan nose. Deviled eggs were tinted orange with sliced sweet pickles for a stem, making them look like miniature pumpkins. Individual pizzas with pepperonis for eyes and a mouth peeking from behind mozzarella strips looked like mummies. A favorite among the children were the rattlesnake bites, which were hotdogs baked in crescent rolls. Cut into pieces and shaped into slithering snakes with red bell peppers sliced into a forked tongue, they were gone in a hurry. Bowls of popcorn, candy corn, and chips were placed throughout the house. And since this was a night for sweet treats, there were desserts such as pumpkin bread in the shape of a pumpkin, severed green witch finger cookies with an almond nail and red jam for blood, and zombie brain cupcakes, which the Brevard kids helped decorate, hence the crazy frosting oozing out of the top. Chloe, a cat lover, said her personal favorite were the chocolate cookies with cat ears and whiskers.

Sully introduced Charley to the veterinarian who had taken care of Rain. Jill Henderson's husband, Don, was also a veterinarian who cared for the Cooper livestock. They were both polite and friendly. As the party wore on, Charley figured she and Sully had visited with just about everyone there. When Sully excused himself to return their empty glasses to the kitchen, Charley was in the foyer as she noticed a late arrival. The woman named Trish Potter stopped Sully in the hallway. Though a pang of concern jabbed Charley, not wanting to stare, she looked away. When she glanced back, Trish and Sully were gone.

"I didn't expect to see you here," came a woman's voice on Charley's right.

Charley turned to the woman who had spoken. "Hello, Trish." Her long black hair was teased into a beehive, and she wore an extreme version of an Elvira, Mistress of the Dark, costume. Her breath reeked of alcohol. "We met briefly in Sully's kitchen."

"Yeah," Trish said. The woman's costume was cut so daringly low cut in the front, her cleavage was on display almost to her nipples. A wide slit up the front of the dress stopped just below the vee in her legs. Charley did not consider herself a prude, but this was not an appropriate outfit to wear to a party with children in attendance. Trish eyed Charley's costume with a definite smirk and asked, "So, you're Sully's bitch tonight?"

"Excuse me?"

"A female dog is a bitch," Trish said. When Charley didn't comment, Trish ran a hand with long black nails over her breasts, reached into a small purse, and pulled out a flask. She tipped it to her mouth and took a precariously close step to the fishpond. "Didn't Sully tell you about the two of us?"

"No," Charley said, feeling uncomfortable.

"Sully and I are a thing, and your whole damsel in distress charade is causing trouble," Trish hissed under her breath and waved the flask before shoving it back into her purse.

Charley didn't view herself as a damsel in distress, and her situation certainly wasn't a farce. "Really?" Charley replied to Trish's statement as to her being with Sully. Though she'd rather wait to see if Trish fell into the fishpond, Charley took a step to leave.

"Stop!" Trish spat and splayed a hand in front of Charley. "Yes, really," she replied to Charley's question. "I'm pregnant, and Sully is my baby's daddy."

The pang of concern became a knife in Charley's heart. She was speechless. She sucked in a breath, and her stomach rolled as she glanced at Trish's flat abdomen. Sully's words echoed in her head: *I always wear a condom.* What kind of woman drank knowing she was pregnant? From across the room, Chloe caught Charley's eye and smiled. Seeing that Charley was talking to Trish, Chloe rolled her blue eyes as if to convey: *pay no attention to her* or *sorry she's here.*

"Does Sully know?" Charley asked barely above a whisper.

"*Bingo!*" Trish said in a snotty voice, glaring at the name on Charley's collar. "He knows as of tonight. Why do you think he ditched you, leaving you standing by the door all alone?" Trish snickered as if Charley was completely naïve and utterly stupid. "He's excited about our baby and agrees you need to go." With that, Trish swung her arm into the air, flinging black trails of fabric on her sleeve in Charley's face. "Vamoose, bitch!"

CHAPTER TWENTY-TWO

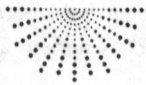

"*H*ave you seen Charley?" Sully asked Cash, who was herding his group of dude ranchers across the wide, front porch where Sully was standing under the festive orange lights. It had rained during the party and was sprinkling again. The night was dark due to the heavy rain clouds covering the moon.

"No, not since Tracy and I were talking to you two earlier," Cash said and turned in the direction of the cars and the hay wagon. "Tracy, do you know where Charley is?"

"No," she said as Sully walked down the porch steps. Tracy was in the passenger's seat of Kellie's car as she replied, "The last time I saw Charley was when she and Carly were eating pizza mummies together."

"I love Charley and pizza mummies," Carly called from the back seat.

"Thanks," Sully said, and then the ladies left with a wave at Cash who was headed toward the hay wagon.

Sully loved Charley, too, and wondered where she was. His dad was out on the driveway and had just said goodbye to Chase and family. At that moment, the headlights from Chase's SUV lit up the darkness where Sully had parked Charley's Mini Cooper earlier. Her little red car was gone.

He remembered giving the car keys back to her. Charley had left without telling him?

"Where's Charley?" his dad asked, walking to him.

"I don't know," Sully replied. "When was the last time you saw her?"

"Ten minutes or so," Owen said, with a wave goodbye at the hay wagon.

"Derek, did you see Charley before she left?" Sully asked as Derek came toward them with twins, Austin and Abilene, in tow.

"No. Last time I saw her, she was talking to a friend of Chloe's," Derek replied.

Waving goodbye to Chase and family, Chloe and Cooper joined them in the driveway near the porch. Then the three Brevard children said good night and hurried inside to their candy.

"Friend is a loose term," Chloe said. "Trish wormed one invitation out of me years ago, but never again. She showed up tonight totally uninvited. Why?"

"Charley's gone," Sully said. "We came together, and I'm confused as to why she would leave without me."

"The last person I saw Charley talking to was Trish," Chloe said. "I thought Charley looked trapped and was about to go intervene, but when I looked back, they were both gone."

"Okay, thanks," Sully said. "I'll call Charley and find out what's going on."

"I hope it's not something to do with another murder in her neighborhood," Derek said.

"Right," Owen agreed. Then to Sully, he said, "I'll give you a ride home, son."

"Thanks for having us tonight," Sully said and shook Derek's hand.

As it started to rain harder, headlights at the end of the driveway suddenly flashed.

"Maybe this is Charley," Chloe said as a car came toward them in the darkness.

"Need a ride, Sully?" Trish asked as she came to a stop in front of them.

Sully took a couple of steps closer to Trish's car as his dad made his way to his own vehicle. Chloe and Derek gave them privacy by going into their house but left the porch light on out of courtesy. Sully's dad got in out of the rain but waited.

"Trish, did you happen to see Charley leave tonight?" Sully asked.

"Who?" Trish asked.

"Charley, the Coopers' cousin," Sully said patiently. "You met her at my house."

"Oh, the dog," Trish said with a contemptuous wave of her hand. "Hop in and I'll give you a ride, Marshal Earp."

"My dad's waiting to give me a ride."

"Come on, Sully. For old time's sake?" Trish asked. "I'll take you straight home. Cross my heart," she said, making a show of running her finger across her barely covered breasts.

"No thanks," Sully said and stepped back from her car.

"I might know why the bitch left," Trish said.

Sully clenched his jaw. "Yeah? Why?"

Trish shrugged and said, "Get in, Sully."

Sully crossed his arms over his chest and said through gritted teeth, "Tell me here, Trish."

"If you don't want to know—" Trish shrugged and started to pull away.

"Hold on," Sully said. He motioned to his dad to go on as he strode around the rear of Trish's car. Owen pulled away, heading onto the highway. Sully yanked open the door to Trish's car and slid into the passenger's seat. "What do you know about Charley leaving the party?"

"Let's discuss it at your house," she said. "I promise not to jump your bones—unless you want me to."

Trish turned her car around and drove down the drive. This was not the car Sully wanted to be in, nor the woman with whom he'd planned to spend the night. Sully called

Charley's phone, but it went to voice mail. Trish turned east, as if keeping her word to take Sully home. They passed Triple C-Central, and after passing Triple C-East, in the far distance up ahead Sully saw his dad turn south and disappear.

As they neared Triple C Ranch-South, despite the pouring rain, Sully rolled down his window. His eyes were peeled for Charley, and he asked Trish to slow down. She sped up. Ponderosa pines whizzed past in a blur, and then Sully caught a side view of Charley's car. It was paused at the end of her gravel drive close to the highway. In the head-lights of Trish's car, he saw Charley behind the wheel. And she saw him. As Trish raced past Charley, Sully called her cell again, but Charley didn't answer. He left a quick message.

"Stop!" Sully told Trish. "Go back!"

She didn't. Where Sully's dad had turned south as Trish should have, she didn't.

"So, how have you been, Sully?"

"Slow down and turn the damn car around, Trish," he ordered.

She didn't. Instead, Trish sped up even more and said, "Here's a trick, let's treat ourselves by going to my house and screwing each other until we pass out."

"Hell no!" he barked. "You're drunk and I'm not inter-ested. Stop the car. I'll walk."

"No! They wouldn't serve me at the wet bar. So, I went to my car and emptied my flask, waiting for you to come out of the house. If I'm drunk, it's your fault," she spat and made a show of stomping on the gas pedal. "You were mine until that bitch came along."

"Bull!" It had been at least six months since they'd last gone out, and he'd been done back then. "I was never yours," Sully said as the car flew down the wet highway. "Is that what you told Charley?"

"Halloween's a night for tricking and scaring people." Trish laughed way too loudly and purposely swerved through the rain from one side of the road to the other. "Oooh! Scared?"

"Stop it!" he said as to her intoxicated, erratic driving. "What do you mean tricking and scaring people?"

Trish took her eyes off the road and said to him, "I told the bitch I was pregnant and you're my baby's daddy."

"Dammit," Sully growled through his teeth as Trish drove ever faster. "You and I both know that's a lie."

"Boo!" Trish laughed. Looking at him instead of the highway again, she hissed, "Tricked her, and now you're scared you can't get the bitch back. Happy Halloween, Sully!"

Sully made a grab for the ignition key to turn off the car. But Trish yanked the steering wheel so hard they careened into the other lane of the road. An oncoming car blared its horn. Sully grabbed the wheel and brought the car back into the correct lane.

"Stop the damn car!" Sully yelled.

Trish shouted no and stomped on the gas again. She yanked the wheel so hard rounding a curve in the road, they fishtailed across the highway. Tires hydroplaned on the rainwater, and they careened over a slippery embankment. Trish screamed as the world flipped upside down. The car rolled over and over down the hill, and the last thing Sullivan Custis saw was blackness.

CHAPTER TWENTY-THREE

"*W*hat in the world?" Charley mumbled as she bumped into something on her pitch-black porch.

Fishing her new apartment key out of her purse, she opened her front door. Stepping into the small foyer, she switched on the porch light. Setting her purse on the wing-back chair in the living room, she backtracked to the door. On the porch, she had knocked over a vase of flowers. Picking up the broken vase and stepping around the spilled water, she gathered up the flowers. Closing and locking the door, she slid the chain into place too. Then she set the pieces of the broken vase on the countertop between the living room and kitchen. She placed the flowers beside the broken glass and noticed the florist's card among the multicolored blooms.

Charley ignored the card and, rubbing her forehead, meandered across the living room. Having taken off her wet beagle cap but still clad in her costume, she dropped onto the sofa. As rain pelted the window, she sat staring blankly at the curtains over the glass.

At Triple C Ranch-West, she'd had the shock of her life. Sully had a girlfriend. He was handsome and charming. He had a huge ranch and a successful business. He'd no doubt had a bunch of women chasing after him and a lot of girl-friends over the years.

Charley wished he would have given her a fair warning about the one named Trish.

Following the trauma of the attempted assault and her mother's murder, Charley had been profoundly comforted by Sully's strong, protective influence. She had fallen hard for him. He had helped her to get past the assault so completely she'd given herself to him. With no promises, no protection, no nothing—she had given Sully her all.

To find out he was going to have a baby with another woman was an enormous emotional blow. She wasn't sure she could handle the situation on her own. But she had no one to turn to. No one to confide in. Not true. She had the Coopers. But, Sully had known them long before she came along. As for her, she'd only known Sully for a short time. She'd been an utter fool.

Charley curled into a fetal position on the sofa, and her thoughts raced.

After Trish had told her to vamoose, Charley glanced around for Sully. He'd been nowhere in sight. Trish had already said he'd ditched her, and that appeared to be true. To head off any awkwardness for the Coopers, Charley had quietly left the house and hurried across the driveway to her car. She'd driven straight to her cabin. How happy she'd been there with Sully. He had seemed so genuine and happy too.

Planning to get out and go into the cabin, she'd opened the car door and then stopped. With the rain pouring so hard, she'd closed the door and sat in the dark car as her thoughts swirled. Should she call Sully? Weren't there two sides to every story? She'd heard Trish's side. Shouldn't Sully have the chance to tell his side? Well, if he had been interested in telling his side, he would have made the effort to do so. But no, her cell phone had remained silent. No calls from Sully. No texts. Maybe there was nothing left for him to say. Trish had said it all.

How was Sully supposed to get home? Starting her car, Charley had turned it around in order to go find him and ask for an explanation. Surely, she deserved that much from him. She'd had to stop at the end of the gravel road where it met the highway as a car came zooming in her direction. When it passed, Charley had clearly seen Sully in the passenger's seat. Trish was driving, and Sully had looked right at her. They'd kept going. And still, he'd not contacted her.

Charley couldn't hold the tears back another minute. And once she'd started crying, she couldn't stop. As she lay on her sofa, her hair grew soaked with tears, her nose ran, and her entire body ached from the sobs racking her.

When she opened her eyes, it wasn't because of the late morning sun filtering in through the curtains at the living room window, but due to a noise at her front door. She immediately stiffened. She was back in the Old Colorado City neighborhood where gruesome murders remained unsolved. She'd promised Sully she wouldn't come back here alone. Oh well. Any deals with Sully were off the table now. She sat up on the sofa and listened. Nothing. She noticed the broken vase and wilted flowers on the countertop. She walked across the room and opened the card.

Please give me another chance. Rod.

If only she could hear those words from Sully. But to what end? To no end. He was going to be a father to his and Trish's baby.

Charley heard the noise again. A shuffling sound. A brush against the door. She cautiously padded to the window and peeked out the curtains. Though her heart was shattered and bleeding, somehow cheery sunlight filled the front yard. She saw no vehicle in the parking area other than hers. She turned, and seeing Rod's card again made her feel even more alone. If Sully were here, he'd roll his eyes and probably pitch the flowers out. She walked to the door.

Keeping the chain in its place, she slowly turned the knob and carefully looked across her porch.

"Hello?" Charley said, seeing no one. "Hello?" She was about to close the door when a flash of black appeared on the doormat. Then a little black nose poked into the opening. Charley looked down into two brown eyes. "Who are you?"

Charley removed the chain across the door and took a quick, visual sweep of the porch. No one was there except for a skinny black puppy staring up at her. When Charley stepped forward, the puppy scampered backward but with a limp. She crouched down and reached out her hand. On three paws, the puppy cautiously hobbled toward her.

"Are you hurt? Where's your owner?" Charley asked, with another glance around. "As much as I might somewhat look the part, wearing this costume, I'm not a dog." She saw no other dogs or puppies anywhere in the vicinity. This one had no collar. "Are you a stray? Like me?"

With the tiniest of barks, as if to confirm he had no owner and was indeed a stray, the puppy then sat down in front of Charley. He lifted his right paw into the air and panted. Charley noticed a couple of pieces of broken glass on the ground from the vase she'd knocked over the previous night. Ever so gently, she picked up the puppy and walked inside, making sure to lock the door behind her.

"You look like you might be a couple of months old. You are seriously underweight and really dirty," she said. "But you're very smart. I'm all by my lonesome up on this hill and you found me."

Taking the little dog into the kitchen, she placed him in the sink and examined his paw. There was blood on it. He pulled his paw back, but she carefully took hold again and saw a broken piece of glass in the center pad. Holding the puppy in place with her left hand, she carefully pulled out the sliver of glass with her right. A bit of blood followed, and Charley dabbed it away with a wet paper towel. She soaped the puppy up with dollops of dish liquid, sometimes used to clean oil off birds or animals, and then thoroughly rinsed him. Wrapping him in a clean, terry cloth dish towel, she dried him as she returned to the living room. There, she released him and the puppy gingerly touched his paw to the floor. Taking a step, he was able to put weight on it. Charley found Bingo's old bowls under the sink and filled one with water. The puppy eagerly lapped up the water as she went to her fridge and took out a carton of eggs.

"Bingo and I used to love scrambled eggs, so even though it's past breakfast time, that's what we'll have," Charley told him. She set the eggs on the counter, took a pan out of the cabinet, and broke several eggs into it. Once she had them cooking, she went into her bedroom, and the puppy followed her. She finally took off her beagle costume, and standing in her underwear, she dropped it onto the floor. "See I told you, I'm not a beagle. Sorry."

When the eggs were scrambled, she gave half to the puppy. He ate while she sat at the table for two in the nook at the end of her kitchen. The puppy finished his eggs in a few gobbles. Charley could only swallow twice before tears threatened again. She gave the puppy the rest of her eggs and returned to her bedroom. Grabbing jeans, a sweatshirt, and underwear, she went into the bathroom. She turned on the shower and cried. She shampooed her hair and cried. She scrubbed her body and cried. She rinsed off and cried. She dried herself and cried. Back out of the shower, she saw the puppy had fallen asleep in the middle of her beagle costume.

Dressed, she went into the kitchen to clean it up, and glancing across the countertop, she noticed her purse in the living room chair. Not one sound from the cell phone inside the purse. What did she expect? Sully wasn't giving her any thought. He was off on a new adventure. Finishing in the kitchen, Charley brushed her teeth and hair.

Could she have missed his call when she was in the shower? Doubtful. But she decided she finally had the strength to look at her phone knowing she'd be devastated not to have a call or text from Sully. With a sigh and steeling herself against shattering disappointment, she walked to the wingback chair in the living room. Picking up her purse, she opened it. Searching through her purse, she became frantic. Her cell phone was not there.

"Oh no," she whispered in dread.

Where was her phone? She rushed out to her car and thoroughly searched it. Her phone was not there either. She'd not had such a sense of aloneness since the day of her mother's funeral. The Coopers had yet to contact her at that time and she'd felt completely isolated. It was one of the reasons she'd accepted a date from Rod Vaughn. Ugh, Rod. That made her think of the broken glass on the porch. She locked her car and quickly cleaned up a few stray pieces of glass. Tossing the shards, along with the broken vase and wilted flowers into the kitchen trash can, she tried to recall where she could have left her phone.

Her costume had pockets! Charley remembered putting the car keys into her purse after Sully had given them to her. Then she had slid her phone into the pocket of her costume. She walked to the sleeping puppy, crouched down beside him, and felt under him for her phone. The puppy nuzzled her, but her phone was not there. With his tummy full, nice and clean, and the glass out of his paw, the exhausted puppy shut his eyes again.

As she paused on her knees beside the puppy, she concluded she had either lost her phone on Triple C-West or outside her cabin. Darn it. She had no choice but to drive back out to the country to see if she could find it. What to do with this little black puppy?

"Come on, Wyatt Earp." Where had that come from? From the handsome man with black hair who was also very smart and who had found her when she was all alone at her country cabin. "You can sleep on the way to Triple C-South."

Charley found the leash and collars she'd used for Bingo in the foyer closet. She grabbed Bingo's dog bed and her purse. After fastening the smallest collar around Wyatt's neck and clipping the leash to it, she gently led him to the porch. She noted happily that he was able to walk on all four paws. Locking her front door, she let the puppy relieve himself in the yard and then placed the dog bed and puppy in the passenger's seat of her car. The only stop she made was at the grocery store to get a bag of puppy food. Then they were back on the road.

She prayed her cell phone would be at her log cabin. That way she wouldn't have to go to Triple C Ranch-West. She wouldn't have to talk to anyone or explain why she left the party without Sully. Then again, they probably knew why. The Coopers thought well of Sully. She recalled Chloe rolling her eyes at the sight of Trish, but surely they were happy for Sully and Trish. They'd evidently been a couple before Charley stumbled onto the scene. But how recently?

She'd been over and over this in her head. Without Sully's input, she was lost.

As Charley passed Triple C-West, she cringed at how naïve she'd been in thinking Sully was available. Thinking Sully liked her. Thinking she loved Sully. Charley clenched her teeth and fought back the fresh tears. She absolutely loved Sully, and her heart was shattered.

Upon reaching her log cabin, Charley let Wyatt out of the car. He pounced around and smelled the flowers, the grass, and the pine trees. Charley searched the parking area where she'd opened her car door the previous night but failed to find her phone. Since she'd not lost her phone when opening her car door, the only other place it could be was Triple C Ranch-West. She had no choice but to drive back there and talk to the Brevards.

"Come on, Wyatt Earp."

Charley smiled through her heartache as the little dog scampered to her. She loaded the puppy up in her car and backtracked toward Pikes Peak. Turning right into the driveway of Triple C Ranch-West, she drove toward the front porch and stopped near the hitching posts often used for the horses from all the Triple C Ranches. With a pat to Wyatt's head, she left him in her Mini Cooper for the moment and walked toward the steps to the porch. There! Next to the steps, on the ground, she saw her phone! Kept out of the rain by the porch roof, she grabbed it up and saw that Sully had called her twice. She listened to his message asking her to call him. Charley noticed Chloe had called her, too, as she started back to her car.

"Charley?" came Chloe's voice before Charley could listen to her message.

"Oh, hi, Chloe," Charley said to her cousin, twisting around to face her. Standing on the porch, Chloe wore her long black hair in a ponytail and a soft smile on her pretty face. Charley explained, "I lost my phone last night and came back out to the country to find it." With a wave, she held her phone up in the air and said, "It was on the ground beside the steps. I didn't want to bother you, so I was going to leave."

"I didn't know you lost it, but I'm glad you found it. I tried to call you this morning." Chloe walked down the steps and said with obvious compassion, "Without your phone, you probably haven't heard the news about Sully."

"Yes, actually, I have heard the news," Charley said. She would no longer be naïve or the last to know. "Trish told me that she and Sully are going to have a baby. He's thrilled."

"What?" Chloe grimaced and shook her head. "I highly doubt that. Sully and Trish were never a steady couple and haven't dated for months as far as I know."

Charley's heart beat a bit faster. "Really?"

"Really," Chloe said firmly. "Sully's not the kind of guy who would lead you on while being involved with another woman, Charley."

Charley paused and then asked, "What did you mean, referring to news about Sully?"

"He and Trish were in a car accident last night."

Charley wasn't sure how much more anguish she could take. "Are they okay?"

"No idea if they're alive or dead. Derek has a call in to Owen."

CHAPTER TWENTY-FOUR

"*O*h, no," Charley whispered in stunned shock. Her arms hung limply at her sides, and her legs felt like jelly. With great effort, she managed a few steps toward her cousin. "Chloe, please let me know as soon as you hear from Sully's dad," Charley said. She hadn't known Sully long but couldn't imagine the world without him in it. "Please."

"Charley, why don't you come in? Let's talk," Chloe said, stepped closer, and hugged her. "If I can help you in any way, you know I will."

"Well—" Charley desperately wanted to do so and hugged Chloe back, but felt she owed her cousin some information first. "I have a little puppy with me. I found him on my porch in the Springs this morning. He had cut his paw and was starving."

"Bring him in. Derek and Cooper went to the stables after lunch, but the twins are watching a movie. Austin and Abilene will love seeing your puppy. Would you like lunch?"

"Oh, no thank you. I'm not hungry."

Chloe looked at her with a knowing expression of concern. "We'll have sweet tea and a snack."

"Okay," Charley said, needing her cousin more than nourishment. "I'd really like that."

"Our cat, Scarlett, and Spike, our German shepherd, who you met at the party last night, are friendly to other animals. Spike's with Derek and Cooper now, and Scarlett's catnapping."

"Okay," Charley said. "I'll get the puppy."

Charley fetched Wyatt from the car, and attached his leash, the puppy scampered to the porch steps. He had a little trouble getting up them, so Charley picked him up and carried him into the house. Fluffy, black Scarlett, sunning herself in a window, woke but was indifferent. The twins, however, were ecstatic and offered to play with Wyatt immediately. Charley followed Chloe to the pretty kitchen and slid onto the bench seat at the breakfast nook table. Chloe poured two glasses of iced tea and set them on the table. With pumpkin bread and two plates in hand, she sat down on the bench seat across from Charley.

"So, Trish stirred up trouble as usual," Chloe said with a raised eyebrow.

"Has she done so in the past?"

"Oh, yes." Chloe nodded. Slicing a piece of pumpkin bread, she put it on a plate and handed it to Charley. "She went out with Cash once or twice years ago, and so I invited her to the Halloween party also...*years ago*. Anyway, as you may have guessed after meeting Tracy, Cash is partial to redheads."

"Tracy is an absolutely stunning redhead," Charley said. "Gracious as she is sweet."

"Yes. We all love Tracy. She has been the perfect match for Cash. He couldn't be happier, and Tracy is devoted to him."

Charley smiled. "That's so wonderful."

"As for Trish, she pulled the *I'm pregnant* trick on Cash too."

"Seriously?" Charley asked as Chloe nodded. "But she wasn't?"

"No, she was not." Chloe rolled her eyes much as she had the previous night.

"But she was so convincing," Charley admitted.

"She was convincing with Cash too," Chloe replied. "He told her that he wanted to see a pregnancy test. And he said if she did have a baby, he'd demand a paternity test."

"What happened?" Charley asked. Though she wasn't hungry, she politely took a bite of the pumpkin bread, because Chloe was eating hers.

"Trish told Cash since it was Halloween, she was just trying to scare him." Chloe frowned. "She admitted she wasn't pregnant right then and there. But it was the last time Cash ever went out with her."

"Wow, I cannot imagine pulling such a horrible trick on a man," Charley said.

"Me neither," Chloe said and glanced at her watch. "I was hoping Derek would hear back from Owen by now." No sooner had Chloe spoken those words than Derek, Cooper, and the German shepherd entered the house through the back door. The dog trotted straight to Chloe. "Hi, boys," she said to her husband and son as she petted Spike. "Cooper, Charley brought her new puppy with her to visit today."

"Cool! Hi, Charley." Cooper asked, "Where's the puppy?"

"In the family room with the twins," Charley said. "His name is Wyatt Earp."

"I'm gonna go see him," Cooper said and took off down the hall.

"Wyatt Earp, like Sully," Chloe said to Charley and looked at Derek. "Coffee?"

"Sure," he said as Chloe stood to let him sit on the bench seat across from Charley. "Hi, Charley. You've heard about Sully?"

"Hi, Derek," Charley said to the former deputy sheriff as he rubbed his forehead. "Yes."

As Chloe fixed Derek's coffee, she asked, "Any news?"

"Yes." Derek sat up straighter as she sat down beside him

with his coffee. "But not from Owen. Since I hadn't heard from him, I called the sheriff's office and talked to a buddy."

"Tell us, please, what you found out, Derek," Chloe urged.

"Yes, please," Charley said. Expecting the worst, her body was nearly numb from fear and anxiety. She crossed her arms over her heart and hugged herself.

"The crash wasn't discovered until early this morning. Trish Potter was driving, and the car went over an embankment at a curve in the road on the way to her house," Derek said. "Because it rolled all the way to the bottom of the ravine, no one saw the wreck until daylight."

So, while Charley lay crying all night, Sully lay at the bottom of a hill? She cringed and silently berated herself. Please God, let Sully be alive.

"Are they alive?" Chloe asked.

Charley dug her nails into her arms as she waited for Derek to answer.

"My buddy at the sheriff's office said Trish died instantly." Derek looked from Chloe to Charley and said, "Sully was in the hospital, unresponsive but alive as of two hours ago."

"Which hospital?" Charley asked, barely above a whisper.

"The medical ICU at Memorial Hospital in the Springs," Derek replied as his cell phone rang. "It's Owen." Derek answered his phone and listened intently. "Owen, I'll go to the place where the wreck happened right now. You know it's not my first crash site and probably won't be my last." He listened again and then said, "I'll call you back and let you know if we find anything or not. Either way, you'll hear from me." He hung up and scooted sideways.

"What did Owen say?" Chloe asked, letting him slide out of the bench seat.

"Owen says Sully is still unconscious, maybe due to a concussion. He sustained a laceration across his side and lost a lot of blood. But the seat belt saved him. Trish was not wearing hers and was nearly decapitated."

"Dear Lord," Charley whispered. "This is all my fault. I should not have left the party without Sully last night."

Chloe instantly said, "No. This is not your fault. You had your reasons for leaving the way you did." She gave Derek a look that said she'd explain later. "Trish was driving the car, not you, Charley."

"Owen said that Sully's Ruger Redhawk was snapped into the holster on his belt when he reached the ER. Owen has the gun. But he asked me to go to the crash site to look for Sully's wallet and cell phone." Derek stood and said, "He says both are missing from Sully's belongings in the hospital."

"May I go with you, Derek?" Charley asked. "It's the very least I can do to help."

"Sure," Derek said as Chloe nodded. "Too bad we don't have something of Sully's for Spike to sniff. He's good at ferreting out things that go missing."

"I have a sweatshirt of Sully's at my cabin that we can take to the crash site," Charley offered and stood up.

"Let's get it on the way." Derek gave Chloe a hug and kiss.

"Charley, the kids and I can keep the puppy until you and Derek get back."

"Chloe, thank you so much," Charley said and hugged her. Chloe's hug was warm and reassuring. Knowing Chloe would understand she was referring to the information about Trish's horrendous tricks on men, she added, "For everything."

Derek led the way to his truck and let Spike into the back seat as Charley slid into the passenger's seat. Derek started the engine, Charley buckled up, and they were off. They stopped at Triple C Ranch-South, and Chloe raced into her cabin. She retrieved Sully's sweatshirt and hurried back out to Derek's truck.

"Owen says a tow truck is coming to clear the crash site

and wanted me to get there before the truck," Derek explained as he headed them toward the scene of the crash.

"Of course," Charley said. "Is Owen with Sully in the hospital?"

"Yes."

"Except for their cousins, Roy and Randy, they only have each other."

"Right. My understanding from working with Owen is that they lost Sully's mom a while ago. But father and son have stayed close," Derek said. "I can identify with that because my mom and I lost my dad years ago. She and I have stayed close too."

"I met your mom at the Halloween party. She's lovely. Does she live in the Springs?"

"Yes, in her townhouse in a complex known as Shadow of Kissing Camels."

"I know where that gated community is. It's beautiful."

They rode in silence then, and Sully's warning replayed in her head. *If it rains, snows, or is icy, these country roads can get treacherous. So be safe and don't speed.*

Derek knew his way around the countryside and drove straight to the crash site. Charley's heart clenched at seeing tire tracks going over the muddy edge of an embankment. They exited the truck where broken tree branches and flattened shrubs descended the hillside. Standing at the edge of the sloping incline, they saw the car which had rolled and flipped, finally stopping far below, upside down against a pine tree. Charley wanted to scream from the stress and tension. Instead, she silently followed Derek and Spike into the ravine.

There, Charley stood amid the totaled car, broken glass, a fender here and a bumper over there. And blood. A lot of blood. Looking at the passenger's door, Derek said it appeared to have been opened with the jaws of life, which Charley knew was a hydraulic rescue tool.

"Here, Spike," Derek said and held Sully's sweatshirt for him to smell.

Spike took off across the rubble, and they followed. The German shepherd searched, sniffed, and pawed the ground. He jumped forward, barked, and dug. Derek and Charley hurried to his side. Derek lifted a fallen tree limb near the passenger's door, and they both saw the wallet that Spike had found. Charley knew Sully carried his wallet in his back pocket. It must have slipped out during his rescue. As Derek held the tree limb up, Charley grabbed the wallet. She took a quick look as Derek dropped the limb back on the ground.

"I think the wallet is intact," Charley said. "His driver's license is here, along with bank cards and cash."

"Good job, Spike," Derek praised the dog. Then he gave Spike another whiff of Sully's sweatshirt. "Can you find his phone?"

Spike was off on a second mission. Derek and Charley searched the area as the German shepherd sniffed the ground. Charley remembered Sully's window being down when he passed her ranch. She told Derek, and he said if Sully was holding his phone, it may have gone flying. They spread out wider from the car. Along with Spike, they hunted for the cell phone. When Spike barked, Charley and Derek hurried to him. His nose was in the dying yellow flowers of rabbitbrush, and his front paws were digging. Charley and Derek began rifling through the branches, and Charley's hand hit something hard. She wrapped her fingers around a black case.

"We found it!" she said excitedly. Pulling her hand out of the rabbitbrush, she and Derek saw that the cell phone screen was unbroken. When Charley squeezed the side button, the phone lit up. "It's got a low battery, but it's working."

"Landing in the brush saved the phone from being broken and kept it dry." Derek patted the dog's head. "Good boy, Spike."

"Yes, good dog, Spike," Charley agreed. "Thank you."

Spike barked, and they climbed back up the hill to

Derek's truck. When they were inside the vehicle, Derek pulled out his own cell and punched in a number.

"Owen, it's Derek. We've got Sully's wallet and cell phone." He listened and said, "Charley Cooper is with Spike and me. The wallet appears untouched, and the phone seems to be okay. Are you still at the hospital?"

"I'd be happy to take the wallet and cell to him," Charley whispered, desperate to see Sully. Letting her make amends was too much to ask, but she could deliver his property.

Derek nodded. "Charley says she would be happy to bring both to you." He listened and said, "Okay, I'll tell her. Any update on Sully?" After a moment, he hung up and looked at Charley. "They're deciding whether or not to send Sully to the Neurosciences Center at UC Health University of Colorado Hospital in Denver."

Charley flinched and squeezed back tears. "I'm going to Memorial Hospital."

"Okay, and Owen would appreciate you bringing the wallet and cell phone."

As Derek turned the truck around, a tow truck drove into view. He gave it a wave, and Charley was relieved to have successfully accomplished their mission before it had arrived. During the trip back to Triple C Ranch-West, Charley's phone signaled a text from Leon saying he had a stomach virus and asking if she could visit him.

"Sully has to make it," she said softly to Derek and texted, *No, I can't*, to Leon.

"Sully's tough just like his dad," Derek replied.

Back at the Brevards' house, Chloe came out on the porch to greet them. She walked down the steps, meeting up with them along the driveway. She was elated they had found Sully's missing wallet and cell phone.

"I'm heading straight to the hospital to meet up with Owen and hopefully see Sully," Charley told her cousin. "I can take Wyatt off your hands and drop him at my apartment."

"Sully said at the party last night that he didn't want you

at your apartment alone," Derek said, as Spike stood at his side.

"Right. I heard him say that too," Chloe said and nodded. "Leave Wyatt here as long as you need to. Take your time and come back here whenever you're ready. Night or day, we'll have a bed waiting for you, Charley."

"Thank—" A sob cut Charley off and she hugged Chloe. "Thank you." As always, Chloe's hug was warm and reassuring. How grateful Charley was for her family. "I don't know what I'd do without all of you."

"Give us an update on Sully when you can," Derek said, draping an arm around Chloe.

"I will. Thank you, Derek, for letting me go with you."

"No problem."

Chloe smiled and said, "Go see about Sully."

CHAPTER TWENTY-FIVE

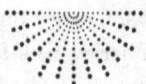

harley all but ran to her car and with a wave, headed down Triple C Ranch-West's ponderosa pine-lined drive. Before turning right onto the highway, Charley glanced into her rearview mirror to see Chloe and Derek walking hand-in-hand up the porch steps. The front door opened, and Cooper appeared holding Wyatt with the twins right behind him. How wonderful it must be to have such a solid, loving marriage with children.

"I wish I could be so happy," she began, pulling onto the highway, "with Sully."

Heading toward Pikes Peak, she made herself drive the speed limit. But the trip from the country into town seemed never to have taken so long. When Charley finally reached Memorial Hospital, she zipped into the parking garage, found a spot, and parked. With another glance in the rearview mirror, this time she cringed. She'd cried all her eye makeup off and searching the wreckage had *wreaked* havoc on her hair. Reaching into her purse, she pulled out mascara and lipstick. After applying some of both, she hopped out of her car. Running her fingers through her hair, she hurried to the parking garage elevator. Punching the down button, she tapped her foot. The doors opened, she hopped in, and pushed the button to the main entrance of the hospital.

When the doors didn't close fast enough, she punched the button twice more.

Finally, she reached the inside of the hospital and found her way to the information desk. She was told Sully was still in the medical ICU. Reaching the waiting area of the intensive care unit, she found the unit itself lay beyond closed doors, as there was a strict limit on visitors. A discreet sign above a button and a speaker said to press the button in order to inquire about admittance. Charley pressed the button.

"Who are you here to see?" came a voice over the intercom.

"Sullivan Custis."

There was a pause, and Charley whispered to herself, "Please, please let me in."

After a moment the voice said, "Bed three."

A click sounded before the door swung open. Charley entered the ICU, where a busy but quiet nurses' station was on the right. Around its perimeter were small rooms consisting of glass doors. Most of the doors were partially open, with hospital curtains over them to provide some privacy. Charley slowed her pace in an effort to gain her bearings. Straight ahead was bed four. She looked left and saw a number three on the room next to it. Just as she was about to take a step in that direction, Owen emerged from the room. The lines on his face said he was worried.

"Hello," Charley said and walked toward him. She blamed herself for Sully being in the ICU and fully assumed Owen held her responsible too. She prepared herself for his icy greeting.

"Charley," Owen said, walking forward and hugging her. "Thank you for coming."

"Of course." Charley hugged him back, and fresh tears stung her eyes. When his embrace lessened, she stood back and asked, "How is he?"

"The same. Unconscious," Owen said quietly. "They've been giving him blood transfusions. I don't know how many units of blood he's had. But he's hooked up to all kinds of machines. He's had and an EEG—electroencephalogram."

"Does the EEG mean they think he has a brain injury?" Charley prayed the answer was no but braced herself.

"At the very least he has a mild concussion," Owen said as they stood outside of Sully's room. "After the accident happened, he oozed blood all night long until he almost bled out."

Charley shivered. "Thank God, someone finally spotted and reported the accident."

"Right, thank God," Owen agreed. "The accident was approximately eighteen hours ago, and with the blood transfusions Sully's received, his physician thinks Sully should have regained consciousness by now. He wants Sully to be alert and oriented within twenty-four hours. So, if Sully doesn't come around in the next couple of hours, they're going to fly him in a flight-for-life helicopter to Denver to their neuro ICU."

"I understand." Charley wanted to collapse to the floor in tears. Instead, she smiled at Owen and patted his arm reassuringly. "May I see him?"

"Yes, of course," Owen said and rubbed his forehead. "I was just going to get something from the cafeteria and bring it back here to eat."

"Before you go, I have Sully's wallet and cell phone," Charley said, taking them out of her purse.

"Thank you for going with Derek to find them," Owen replied. "Can you hold on to them for me for now?"

"Yes, of course, Owen."

Charley put Sully's wallet and phone back into her purse. Owen took a few steps to Sully's open doorway and pulled back the curtain to allow her to enter. Sully lay in the narrow bed, and as Owen said, he was hooked up to several machines. Charley's heart nearly stopped seeing the strong, muscular man unconscious, pale, and unmoving in the bed. There was a bandage on his forehead, and his right hand was scraped. Owen said something from the crash had punctured his left side causing the blood loss. Charley walked into the room and stopped at Sully's bedside. There was an empty chair pulled close, and she figured it was where Owen had been sitting beside his son.

"Have a seat, Charley," Owen said from behind her. "I'll give you some privacy with Sully. May I bring you something to eat from the cafeteria?"

"No, thank you," she replied, never taking her eyes off Sully. "I'm not hungry."

"I'll be back in a little while."

"I'll be right here," Charley said.

Owen left her, and Charley sat unmoving in the chair beside Sully for several minutes. Slowly, she placed her purse on the floor and gripped her hands together in her lap. Even in his current condition, Sully was outrageously handsome. Despite what he'd been through, his thick black hair fell into place on his head and the stubble of his black beard as always gave him that rugged, sexy look. His breathing seemed shallow, but steady.

A nurse, who appeared to be in her mid-forties, entered the room with a bag of blood. She smiled at Charley and said hello. Then she went about her work of hanging the bag on the IV pole beside his bed and attaching it to the needle already in his left arm. The nurse noted that the patient had a slight fever, but that was to be expected as his body tried to fight the injuries and heal. When the nurse left the room, Charley scooted closer to Sully.

Sully's right arm lay lengthwise alongside his body, and she gently placed her hand atop his much larger, scraped hand. It was warm to the touch. Flashes of Sully touching her face, holding her close, caressing her breasts, and spreading her legs with that hand replayed across her mind. Charley bowed her head and wondered if he'd wake up and touch her like that again. Would he even want to? Deep in her very soul, she prayed he would. But if he woke, no, *when* he woke, he might blame her as she blamed herself for the accident. She slipped her other hand underneath his and softly squeezed.

"Sully," she whispered, looking at him. "I'm so sorry. Please wake up. Even if you never forgive me, you need to wake up. You have your whole life ahead of you." He didn't move, didn't open his eyes. Holding his hand with both of hers, she said, "If you do give me the chance to make it up to you, I will never let you down again. Never ever."

There was no response. The monitors did their job with red lines on black screens. The blood dripped red out of the bag into Sully's blue vein. The clock on the wall ticked. Nurses' voices drifted to her from their nearby station. Everything seemed overwhelming, tenuous, and surreal. She let go of Sully's hand only long enough to text Chloe, letting the Coopers know she was safely at the hospital with Sully and Owen. But Sully's condition remained the same.

After pressing send on the text, Charley bowed her head and prayed. An hour later, Owen returned and handed her something in a Styrofoam box. Despite how little she'd eaten, she had no appetite. But as she'd done in taking a couple of bites of the snack at Chloe's house to be polite, she took the box and found a ham sandwich inside it. She thanked Owen as he pulled up a chair at the end of the bed and sat. Charley glanced at the clock on the wall. In another hour, Sully might be transferred to a Denver hospital. At Owen's urging, she nibbled on the sandwich. But it was mostly to please Owen, who by some miracle seemed concerned about her welfare.

"Hello," said a man, wearing a white lab coat, light blue scrubs, and stethoscope around his neck as he entered the small ICU room.

"Dr. Sankari, this is Charley Cooper, a friend of my son," Owen said politely and stood up. "Charley, this is Sully's physician."

"Hello," Charley said to the doctor.

Dr. Sankari acknowledged her with a polite nod. Walking to the opposite side of Sully's bed, he put his stethoscope in his ears and listened to Sully's heart as he felt the pulse in his wrist. He looked at the monitors and glanced at the bag draining blood into Sully.

"Mr. Sully, are you going to wake up for us? If you would do so, I would not be worried, as your vitals are normal and your bloodwork is coming around," Dr. Sankari said kindly, holding Sully's left hand in his. Sully didn't move. Looking at Owen, the doctor said, "The hospital in Denver has a bed, Mr. Custis. I'm going to play it safe and request the helicopter."

"I understand," Owen replied, his broad shoulders sagging just a little.

Dr. Sankari walked out of the room, and Owen went with him. Charley heard their voices and that of Sully's nurse discussing the transfer. Charley closed the Styrofoam box and set it aside. Now that she was alone with Sully once more, she took his hand in both of hers again. Closing her eyes, she bowed her head and prayed.

"Sully, please wake up," Charley said upon raising her head. His green eyes remained closed, and except for breathing, his body stayed motionless. "I know what Trish told us was a lie," she whispered. "I was wrong not to ask you about it. I should have stayed and found you instead of running away." She swallowed hard and continued, "I'm not usually scared so easily. But what she said hit me so hard because I love you so much, Sully." A small sob escaped Charley after telling him she loved him for the first time. "I love you with all my heart. Please give me the chance to prove it."

The nurse entered the room again, and after checking the blood hanging on the IV pole, she turned to Charley and said kindly, "You'll need to leave in a few minutes."

Charley nodded and the nurse left. Charley stared at Sully, willing him to open his eyes. But he didn't. She sniffled and said, "A little black puppy showed up on my porch this morning. He wants me to adopt him." She wiped tears off her cheeks. "I think he could be a Labrador retriever.

Your favorite kind of dog. When you wake up, I'll introduce you to him. I named him Wyatt Earp."

Charley watched Sully carefully, but there was no response. She bowed her head again, and tears rolled down her cheeks. A moment later, Sully's nurse was back. She explained they were going to prepare him for his flight to Denver and it was time for Charley to leave the room.

"All right," Charley whispered. She stood, and still holding Sully's hand leaned over him. She placed her lips to his forehead, opposite the bandage over his right brow, and lightly kissed his skin. At that instant, she thought she detected his fingers move ever so slightly within her grasp. She straightened her stance and said, "Sully?" His eyes stayed closed. She glanced away from him long enough to say to his nurse, "I think his fingers moved."

"Probably involuntary," the nurse said with compassion.

"Sully, it's Charley," she said. "Can you hear me? Sully, please wake up."

CHAPTER TWENTY-SIX

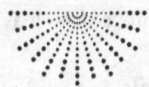

*S*ully heard her voice from a distance. He forced his eyes open and saw her. Charley. He blinked. She was smiling at him through her tears. At least he thought this was really her. He'd had a reassuring, but all too brief dream about the two of them. However, there had been a nightmare too. Was she here, or was this another fantasy? Had there been a car crash? He was confused and closed his eyes.

"Sully? Come back to me."

Sully opened his eyes at Charley's urging. He blinked again. Where was he? He noticed his dad standing at the end of the bed with a nurse at his side. He looked back to his right.

"Charley," he managed, his throat dry and his voice raspy.

"Hi," Charley said, wiping away the tears on her pretty cheeks.

Sully realized she was holding his right hand. Yes, he remembered hearing her ask him to wake up. Feeling happy and hopeful, he had opened his eyes to find she was not just in his dream. She was real, and she was here. He gave her hand a squeeze.

"Hi," Sully whispered, looking up at her. Her blue eyes

were puffy, and her dainty nose was pink, but never had she looked more beautiful.

"Glad you're back with us," his dad said, walking around the side of the bed and standing closer to Charley. "How do you feel, son?"

"Okay," Sully replied.

"I'm going to let Dr. Sankari know his patient is awake," the nurse said with a smile before leaving his room.

"I'm in the hospital?"

"Yes," Charley and his dad said at the same time as they smiled at him.

Sully shifted in the bed and grimaced. With stiffness and pain, his body quickly reminded him that he had indeed been in a car crash.

"You've got bruises and scrapes, but amazingly no broken bones," his dad said.

As his memory of the crash returned, Sully grimaced and asked, "How long was I out?"

Owen looked at his watch. "The wreck happened around nine p.m. last night, and it wasn't discovered until daylight. It's six p.m. now, so twenty-one hours."

"You lost a lot of blood," Charley said as she and his dad stood close together.

"Sit down," Sully said, not wanting them to leave. Owen pulled up an extra chair next to Charley, and when they were both seated, he asked, "Is the blood loss why I was out so long?"

"That and a mild concussion is what Dr. Sankari initially thought," Owen told him. "But when you didn't wake up after receiving several pints of blood, he became concerned the cause could be neurological. Dr. Sankari was planning to send you to a specialty unit in Denver."

"Okay," Sully said, trying to make sense of it all. He tightened his grip on Charley's hand and smiled at her. "I don't need to go to Denver."

His dad paused and then said to him, "Trish Potter didn't make it."

Sully flashed on a dark recollection of Trish lying, laughing, and stomping on the gas pedal. He recalled the rain and grabbing the steering wheel to bring it back into the correct lane. An oncoming car blared its horn. Trish claimed to be trying to scare him with a cruel trick. He remembered her jerking the steering wheel on a curve and fishtailing across the road. She lost control of the car and they had careened toward an embankment. He heard Trish scream and saw her fling her arms across her face. There was a sense of being airborne, and then jarring images and a severe pain along his ribs had melted into silent, merciful blackness.

"I remember most of it," Sully said. "She was drunk."

"It wasn't your fault, and there was nothing you could have done," Owen added.

"I shouldn't have gotten into her car," Sully said, still holding on to Charley's hand.

"It's my fault," Charley told them and tenderly covered Sully's hand with her other one. "You wouldn't have gotten into her car if I hadn't left the party without you."

"No, that's not true," Sully said. "I could have ridden home with Dad."

Owen nodded. "Right, I was waiting for you. It's my fault for letting you get into the car of someone under the influence. I've kicked myself a hundred times."

"You couldn't have known she was intoxicated," Charley said in Owen's defense.

Shaking his head, Owen smiled his appreciation at Charley and said to Sully, "I wish I had followed you instead of being ahead of you on the highway."

"The more she and I argued, the more Trish lost control," Sully said. "I'm a grown man, and if there's any blame, it sits squarely on my shoulders."

"Sully, I'm so happy you're alive," Charley said softly, changing the direction of the conversation.

"Me too," Owen said. "You're the most important thing I have left in this world, son."

"I'm happy to be here," Sully said as a man in a white

coat and a stethoscope around his neck, walked into the room with the nurse following close behind him.

"Mr. Sully," the man said, stopping on the opposite side of the bed from Charley and Owen. With a smile he added, "I'm happy to see you're back with us. I'm Dr. Asif Sankari."

"Thank you, Dr. Sankari," Sully replied. "Can I leave now?"

"No, sir. Not today," Dr. Sankari said, looking from him to the monitors. Taking his wrist, the doctor felt Sully's pulse and nodded. "I want to run a couple of tests and draw another set of labs. If those look good, I'll have you moved out of the ICU to a regular room."

"Can I go home tomorrow?" Sully asked as the doctor released his wrist.

"You're on IV pain meds and antibiotics due to the thirty-two internal and external sutures in your left side."

"A stitch for each year of my life," Sully muttered as Charley gave him an encouraging smile.

Still on the opposite side of the bed and keeping the sheet in place over Sully, the physician lifted the side of his gown and examined the wound. "Looks good." He nodded and put the gown back in place. "We'll decrease the analgesics and see how you do overnight," Dr. Sankari said in regard to the painkillers. "Your temperature is almost back to normal, and you've had your last transfusion of blood. But you just about bled out, young man."

"I saw proof of that at the crash site," Charley said to the doctor and then looked at Sully.

"When you run out of blood, you run out of time." Dr. Sankari said, "I've canceled the transfer to Denver. I'll see you tomorrow morning, hopefully on a discharge floor and we'll go from there."

"Thank you," Sully said.

"Yes, thank you, Dr. Sankari," Owen said and stood to shake the doctor's hand.

"You're welcome," Dr. Sankari said and exited the room.

"What can I get for you?" the nurse asked him. "Are you thirsty?"

"Yes, and hungry," Sully said.

"Good, I'll go ask Dr. Sankari what you can have," she said and left them.

"I talked to your cousins, and both Roy and Randy said for you not to worry about a thing," Owen told him. "They have your horses and the store under control."

"Thanks, Dad. Yeah, they're good at taking over."

"Maybe I should go and let you two visit," Charley said, but when she tugged on her hand that was underneath Sully's, he held on tight.

"No, please stay, Charley. I want to talk to you," Sully said.

Bringing a container of water with a straw, the nurse pulled a bedside tray over the top of Sully and then raised the head of his bed so that he was in more of a sitting-up position. Sully drank from the water container. A phlebotomist entered on the nurse's heels and explained Dr. Sankari had ordered blood work and prepared Sully's arm for a stick. As she took the blood, his nurse told Sully the physician said he could return to a normal diet. Then the phlebotomist took the blood she needed and left with his nurse.

"I'm going to step into the waiting room and make a couple of calls," Owen said with a look of relief and a big smile. "I want to let your cousins and the Coopers know that you're back among the living, Sully."

"Owen, could you please let Derek and Chloe know I'm here with Sully, but I'll be out to take the puppy off their hands later?"

"Will do," Owen said with a happy smile. "Be back in a bit."

"What puppy?" Sully asked when his dad was gone.

"A puppy adopted me this morning," Charley said, keeping Sully's hand clasped in hers. "I named him Wyatt Earp."

"Where was this puppy?"

Charley hesitated and then squared her shoulders. "On the porch of my apartment."

"Charley." Sully sighed. "I didn't want you to go there without me."

She looked away and said, "I was upset last night and not thinking all that clearly."

"I called you. Twice."

"I temporarily lost my phone. I didn't realize it until today," she explained earnestly. "I found it outside at Triple C-West. I listened to your message and was about to call you when Chloe came to my rescue."

Sully nodded. "I want to hear more about Wyatt, but let's discuss what happened last night first."

"Sully," Charley said with a shake of her pretty head and a shrug of her slim shoulders. "I jumped to conclusions last night when I should have calmly stood my ground and objectively listened to your side."

"Tell me what Trish said to you."

"It doesn't matter."

"It does. I want to make sure we got the same lies. Tell me."

Charley raised her chin and said, "That you were the father of her child and happy about it. She said you wanted me to leave and that's why you ditched me at the party."

Sully sighed. "Does ditching you sound like me or something I would do?"

"No, but I was in shock and when she told me to vamoose, I did."

"I hadn't gone out with Trish in six months, Charley," Sully said. "The first time I'd seen her in all that time was the day she showed up in my kitchen when you were there."

Charley nodded. "Chloe told me that Trish pulled the same pregnancy scare on Cash a few years ago."

Sully smiled with empathy and said, "I'm so sorry you were hurt like that. I got into her car only because she said she knew why you left the party."

"I'm okay. But her trick backfired this time and cost Trish her life."

"Not to speak ill of the dead, but Trish is the one on whom the blame falls for what happened to her."

"Certainly not you or your dad," Charley was quick to agree.

"Certainly not on you either," Sully said. "So, no more self-blame among us, okay?"

"Okay," Charley said softly and gently squeezed his hand.

"Just to be clear—" Sully began as he studied the gorgeous girl, and then thinking he might be overstepping, he didn't continue.

"Just to be clear about what, Sully?" she asked. "This is a day for truths, please tell me."

A hospital employee with different-colored scrubs entered the room with a tray. Her name tag indicated she was from dietary, and she asked, "Mr. Custis?"

"Yes," Sully said.

"Dinner," the dietician said. She set the food on his tray and removed the warming lid.

"Thank you," Sully replied. When she was gone, he looked at Charley. "Just to be clear, I would like to have a child someday."

"So would I."

"But with the *right* woman. The one I love."

"Eat." Charley pulled her hand free. Then, with a hint of a flirt in her voice, she said, "Maybe you'll meet her."

"Maybe I have." Sully grinned as Charley blushed. He twirled pasta around his fork and then ate it as she took his phone and wallet out of her purse. She placed the items on the bed alongside his hip. Looking at them, he asked, "Did I lose those?"

"Yes. Your dad asked Derek to see if he could find your wallet and cell at the scene of the crash. With help from Spike, we did."

"Thank you, Charley. I'll thank Derek when I see him,"

Sully said as Charley received back-to-back texts on her phone. He watched her frown. "What's wrong?"

"Frick, also known as Rod, sent me flowers and wants to know if I'll have lunch with him," Charley said. Sully knew the use of *Frick* was her way of trying to make light of the texts. "Frack, alias Leon, says he was sick but is feeling better now and wants me to come see him."

Sully asked, "What do *you* want to do?"

NO ANSWER TO HIS MOST RECENT TEXT. HE HAD REACHED OUT to Charley because she wasn't reaching out to him. It had been another stab to his heart to see her drive off with the cowboy in the dark of night. He'd been by her apartment. Her car wasn't there, but he'd knocked on her door anyway. No answer. Her flower shop still had the Closed sign hanging on the door. The voices said she was with that rancher in the big truck. Where did that guy live? He was sure they were having sex, and that turned his gut inside out. Charley belonged to him. He needed to step up his game, but with his current level of anxiety he might push her too hard. But having Charley satisfy his needs was an urgent and unrelenting priority. The deadening bliss of another kill lured him. Grabbing a handful of toadflax, he walked into the fading light of day.

CHAPTER TWENTY-SEVEN

"*I*'ll politely text them both no," Charley told the handsome man in the bed, wearing a frown on his face as he waited for her answer.

Sully grumbled, "Don't be too polite."

"You're my only concern, Sully." That made him smile and maybe blended a little color back into the healthy tan of his cheeks.

"Where will you be until I can get out of here?" he asked and took another bite of pasta. "It's dark outside."

"Chloe invited me to stay with them on Triple C Ranch-West."

"Yes." Sully nodded. "Please take her up on that."

"I will. I have puppy food in my car, and I need to see how Wyatt is doing."

"Good," Sully said with a nod. "I'll be able to rest tonight if I know you're with the Brevards. Now, tell me about this dog. Where did he come from?"

"I don't know." Charley splayed her hands and recounted how she'd heard the noises outside her front door and found the puppy. "He was filthy as if he'd been dumped in the nearby woods, and he's skin and bones. I was afraid if I didn't take him in, he'd wander down the hill and into the traffic on Colorado Avenue."

"I wonder if he belonged to one of the murder victims found in the cave tunnels."

That hadn't occurred to Charley, and she tilted her head in thought. "That would explain why he was so dirty and hungry."

"I'm guessing since you named him, you're planning to keep him."

"You and I both like dogs. Maybe I could share him with you," Charley said, and then feeling vulnerable looked away. "He deserves a safe home."

"He does," Sully said. "I can't wait to meet Wyatt."

Finding a grin on Sully's face, Charley smiled back. Owen was smiling, too, as he entered the room again and said that he'd contacted Roy, Randy, and the Coopers.

"Your cousins are relieved and happy you're okay, Sully. Randy said to tell you he will keep the horses and skeet customers covered. Roy says his girlfriend, Mindy, will also help out in the store with the customers until you're well enough to come back to work."

"Good to know. Those guys are great. Thanks, Dad."

"I called Derek Brevard, so all of the Coopers are aware by now that you survived and are on the road to recovery." Turning to Charley, Owen said, "Chloe said to tell you she'll have a warm dinner waiting for you whenever you get back out to Triple C-West, Charley."

"Thank you, Owen," Charley replied. Then to Sully, she said, "I should get going and let you rest, Sully. And I've left that puppy for the Brevards to care for long enough. I don't want us to wear out our welcome."

She could tell Sully was about to protest her leaving when an overhead announcement advised everyone that visiting hours in the ICU were over in ten minutes. Sully's nurse entered as the message ended and stated that Dr. Sankari was happy with his latest labs.

"I'll call you later, if that's okay," Sully said and reached for Charley's hand.

Charley took his hand and nodded. "Yes, please." When

he tugged on her hand, she stepped closer. Impulsively, she leaned down and gave him a gentle hug and kiss.

"Thank you," Sully whispered in her ear.

When Charley stood up and met his gaze, the look in his green eyes and on his face conveyed a multitude of meanings behind his words. She guessed first and foremost he appreciated her believing he was innocent of the charges Trish had leveled against him. Maybe his thank you included finding his wallet and phone. And perhaps, she hoped, he was thankful she'd come to him in the hospital. Wild horses couldn't have kept her away.

"Yes, thank you, Charley," Owen seconded with a heartfelt smile.

"My pleasure," Charley said simply, letting it cover everything for both men. She felt Sully squeeze her hand before letting go. Picking up her purse, Charley walked to the doorway, and turning to Sully with a wave, she said, "Good night."

As heavy as her heart had been for nearly twenty-four hours, Charley's heart danced a happy jig in her chest now. She smiled all the way through the hospital and outside to the parking garage. Once she reached her car, she got in and locked the door. She paused to send two texts. To Leon, she said she hoped he was feeling better and explained that Sully was in the hospital after a serious car accident. In addition, she explained to Leon that she had an obligation to take a puppy off the hands of her cousin and couldn't visit him. To Rod, she turned down his offer of lunch, firmly reminded him that she would never accept another date and told him not to contact her again. Having realized she hadn't blocked Rod's number, she did so now for certain. Then Charley started her Mini Cooper and left the hospital garage. She headed for the interstate, and halfway to the country, her cell phone rang. Keeping her hands on the wheel, she answered.

"So, when will you be back?"

"Sully." She giggled happily. "I haven't even reached Triple C-West yet."

He chuckled, and his deep voice was music to her ears. "That doesn't answer my question."

"When do you want me back?" she asked, her headlights shining on the highway and thickening ponderosa pines.

"Now," he said. "I'll scoot over in this bed, and you can spend the night with me."

"I'd like nothing better," she admitted. "But I think your doctor and the nurses might object."

"I don't care," he said. "I want you with me, Charley."

Those words made Charley deliriously happy. "I want to be with you too."

"Do you mean that?"

"Yes, I do. How about I come by tomorrow and see if they'll let me take you home?"

"Promise?" he asked.

"Promise."

Even after their conversation ended, the smile didn't leave Charley's face. She soon pulled under the Triple C Ranch-West wooden archway and parked in the drive near the lovely home. Grabbing the puppy food, she all but skipped up the steps and rang the bell. Chloe answered the door and gave her a big hug. The twins were already in bed, but Cooper appeared in the foyer, holding the puppy, with the German shepherd at his side.

"Time for you to be getting ready for bed too, Cooper," Chloe said. "You have school tomorrow."

"Aww...Mom," Cooper began. He was a miniature of his father. "Do I have to? I'm playing with the puppy."

"You can take Wyatt and Spike outside to go potty, but then it's up to bed."

Cooper and the two dogs scampered out the front door, and Charley said to Chloe, "Thank you so much, Chloe. I don't know how I would have made it through today without you and Derek and the kids."

"That's what family is for, Charley. We were so relieved to hear the good news about Sully from Owen earlier," Chloe said as they stood in the foyer near the arched bridge over the pretty fishpond. How calm Charley felt now opposed to the anxiety that had enveloped her the previous night when standing near this spot. "Sully is stable but they're keeping him overnight?"

"Yes," Charley said and repeated what the doctor had told them earlier. "Sully hopes to be moved out of ICU tonight and discharged tomorrow. I said I'd check on him and take him home when his doctor releases him."

"Good," Chloe said. "Are you hungry?"

"I'm suddenly starved."

"Wonderful. I have dinner for you," Chloe said as Cooper, Wyatt, and Spike trotted back inside the house.

"Cooper, thank you so much for taking charge of Wyatt," Charley said.

"You're welcome," Cooper said politely, picking up Wyatt and scratching his furry head. "It was fun. He's a nice puppy."

"Hi Charley," Derek said, walking into the hallway from the family room. "Great news about Sully."

"Yes, the best, Derek," Charley replied, smiling.

"Let's go, Cooper," Derek said. "It's your turn to read the story tonight."

"Can Wyatt sleep with Spike and me?"

"Up to Charley," Chloe said.

"Sure," she said and watched as Derek, Spike, and Cooper, carrying Wyatt, started up the staircase to the second-floor bedrooms.

"Since the master bedroom suite is downstairs, Spike likes to sleep upstairs to be near the kids," Chloe said and motioned for Charley to follow her to the kitchen. There they were joined by Scarlett, waving her fluffy black tail. Charley petted Scarlett as Chloe walked into the pantry. Chloe came back out with a bottle of red wine and lifted it into the air. "A glass of wine?"

"Yes. A glass of wine would be fantastic," Charley said as Scarlett jumped onto a windowsill in the breakfast nook and groomed herself. Chloe opened the wine and poured two glasses. They touched their glasses and Charley suggested, "To Sully?"

"To Sully," Chloe agreed. They each took a drink and then Chloe set her glass down and removed a dish covered with tinfoil out of the oven. With the tinfoil off the delicious smells of baked steak, mashed potatoes, green beans, and a corn muffin wafted Charley's way. When they were sitting opposite each other at the table, Charley ate, and after a moment Chloe said, "Charley, if it's none of my business, just say so. But what are you going to do about your flower shop, and more importantly about Sully?"

"I don't know if I want to reopen my shop in the same location or sell the property and move. Sully and I joked about him being my business manager, so I guess I should consult him."

"I bet he'll say to move your shop to the country. I would second that."

"What I do know for sure is how I feel about Sully," Charley admitted.

Chloe smiled and said, "You've fallen hard for him, haven't you?"

"Yes," Charley hesitated and then said quietly, "I haven't told Sully yet, but I'm in love with him, Chloe."

"Tell him. Don't play games or waste time. By the way, I've seen the way he looks at you. I think he feels the same," Chloe said, but Charley wasn't convinced Sully's feelings about her were nearly as strong as her own and shrugged. "When he realized you had left the party, he was worried about you and determined to find out what happened."

"I told him I should have stood my ground and listened to his side."

Now Chloe shrugged. "We live and learn. I can tell you that my life changed forever for the better after I listened to Derek's side of things back in the day."

Chloe told her more about that time in her life as Charley finished every bite of her dinner. Chloe carried Charley's empty plate to the sink and loaded it into the dishwasher as

Derek entered the kitchen. The three of them spoke for a few minutes, and then Charley yawned.

"Sorry," Charley said with a laugh. "I'm exhausted."

"Let's get you settled in upstairs," Chloe said.

Charley left the kitchen and walked down the hall. In the foyer, she paused to wait for Chloe. Over her shoulder, she saw Derek pull Chloe into his arms. Chloe wrapped her arms around his neck, and as she stood on tiptoes to kiss him, he patted her fanny. Oh, how Charley wanted that with Sully and so much more. She looked away and moved forward to the bottom of the staircase. Chloe joined her a moment later with a peaceful smile on her lovely face.

Yes, what a perfectly wonderful life.

THAT REJECTION TEXT FROM CHARLEY HAD DISTRACTED HIM AND he'd shrieked as the woman's knee slammed into his groin. Instantaneous sickening pain almost made him puke. With long, brown hair, she had been the closest match to Charley that he'd ever caught. The voices said she was a noxious whore like his mother. They deserved toadflax, not flowers. How stupid could she be walking the streets with a killer on the loose? The irony made him laugh. He'd pulled up alongside her and made an offer. Sure enough, for twenty bucks, this one had willingly accepted *a ride*. Not until his hands had tightened around her throat did she fight back. She'd clawed, hit, and kicked her way out from under him. Also like Charley, she'd escaped. For now.

CHAPTER TWENTY-EIGHT

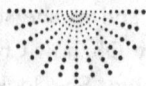

"Good morning," Charley said, opening her bedroom door bright and early on Triple C-West.

"Good morning," Abilene said, holding Wyatt Earp.

"Hi," Austin, her twin brother said. "I knocked on your door so that we could tell you we like your puppy."

Cooper caught up with his siblings, and Chloe was right behind him. She shooed the children, along with Spike and Wyatt, down the hall to the top of the stairs.

"Come to the kitchen whenever you're ready, Charley. Derek's already gone to the stables. I'm going to feed the kids some breakfast and get them on the school bus."

"Okay," Charley said, watching them trek down the staircase. "I'll be right there."

With a laugh, Chloe said, "We can have our breakfast in peace after they leave."

Charley shut her door and put the same clothes back on that she'd worn the previous day. She had no makeup with her and really wanted a shower and a change of clothes. She couldn't go see Sully again looking as bad, at least in her opinion, as she'd been the day before. So, she made her bed, grabbed her purse, and hurried downstairs. Finding Chloe and the kids in the kitchen, Charley poured herself a cup of coffee and picked up Wyatt. She took him out to the front yard. As he did his business and played, she sat in a rocker on the porch.

Wyatt was back in Charley's lap when the kids came bustling out of the house. Shouting and waving goodbye to her, they piled into a golf cart parked beside the house, and Chloe drove them to the end of the drive. Spike raced alongside them. Within three or four minutes, a big, yellow school bus stopped in front of the Triple C Ranch-West archway and the children boarded. Chloe waved, and Spike barked. The dog jumped onto the passenger's seat of the golf cart, and Chloe returned to the house. Spike hopped out and stopped next to Charley and Wyatt.

"I want all of this someday," Charley said to her cousin as Chloe walked onto the porch.

Chloe smiled and said, "That same school bus just picked up Colton and Courtney Cooper. And before Triple C-Central, it goes right by Cash's, yours, and Sully's ranches."

Charley stood, put Wyatt down, and hugged her cousin. In the kitchen, Chloe poured coffee, served along with yogurt and blueberries and a side of toast for breakfast. The dogs ate in the mudroom as Scarlett, who had evidently already dined, sunned herself in the windowsill. As Charley finished her coffee, she received a text from Sully. When Chloe cocked a questioning brow, Charlie smiled.

"Sully's awake. He says they moved him out of the ICU last night as planned. He's on a discharge floor now, has no temperature, and feels good. The nurse just told him that his doctor will be making rounds soon. Sully will know then if he'll be discharged." Charley texted back and said, "I don't know why I'm so nervous, but I can't wait to see him."

"Because you've admitted out loud that you're in love with him, and in your heart you're hoping he's in love with you too."

Charley raised both of her eyebrows, sighed, and admitted, "That sums it up perfectly." They both laughed, and Charley said she was going to head to her cabin with Wyatt. "I need to try and look a bit more presentable today than I did yesterday. Or I might lose Sully before I can win him."

"I highly doubt that," Chloe said. "I think you've already won him." After breakfast, Chloe walked her back out to her car with Wyatt and Spike as escorts. "Please keep us posted, and if Sully isn't discharged, come spend the night again."

"Okay, I sure will. Thank you, Chloe. I love you all."

"The entire Cooper family loves you too, Charley."

Charley hugged her and promised to keep them posted. Putting Wyatt and his puppy food into her car she got in after him, and with a wave, headed down the drive. She met up with Derek in his truck as he turned off the highway and into the driveway.

He stopped, rolled down his window, and said, "Be careful and say hello to Sully."

"I will. Thanks again for taking me to the crash site yesterday, Derek."

With a nod, he raised a hand in goodbye and Charley waved back before heading east on the highway leading to her cabin. She talked to Wyatt as she drove, telling him about Sully. She waved at Chase and Jade Cooper, who were also in a truck, and heading west. Triple C Ranch-East was next, and everything looked quiet. The parking lot of the Lodge, however, was packed. Despite the fact they were busy, she'd heard Cash say at the Halloween party that he was taking some time off from the dude ranch during the holidays due to the expected Thanksgiving arrival of the new baby boy. How exciting and wonderful.

Charley reached her cabin, and heading inside with Wyatt, she planned to make fast work of taking a shower and changing. Humming a happy tune, she was excited to get back to the hospital and check on Sully's discharge status. But when she looked through her clothes, she couldn't find the freshly laundered sweater and jeans she'd planned to wear. That was frustrating enough, but in the process of taking things out of her duffel bag, she dropped her hairdryer onto the bathroom floor, and it decided not to work. The shower would be postponed.

"Wyatt, it's broad daylight. We're going to make a quick trip in and out of my Old Colorado City apartment," Charley said.

Locking the cabin, she took the puppy back to her car. Placing Wyatt in his dog bed on the passenger's seat, they zipped west down the highway. "I love Pikes Peak," she said, admiring it in the distance.

Wyatt gave a puppy-sized barked as if he agreed. Reaching the corner of her shop on Colorado Avenue, everything appeared normal. In the parking pad area at the duplex, Charley looked in all directions before exiting the car.

Wyatt relieved himself, and Charley said, "Wyatt, I think someone may have done some housetraining with you before you were abandoned." Charley wondered again if that person had since been murdered.

They hurried inside, and she locked the door. Giving Wyatt water, she made a mental note to take his dog bowls with her this time. As Wyatt curled up on a thick rug for a puppy nap, Charley found the clothes she wanted to wear and took her shower. After shampooing and blow-drying her hair, she dressed. With a dab of makeup, she felt like her old self.

Just as she finished dressing, her phone sounded, and when Wyatt looked up, she said, "A text from Sully. He's being discharged." She texted back that she was on her way to pick him up and walked to the front door. She opened it without the chain in place and gasped. "Rod."

"Hi beautiful," he said and held out a bouquet of flowers wrapped in cellophane. He always seemed to have a smirk on his somewhat round face. She knew he came from money. A trust fund baby, he'd claimed, and perhaps the reason why he was accustomed to getting whatever he wanted. "I see you got my other flowers, since they're not out here on the porch."

"Yes, I did. But I'm just leaving, so—"

"So, I'm only staying for a minute." He pushed past her and with his foot nudged Wyatt out of his way. The puppy evidently didn't move far enough or fast enough to suit Rod, and the second shove he gave Wyatt seemed a bit rough to Charley. "I called, but you didn't answer."

"Come here, Wyatt." Charley picked him up and cuddled him. She didn't tell Rod that she'd blocked his number.

"I don't see the other flowers, baby," Rod said.

"The vase broke, and the flowers didn't make it."

"You couldn't save my flowers even though you're a florist?"

"Even though."

Rod scowled at that but quickly masked it with a smile that didn't reach his eyes. "Then it's a good thing I brought replacements." With that, he laid the flowers on the counter, leisurely walked to the sofa, and plopped down as if he had no intention of *only staying for a minute.*

"I'm headed to the hospital to pick up a friend, and I need to get going."

"The guy with the guns? The guy I saw in your flower shop? With the big truck?"

"Yes." Charley cautiously remained near the front door. Someone had vandalized her car and property, and she still thought it might have been Rod.

"Tell you what, you get rid of that cowboy, and I'll take you anywhere you want to go, do anything you want to do." Lounging on the sofa, like he owned it and her, Rod spread his arms wide. "Go anywhere and do anything in the world. No pressure."

"Rod, you're pressuring me right now," Charley said, holding Wyatt to her heart and keeping one hand on the new doorknob Sully had installed. She knew Sully would be livid to find out she'd put herself in this predicament. "I don't know how many times I have to say this, but I'm not going to go out with you again. You need to leave or I will call 9-1-1."

"The hell you will." Rod lurched off the sofa with such force that Charley took a step back. She had a fleeting sense of déjà vu as he came toward her.

"Trust me, I will." Charley's phone rang, and she placed Wyatt on the floor, then dug into her purse. Keeping an eye on Rod, she answered her cell without looking at the caller. "Hello Leon, yes, I'm in my apartment. Come on up the hill."

"When that hotshot rancher dumps you, don't come crying to me." Rod charged across the living room, kicking Wyatt along the way as he stomped out the door. Wyatt whimpered and rolled sideways. Rod met up with Leon, who was riding his scooter into the parking area, and shouted for him to go to hell. Over his shoulder, Rod hollered, "That goes for you, too, Charley!"

Charley shoved her phone in her pocket and collected Wyatt to make sure he was okay. He was, and when she looked up, a flash of something on the sofa caught her eye. Rod's gun lay on the middle cushion! Dear God! As Rod got into his Mercedes and skidded over the gravel, she hurried across the living room. She had the presence of mind not to pick up the gun with her bare hands. With the puppy still in her arms, she raced around the counter and into the kitchen. She put Wyatt on the floor, grabbed a dish towel, and hurried back to the living room. She tossed the towel over the gun a split second before Leon entered the tiny foyer of the apartment. She turned and faced him.

"I thought I saw the tail end of your car on the parking pad," Leon said, looking over his shoulder to the gravel area. "That Rod guy is a real piece of work."

"Are you feeling better, Leon?" Charley asked from across the room. When Leon turned to her, she gasped. "My gosh! What happened to your face?"

"Oh, you mean the scratches?"

"Yes. They look raw and deep."

"I had a bad fall."

"Oh," Charley said. Wyatt scampered to her, and Charley picked him up. "I thought you had a stomach virus."

"Dizziness from the virus is why I had the bad fall," he replied, lingering in the foyer as she stayed near the sofa. "But I'm okay."

"Good." Charley found it odd that Leon didn't acknowledge the puppy. Maybe he just didn't like dogs.

"Since you're closed, I'll continue working on my uncle's car today."

"Your uncle had a car? I thought he bought you the scooter for transportation."

"He did because his car needed work," Leon said and touched his face as though it still hurt. "I'm hoping to get his car running reliably today."

"That's great, Leon," Charley said. She had to get out of here before Rod realized he'd misplaced his gun and came back to look for it.

"I'd like to show you the car."

"Leon, I apologize, but I've got to cut our visit short. I have a prior commitment and I need to be on my way."

"You do?" In addition to the fresh wounds on his freckled face, Leon appeared pale and more gaunt than usual. The last time he'd exhibited even a slight smile was the day he'd said she should rename her store the *Little Shop of Horrors*. Today his expression was completely bland again. "If I get the car running, maybe I can pick you up later. For dinner?"

"I can't today." Charley remembered Sully finding out from Owen the caliber of bullet in Rod's gun. She would take his gun straight to Sully and Owen. She knew that since CSPD was in possession of the report on the bullet taken from her mother during the coroner's autopsy, they could test Rod's gun. Rod Vaughn could either be eliminated or confirmed as a suspect in her mother's murder and thus, the man who attacked her. When the cell phone in her pocket rang, she jumped. "Hello?" It was Sully. She couldn't explain what she was dealing with in front of Leon but tried to sound as normal as possible. "Sully, I promise I'm on my way. Right now."

"Charley, we need to talk," Leon said and closed the front door.

CHAPTER TWENTY-NINE

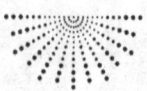

"*W*here is Charley?" Sully asked his dad while sitting in the hospital bed, fully dressed.

"Was she driving from Triple C-West?" Owen replied, having just returned from the country with a change of clothes for Sully. Sully's boots had survived the car crash, but the torn and bloody clothes he'd had on in the ER had been thrown out. "It's Tuesday, a workday, and the traffic could be slowing her down."

"I assumed she was with Chloe on Triple C-West or maybe at her log cabin." Sully rubbed his forehead. "I told her I didn't want her in Old Colorado City without me."

"I fully understand your concern." Owen nodded. "So far, Burt Groves has no solid leads on the person who attacked Charley and shot her mother."

"Talk about kicking yourself a hundred times," Sully said. "I wish we'd bought Vaughn's gun when given the chance."

"And maybe you would have if it had been you in the gun store when Vaughn came in that day instead of Roy."

"Maybe."

"Burt told me CSPD has DNA on the guy who is strangling and stabbing women, but none of the suspects they have interrogated so far have been a match," Owen said and rubbed the crease in his brow. "The cops need a break in the Cave Killer case. Right now."

"Yeah," Sully grumbled. "Anything new that might suggest the Cave Killer also murdered Charley's mother and attacked Charley?"

"The police haven't ruled that out. But personally, I don't think it's the same guy because the MOs don't match," he said, referring to the method of operations: one involving a gun and an attack versus a knife and strangling.

"I agree about the MOs. Dammit." Sully nodded and repeated, "Where is Charley?"

"Charley is an independent and brave young woman, Sully," Owen said, taking a seat beside Sully's bed. "She's been through a hell of a lot in a short time. Don't underestimate her capabilities. And she has that SIG Sauer P365 you gave her."

"Yeah, she does," Sully said. "But if I knew she was at her apartment right now, I'd leave the hospital, discharged or not and go get her."

"Since you're not officially discharged yet, give Charley a few more minutes."

"I'm going to call her again."

Sully picked up his cell, just as the nurse entered the room with his discharge paperwork. He placed his cell on the bed and tried to pay attention to the instructions. The hospital had already made an outpatient follow-up appointment for him with Dr. Sankari. He was told the external stitches would dissolve. Sully was informed to immediately call the doctor or return to the ER with any pain, dizziness, shortness of breath, passing out, or bleeding. Sully signed the paperwork indicating he understood and swung his legs off the bed.

"Mr. Custis, you're discharged and good to go," the nurse told him.

"I'm expecting someone to meet me here, so may I wait for a few more minutes?"

"Of course. Take your time," the nurse said.

"Thanks." Sully picked up his cell again and scrolled for Charley's number.

"Hi," Charley said, passing the nurse and bopping into his room.

"Charley, where have you been?" Sully all but barked.

"Hi, Charley," Owen said with a fatherly frown at Sully. "Great to see you."

"Great to see you guys too!" Charley hurried across the room to Sully. Still sitting on the side of the bed, he pulled her into his arms and tucked her between his knees. As he held her to him, she asked, "Are you discharged?"

"Yes," he replied. Charley's smile warmed his heart. "What took you so long to get here? I was worried. Where have you been?"

"I'll tell you all about it," Charley said and eased back. "I have something in my purse that you won't believe."

"What?"

"I can't show you here," she whispered, her beautiful blue eyes sparkling. "I'm probably lucky hospital security didn't detect it and confiscate it from me. But I couldn't take a chance of leaving it in my car."

"Is it your new puppy I heard about from Sully?" Owen teased.

"No, but Wyatt's in my car."

"I can't wait to hear all about it." Sully gathered his discharge instructions, stood up, and grabbed her hand. Mere minutes ago, he'd been filled with dread, and now that her dainty hand was securely locked in his, he was on top of the world. He grinned. "Let's go, city slicker."

Owen was already heading out of the room. Sully and Charley followed him to the nearest elevator. Taking it down to the main level, they exited the hospital and started toward the parking garage. What a difference a day and a half could make. And if he could help it, Sully didn't intend to let Charley out of his sight again.

"I got here shortly before you did, Charley," Owen said

as they reached the elevators to the parking garage. "I'm on the fourth level of the parking garage."

"Me too," she replied as they entered the elevator.

"So, what's in your purse?" Sully asked as Owen pushed button four.

Before she could answer, a middle-aged couple joined them on the elevator. Charley kept quiet but grinned up at Sully as though she had the best secret in the world. He couldn't imagine what it was. He narrowed his eyes in question and then he winked at her. When the couple exited the elevator on level three, they were alone again.

"A gun," Charley said as soon as the elevator door closed.

"Yeah, Dad and I were just talking about your new gun," Sully said and smiled down at her. "I'm glad you have it with you."

"Actually, my gun is locked in the glove compartment of my car."

"There's my truck," Owen said as the elevator door opened on four.

"What gun are you talking about?" Sully asked as they exited.

"Just you wait and see," Charley said.

Owen led the way to his truck. They stopped on the driver's side with Charley's back to the truck door. When Sully and Owen stood in front of her, she was blocked from the vision of any passersby. Sully and his dad watched as she removed something wrapped in a dish towel from her purse. When Sully stuffed his hospital papers in his back pocket, she carefully placed the parcel in his hand. Being an El Paso County Sheriff's son, he knew how to unwrap it. Without touching his fingers to the item, he revealed a gun. When it lay on top of the towel in full view, Sully looked at Charley. Eyes wide, she nodded.

"I know I'm not gonna like the story that goes with how you have this gun," Sully said. "But this is Rod Vaughn's poor excuse for a gun, isn't it?"

"Yes," Charley said enthusiastically.

"Detective Groves and CSPD may have just caught the break we said they needed, Sully," Owen said with a gleam in his eye.

"Yeah, just like when a suspect leaves a glass with fingerprints behind, the cops can use this gun which Vaughn left behind," Sully said.

"And he left the gun behind in Charley's house, no less. She has every right to turn it over to the police," Owen said and smiled at Charley. "Excellent work."

"Yay," Charley said softly. "The bullets may not match, but at least we can find out one way or the other now."

"About damn time," Sully growled.

"If this Vaughn guy figures out where he lost his gun, he will come looking for Charley, Sully," Owen said. "Speaking of which, I brought your gun, which was still in your holster when you reached the ER."

"Yep, I'm thinking Vaughn will be looking for Charley." Sully took his gun from Owen.

"Don't let her out of your sight," Owen said.

"Damn straight," Sully agreed and gave Charley a stern look. She smiled at him, and his heart beat faster with love and concern.

Hearing a tiny bark a few vehicles away, Charley saw the puppy's nose in the window of her Mini Cooper and said, "There's Wyatt Earp."

"Sully, you go with Charley," Owen suggested. "If you give me that gun she found, I'll take it straight to Burt Groves at the police department." Sully handed the gun over to his dad, and then turning to Charley, Owen added, "Groves may give you a call because I'll have to tell him how I came to be in possession of the weapon."

"Of course," Charley said. "No problem."

"Take care of our boy," Owen said to Charley with a nod of his head at Sully.

"I intend to," Charley replied and looped her arm through Sully's.

Owen got into his truck, and Sully slid his hand into Charley's. With a wave, Owen was already gone as they reached Charley's car a few spaces away. She carefully unlocked the driver's door and scooped up the puppy. She held him, and Sully petted his head.

"I think you're right about him being a Labrador retriever," Sully said as he took the little puppy from her and scratched his furry head. "He looks exactly like the black Lab I had when he was a puppy." The puppy licked Sully's hand, and he gave him back to Charley. As she juggled the puppy into her arms, Sully suggested, "Let's go home."

"Good idea."

Sully offered to drive. Though he fully trusted Charley to get them home safely, after his recent accident, he preferred to be the one behind the wheel. Charley, hugging the puppy, agreed and they got into the car. Sully backed out of the parking space, and once they had exited the garage, he headed away from the hospital. Driving east toward the country, he looked at the gorgeous girl and the cute puppy and grinned.

"Your cabin or my house?" he asked.

"I packed some extra clothes along with Wyatt's food and dog bowls," Charley said. Sully detected a blush on her cheeks. "Your house?"

"Yeah," Sully agreed, reached across the console and petted Wyatt's head before taking Charley's hand. He cocked a brow and said, "Now, tell me how you happened to be in your apartment to get Vaughn's gun and pack your clothes."

Charley made a playful show of swallowing hard and then flashed him an innocent grin. When he fought back a smile and narrowed his eyes, she told him how she'd thought it would be safe to take a quick shower and grab what she needed at her apartment.

"It was broad daylight after all," she explained.

"And crimes are never committed during daylight hours," Sully scolded.

"Well anyway—" Charley held up a dainty hand to placate him as the Mini Cooper sped them toward home. "Right after Rod bailed off the sofa, Leon showed up on his scooter."

"What?" Sully said. "You had to deal with both of them at once?"

"Yes, then Rod took off telling us both to go to hell."

"Vaughn throws tantrums like a two-year-old," Sully said. "I can't wait to hear what CSPD ballistics says about his gun. What did Lerfeld want?"

"First, he told me that he was working on fixing up a car that belonged to his uncle." Charley tilted her head and said, "He wanted to show it to me at his house, and I said no."

"You told me you were on your way when I called you, but Lerfeld was still there?"

"Yes," she said. "Leon said we needed to talk and asked me if I was serious about you. Apparently, he still has the little crush on me."

"The *big* crush on you," Sully corrected and cocked a brow. "What did you say about being serious?"

Charley squared her shoulders, looked him in the eye, and replied, "I told him yes, I am serious about you."

Sully grinned at her and said, "I feel the same about you, Charley."

"Really?"

"Hell yes, really."

With that and a smile, he turned onto the highway that led to the Triple C Ranches. When they eventually neared Charley's ranch, Sully spotted the silver Mercedes on the gravel drive. The vehicle was facing the highway. "Well, well. Looks like Vaughn realized he lost his little gun. He must have returned to your apartment, but luckily you were already gone. So, he's come looking for you out here. Just like my dad said he would."

"Sully!" Charley sucked in a breath, her blue eyes wide. "What are we going to do?"

"I'll handle it," Sully said. "Call the sheriff." He gave

Charley a private number to the El Paso County Sheriff's office and she called. "Tell them you're with me. Tell them Rod Vaughn, a man who's been stalking you, is at your cabin and you're afraid to go home."

"Okay," Charley said and dialed.

As Charley made the report to the sheriff's office, Sully knew Vaughn had recognized Charley's Mini Cooper because the Mercedes appeared in the rearview mirror. Sully sped up, and Vaughn did as well. Damn. He'd just been discharged from the hospital after an accident on this high-way. But the roads weren't slippery today. Sully didn't head toward his ranch. Instead, in a clear stretch of road and with no other cars in sight, Sully turned the wheel, screeching the tires and making a lightning-fast 180-degree U-turn. He stopped exactly in the middle of the highway. Vaughn came to a skidding, sloppy halt off to one side of the road. Sully aimed his Ruger out of the window and shot both tires on the driver's side of Vaughn's car. Raising his chin at an astonished Vaughn, Sully pressed on the gas, and they flew back down the highway.

"That seemed fair," Sully said. "I guarantee you he's the one who slashed your tires."

"I agree. But what about the bullets in *his* tires?" Charley asked with concern. "Will the police be able to trace them to your gun?"

"This gun can never be traced to me," Sully replied as he placed it on the console. When Charley opened her mouth, certainly to inquire as to why the gun couldn't be traced, he said, "Don't ask, city slicker."

CHAPTER THIRTY

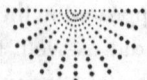

"I told your dad I intended to take care of you," Charley said to the handsome man as they walked through the foyer of his house. "You need to rest."

"That's why I'm taking you straight to my bedroom."

"Ha! Ha!" Charley giggled as tingles zipped through her entire body. Sully was carrying Wyatt and his dog bed since she refused to let him carry her suitcase. "What you need to do is go to the bedroom, lie down, and behave."

"I'd rather *do* you than behave."

"Oh, no you don't. Not today." Walking behind him, Charley made her way into his bedroom and set her bag on the hardwood floor. Sully put Wyatt and the dog bed down, and she said, "Because of your concussion and stitches, I'm not taking any chances with you."

Sully pulled her into his arms. "You've already taken a bunch of chances with me, baby."

Charley grinned. "I mean with your health." Sully's head lowered and when his lips met hers, she gently wrapped her arms around his waist. But because of his stitches, she didn't hold on too tightly. He began backing her toward his bed and stopped only when her legs met with the mattress. When she opened her eyes, the love she felt for him surely showed on her face. "Sully, I'm serious about taking good care of you."

"I want to take care of you too. Again, I'm asking you to please stay here in the country with me, Charley. Forever." With a shrug and a coaxing grin, he said, "For as long as you like."

And once again, she thought that wild horses couldn't drag her away. "I will consider it if you let me make you some lunch," she bargained.

"I am hungry," Sully said with a chuckle and stepped back. "I'll go to bed when you do. Let's go to the kitchen and eat."

"What do you think Rod Vaughn's next move will be?" she asked.

On their way out of the bedroom, the puppy followed them, and Sully scooped him up. In the kitchen, Sully said, "If Vaughn is the guy who attacked you and shot your mom, he's running on high alert, and anything is possible."

Sully sat on a barstool at the island with the puppy in his lap, and Charley asked, "I told Detective Groves about the tattoo on the man who attacked me, didn't I?"

"Yes, you did."

Looking in the fridge, Charley asked, "What do you want to eat?"

"You. C'mere." Sully crooked his finger, and Charley walked to him. She took the puppy from him, and Sully wrapped his arms around both of them. "This feels right."

"It does," Charley said and cupped a hand to the back of his neck. "It did from day one."

"Yeah," he nodded. "From day one."

He kissed her, then let her go long enough to fix bacon and cheese omelets. Having closed her flower shop and with Roy manning the gun shop while Randy took care of the horses and skeet shooting, they enjoyed lunch and then a restful afternoon together in the cozy den. They didn't turn on the news. Instead, Sully sent Randy a text, and Randy answered saying only Storm and Rain were in the stables. So, they took Wyatt on a walk to introduce him to the horses. The puppy bounded around the hay, and when Sully lifted him up to Storm and Rain, the puppy rubbed his little face against those of the horses.

While they were in the stables, a sheriff's deputy showed up to touch base with them about the report Charley had made. The deputy had gone to Triple C Ranch-South, but Rod Vaughn had not been there. The deputy reported that a fellow officer had stopped by Charley's Old Colorado City property and there was no evidence of a break-in or anything amiss. That was a relief to both Charley and Sully. The deputy gave them his name, asked Sully to be sure and tell Owen hello, and then left.

"Let's go to Coopers' Lodge for dinner," Sully suggested once they were back in the den on the leather sofa. Before Charley could answer, his cell phone rang. "It's my dad." He answered the call and listened. He made a half-turn, looked at Charley, and placed his hand on her knee. "So, not only is the caliber the same, the bullets are a match," he said to Owen, as well as letting Charley know. "I'll be damned."

Charley sat quietly, but inside, her nerves jangled. Wyatt lay in her lap, and she hugged the little puppy remembering how Rod had kicked him. She listened as Sully asked if CSPD had Vaughn in custody. Not yet, but Detective Groves was getting ready to pick him up. Charley's heart thudded with anxiety. Sully thanked his dad for the update and clicked off his phone.

"Dear God, Sully," Charley whispered. "What is wrong with Rod Vaughn?"

Sully rubbed his forehead and said, "I think he's been relentless in trying to get you to go out with him again so that he could change your opinion of him." Wrapping his right arm around her and the puppy, he said, "He hoped if he could win you over, you wouldn't suspect him of the crimes he committed against you and your mother."

"But he's made himself look worse instead of better."

"Because he's an entitled jerk used to getting his way," Sully said bluntly. "When you refused to go to bed with him, he came to your apartment fully intending to take what he wanted. Your mother, hearing you scream, saved you."

Charley shuddered. "I will always be grateful to her for that."

"Vaughn didn't have the safety in place on his gun the day I took it from him. I doubt he had it on that day at your duplex. He panicked and shot your mom during his escape."

"Yes." Charley nodded. "I scratched him when I tore the neck of his hoodie and saw his scorpion tattoo. The police have a record of his DNA, from under my fingernails, on file. I wonder if they have tested that DNA against the Cave Killer's."

"If Groves hasn't done so already, you can bet he will," Sully said with a hug. "Come on, let's go to the Lodge. If Cash and Tracy are there, we can give them an update."

Sully suggested they keep Charley's car safe and out of sight by parking it in his garage. While she fed Wyatt, Sully moved her car. A few minutes later she and Wyatt went outside so the puppy could relieve himself. As they walked across the backyard toward the garage, Charley saw Sully talking on his cell phone. He smiled at her and motioned her toward him. As Wyatt played in the yard, Sully mouthed the word *Dad* and then hung up from the call.

"What's the latest, Sully?"

"Groves hasn't found Vaughn yet," Sully replied, taking her hand and walking her back toward the house. "The cops put out an APB for him, meaning an *all-points bulletin*. They've let the Colorado Springs and Denver airports know not to let him on a plane."

Back inside the house, Wyatt ran to his dog bed, as Charley smiled and said, "He's going to be too big for that beagle-size bed before we know it."

The sun had set, and the temperature was crisp so they

put on jackets before going back out to Sully's truck. He drove to Triple C Ranch-East, and they parked alongside other vehicles of folks there for dinner. They spotted Cash just coming out of the Lodge as they walked toward the entrance.

"Sully! Hey, buddy!" Cash said, coming forward and sticking out his hand. "So good to see you. Hi, Charley," he added with a smile. "How're you feeling, Sully?"

"Good. Supposedly I suffered a mild concussion, and I've got a bunch of stitches, but I have a great nurse." With his hand going to his ribs, Sully grinned at Charley.

"My main job is trying to keep him quiet and resting," Charley said. Thinking of Sully shooting out Rod's tires, she rolled her eyes. "It's not easy."

"Yeah," Cash said with a chuckle as they paused under the welcoming portico of Coopers' Lodge. "Good luck with that."

"How's Tracy?" Charley asked, knowing her due date was about three weeks away.

"She *is* quiet and resting," Cash echoed the last three words. "She won't be back here to work here at the Lodge until sometime after the first of the year. She and Carly are spending some extra time together before the baby comes."

"Please tell Tracy and Carly we said hello," Charley said.

"I sure will. Anything new in Old Colorado City?" Cash asked.

Charley wasn't sure how much to reveal since the information they had on Rod Vaughn was from Owen through his police contacts. So, she deferred to Sully with a glance.

"Off the record, Cash, the guy you briefly met at Triple C-South named Rod Vaughn, owns a gun that is somewhat unique in that it has a firing issue. That gun's bullet matches the bullet that killed Charley's mother," Sully told him.

"Damn!" Cash replied with a concerned glance at Charley. "Is Vaughn in custody?"

"He will be as soon as the cops can find him," Sully said.

"They've also got his DNA on file," Charley added. "I hope they catch him soon."

"Me too," Cash agreed. "Along with the gun, the DNA will be damning evidence."

"That's almost exactly what my dad said," Sully told him.

The scorpion tattoo wasn't mentioned, but Charley and Sully promised to keep Cash posted. In turn, he promised to let them know when Tracy went into labor. Either way, they were invited to Triple C Ranch-Central for Thanksgiving dinner. They were to bring Owen along, too, if he'd care to join them. As for this evening's dinner, they bid Cash goodbye and continued into the Lodge. Sully waved at a couple of neighbors he knew. Charley didn't know anyone, but then dining customers came from far and wide, as well as the Springs, to eat here. She and Sully both had the prime rib special, and it was delicious. Though she'd wanted to treat him, Sully wouldn't hear of her paying, and he left a generous tip as well. Back in Sully's truck, they returned to his ranch. There in the light of the front porch, Roy and Randy stood talking to Owen.

As they exited the truck, Owen called, "Hello."

"Have they caught him yet?" Sully took Charley's hand as they walked to the porch.

"Not yet," Owen replied. "But when I was driving by your ranch, I saw Roy and Randy and figured I'd bring them up to date."

"We stopped by to see how you're doing," Roy said. "Everything is good at the store."

"As you know, I took a group of skeet shooters out earlier," Randy said. "The horses are in the stables, brushed down, fed, and settled in for the night, Sully."

"Thanks guys," Sully said. "I'm feeling better, and I'll be back at the store in a couple of days or so to check on things."

"If Charley thinks he's up to it," Owen added with a chuckle.

"That's right, Owen," Charley agreed.

Charley was glad for their families, dinner, and the distractions, because inwardly she remained on edge. A murderer and would-be rapist was on the loose, and she'd once been his victim. Were the young women in Old Colorado City his victims as well? She felt the familiar shudder, and maybe Sully sensed it because he wrapped his arm around her and said good night to his dad and cousins. With a wave goodbye, she and Sully went into his house.

After changing into comfortable clothing, they watched a movie on the big flatscreen in the den. As the movie ended, Charley saw Sully yawn. She coaxed him into the bedroom and he a tugged her into bed with him. Wyatt curled up in his cozy dog bed, they all fell asleep.

Charley saw the intruder as soon as she left the bathroom. He wore a black ski mask and hoodie. He grabbed her and shoved her onto the bed. He tore at her robe. She scratched him and screamed.

"Charley, wake up. You're with me. You're safe."

Charley opened her eyes. Her heart was slamming against her ribs. Moonlight showed her that Sully was in bed beside her. She whispered his name like a prayer. He pulled her into his arms, and she clung to him. Taking a deep breath she fought against the terror. When her trembling calmed, she rolled to her side, and Sully's muscular body molded to the length of hers. He kissed the back of her head, and his arm came around her, protecting her. Charley breathed a sigh of relief and closed her eyes.

HE WAS OBSESSED WITH HER. SHE SEEMED OBLIVIOUS. HE WAS tired of getting nowhere. He burned for her and needed the blissful numbness. Bipolar, narcissistic, borderline personality disorder, and schizophrenia. Those diagnoses had been thrown at him over the years. He spat on the floor. How insulting. He wasn't mentally ill, just a normal man with normal needs. The voices kept repeating that he was losing it. Medicine helped control the voices, but he resented taking it. True, he had been careless. The last victim, the one who looked like Charley, had escaped. That had unnerved him. Why hadn't Sullivan Custis died in that recent car crash? He should have died! The fact that Custis was alive was not going to stop him from pursuing Charley. He would not stop until Charley was his. Or until one of them was dead.

CHAPTER THIRTY-ONE

"They caught him," Sully told Charley as he walked into the kitchen two mornings later. She was so beautiful, intelligent, and adorable, no wonder Rod Vaughn had lost his mind over her. Sully was crazy about her too. "Colorado Springs police got a tip on his whereabouts."

Clad in her red boots, a white sweater, and blue jeans, Charley was an all-American girl. His girl. With her loose braid down the center of her slender back, she turned to Sully with two cups of coffee in her hands.

"Thank God." Charley placed the cups on the quartz counter of the island and walked into his embrace. She twined her arms around his neck and asked, "Where was he?"

"Hiding at the ex-girlfriend's place. Evidently, Vaughn was freaking her out." Holding Charley to his heart, she felt delicate and vulnerable. Sully knew he would do anything in his power to keep her safe. "She wanted rid of him and tipped off the cops."

"Will they be able to keep him in jail?" Charley asked, hugging herself to him. "Will there be a trial? I'll probably have to testify. I'll gladly do so."

"Me too," Sully said. Then, both Sully and Charley

picked up their cups of coffee and sat down on barstools at the island. "My dad says Burt Groves told him that Vaughn had a bad attitude as soon as they showed up at the girl-friend's apartment. Apparently, he had knocked her around before the cops got there."

"Yes, we've seen his bad attitude."

"They cuffed him and hauled him off to jail. During the initial interrogation with Groves, Vaughn claimed he vandal-ized your property and slashed all four of your tires only because I had shot out two of his tires first."

Charley's blue eyes snapped with fire. "That's a lie!"

"I know, and Groves wasn't fooled or sidetracked," Sully said with a shake of his head. "Instead, Groves started nailing Vaughn with the evidence they have on him: the confirmation from ballistics, his fingerprints on the gun that killed your mother, and his DNA proving he was your attacker. Vaughn lost the attitude, waived his right to an attorney, and immediately started begging to make a deal. He knows they have him."

"And the scorpion tattoo?" Charley gently touched her collarbone. "Does he have one?"

"Oh yeah, he does." Sully nodded. "With a couple of fresh scars across it right where you said you scratched him."

"Good. What a despicable person he is," Charley said softly. "Do the police think Rod Vaughn is also the Cave Killer?"

Staying close on the barstool next to her, Sully splayed his hands. "They hope his DNA will match and show that he is the Cave Killer, but—"

"But what, Sully?"

A knock on the back door caused Charley to jump. Sully placed his hand on hers and then got up to answer the knock.

"Hey, Dad. Come on in and have a cup of coffee with us."

"Morning, Charley," Owen said, entering the kitchen. "Coffee sounds good."

"Hi Owen," Charley replied with a smile, but Sully heard the tension in her voice. Even so, she hopped up and took a coffee cup out of the cabinet.

"Have a seat, Dad," Sully said. His father nodded, but he walked to Charley and gave her a hug first. Then, as Charley came to them with Owen's coffee, she grabbed her cup as well and they moved to the kitchen table. Sitting next to Charley and across from his dad, Sully said, "I was just about to tell Charley that Vaughn denied any part of the Old Colorado City murders."

"Yeah, and we know the MOs don't match," Owen grumbled and frowned. "Those women were strangled and stabbed. None were shot, and none were sexually assaulted. The cops have notified the last victim who narrowly escaped being killed. They're putting Vaughn in a lineup for her this afternoon. But she says the guy wore a ski mask, so I don't know what good it will do." Owen shrugged and said, "Anyway, she says she scratched the Cave Killer, so they have fresh DNA which will link him to the other murders. But Groves doesn't think it will be a match to Vaughn."

Charley summed up, "So the man who murdered my mother may be in custody, but a killer could still be roaming my neighborhood."

"Could be." Sully clenched his jaw as his dad nodded. "What about bail? Will a judge let Vaughn out?"

"On murder and attempted rape charges involving two separate victims, the judge will keep him locked up," Owen said with confidence. "The prosecutor will point out that Vaughn has the money and means to flee the country. Not to mention, he's not been completely ruled out as the Cave Killer."

"I don't think Rod Vaughn is the Cave Killer," Charley said, looking away from the men and out the kitchen window.

"I agree but what makes you say that?" Sully asked.

"Like you and I were talking about Sully, I think Rod's attack on me was strictly personal and my mom got in the way. Rod is selfish and mean." Charley met Sully's eyes again and said, "I think the man responsible for the stranglings and stabbings is truly crazy."

Owen nodded his agreement and replied, "Charley, let's fast forward real quick. If you're on the witness stand testifying, avoid the word crazy in a court of law. Don't give the defense a way to get their client off using insanity as an excuse. Change the word crazy into the word criminal."

"Good advice," Sully agreed.

"Yes. I'll remember that," Charley said. "Vaughn and the Cave Killer *are* criminals."

Owen smiled with concern and compassion. After another swallow of coffee, he turned to Sully and asked, "How are you feeling today?"

"Good. The headache I had is gone, and my energy is back."

"But I'm still doing my best to make him take it easy," Charley assured Owen.

"That's true." Sully grinned at Charley and cocked a brow, silently reminding her that she'd made him take it easy since they'd been home. But later, he planned to make love to her.

Owen took a call and then said, "Derek Brevard needs me on Triple C-West. Today we're working with some CSPD officers and the Percherons they've bought."

"Sounds like you'll be in good company," Sully said.

"Yes, indeed," Owen agreed with a jovial chuckle. "Cops are my peeps." Finishing his coffee, he stood up and said, "I'll keep you two posted on CSPD developments." With a nod at Charley, he told Sully, "While she makes you take it easy, you keep a close eye on her."

"You know I will," Sully said and winked at Charley.

"I'll take really good care of him, Owen." Charley stood to hug him. "Thank you."

Owen headed out of the house, and Sully smiled at Charley. "How about we take it easy in my bedroom?"

To Sully's surprise, Charley said, "I was just thinking the same thing." She tilted her head in the direction of his bedroom. "Come on, country boy, I'll take *really* good care of you."

Sully chuckled and made a grab for her. Charley giggled and dashed away from him out of the kitchen and down the hall. Pulling the tee shirt out of his jeans as he entered the master bedroom, he found Charley using his bootjack to pull off her boots.

"That's how it's done, country girl."

Charley peeled off her sweater and socks. She carefully pulled his tee shirt over his head and tenderly placed a hand over the bandage across his ribs. Leading him to the bed as he stood beside it, she unbuckled his belt and undid his fly. Hot blood pounded fast into his lower body. Ever so gently, she finished undressing him, kissing his slowly exposed flesh as she did so. Sully groaned with pleasure as her warm, wet mouth closed around his hardened inches. Kissing her way back up the middle of his naked body, she nibbled each shoulder and his neck before easing him into bed.

Stacking his hands behind his head as he lay on his back, he watched Charley pull her jeans down and off. She undid her bra and dropped it across his chest. Then, turning her back to him, she pushed her panties to her knees and then to her feet. The outrageously sexy sight she presented heated his blood to boiling. As she stepped out of her panties, he groaned and reached for her. She dodged his hand. When she turned to him, her panties joined her bra. Sully swept them off his body to the bed, and this time he snared her hand. He tugged, and she cautiously straddled his hips. Starting between her spread legs, his gaze traveled up her flat abdomen to her full breasts. She was sensational, and he smiled with anticipation. He cocked a brow, letting her know what he wanted. With a smile, she lifted herself to her knees. As he placed himself to her velvety folds, she began deliciously impaling herself inch by hard inch. She undid her braid, and when she brought her head forward, her long brown hair brushed against his chest in silky waves.

"Mmm, Sully," Charley moaned softly.

He'd taught her how to ride him cowgirl style, and she was damn good at it. Charley sped up and as they thrust against each other, Sully placed his hands on her waist to help her raise and lower. He watched her nipples bead and felt her body reacting internally to his. In a few heated strokes, their lovemaking culminated in the gripping and squeezing spasms of Charley's orgasm which triggered his ecstasy. With hard, pounding pulses, Sully released himself deep within her. It was incredible. She was incredible. As another sensual moan escaped her, Charley arched backward, then forward, and smiled down at him. As his heartbeat slowed, Sully pulled Charley's exquisite body down to his. With her soft breasts molded to his chest, her warm flesh covering his wound, and her thighs pressed against the outside of his, Sully felt healed.

He whispered, "Thanks for taking *really* good care of me, Charley."

CHAPTER THIRTY-TWO

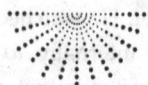

"*W*yatt? Where are you? Wyatt?" Charley called for the puppy the week of Thanksgiving. He popped out from under the sofa in the log cabin and scampered to her. She was certain he was already twice the size he'd been when she'd first found him. Clad in a sweatshirt, jeans, and tennis shoes, Charley was wielding a broom as she swept the living room floor of her cabin. Receiving a text, she read it and walked out to the porch. "Sully, the moving van is on its way," she called excitedly. "The delivery truck won't be far behind it."

"Okay," Sully called with a wave. He had just placed the last of their few remaining smaller possessions from the cabin on the back seat of his truck. It was chilly again today, and he wore a denim jacket lined with wool over a brown flannel shirt. His jeans were snug against his thighs, and he wore brown work boots. Even watching him move at a distance, Charley could almost feel those muscles in his hard body. Thankfully, his concussion had been cleared by his physician. His wound would leave a scar, but it had healed. Charley was so in love with Sully that she pictured running to him. The puppy did so, scampering past her, full speed ahead.

With the beautiful log cabin facing the main road, the

short drive leading straight from the highway to the welcoming porch, and oodles of land for parking spaces, ten thousand acres to be exact, Charley had decided to move her flower shop business to the country. She'd received a *hell yeah* from her handsome, sexy business manager. With Sully by her side in Old Colorado City, she'd packed up her clothes and any other personal items she wanted to keep from the duplex. The two apartments would be sold furnished.

That job having been accomplished, she'd put the Old Colorado City shop and duplex up for sale with a realtor friend whose office was also located on Colorado Avenue. Per Sully, her decision was an excellent step in a safe direction. As to the direction their relationship was headed, they continued to make steady progress. All these exciting new changes had helped Charley keep her mind off deaths and murderers.

Rod Vaughn was still in jail. The eyewitness who had escaped the suspected Cave Killer had viewed Rod in the lineup but as anticipated, could not positively identify anyone due to the attacker's ski mask. Shortly thereafter, DNA results confirmed Vaughn was not the Cave Killer.

Regarding the death of Charlotte Fleming, Rod had plea-bargained his way down from first-degree murder to second-degree murder with a signed confession. Colorado had repealed the death penalty in 2020, but by all accounts, Rod Vaughn would be going to prison for fifteen years to life. Though Charley's mother was dead with no second chance offered, Rod Vaughn however, would be allowed to live and could be eligible for parole at some point. Fair or not, that's the way it was according to the law.

The Cave Killer's victim who had survived had even worked with a CSPD sketch artist. But there was nothing which made the man stand out. The artist's rendering of the woman's description of her attacker was generic enough to fit countless men. In any event, there had been no additional stranglings in Old Colorado City since Rod Vaughn's capture and confession. Odd.

"Good thing I got my uncle's car up and running," Leon said, walking from the older model vehicle to the cabin porch. Even wearing a jacket, his arms appeared thin, wrapped around a box of delicate plants which he'd insisted on transporting from Charley's shop. "Would have been difficult trying to help you move with just my scooter."

Charley nodded, even though he'd only transported the one box. Sully hadn't necessarily wanted Leon's so-called help. But Charley had pointed out that Leon had backed off since she'd admitted to him the feelings she had for Sully. Maybe Leon had thought there was hope for the two of them and realizing there was none, had accepted just being friends. Leon had not acted out of place with her, and he was pleasant enough to Sully as well. Leon walked onto the porch and passed Charley on his way into the cabin. Sully, who had scooped up Wyatt, swaggered toward her as only he could. He stopped on the porch and gave her a kiss.

She and Sully had been busy transforming the great room of the log cabin into a shop soon to be filled with flowers and plants. Two ceiling-to-floor decorative screens hid the kitchen from view and converted part of it into her office area. Not only did the kitchen provide water for her plants and flowers, but she had kept it intact, knowing it would come in handy for lunchtime breaks and bookkeeping, on her laptop, between customers. For now, the bedroom would be used for making wreaths, arranging flowers, working on plants, and storage. Later on, if need be, a wall could be knocked out to enlarge the flower shop.

The movers were dropping off displays and merchandise from her shop and picking up the living room and bedroom furniture in the cabin. The Coopers had insisted Charley keep her father's furniture. Sully had a large, unfurnished family room and bedroom in the basement at his house and the furniture was perfect for it. Since the cabin had more square footage than her shop in Old Colorado City, Charley had also ordered some new displays, wall hangings, pottery, and silk arrangements to add to the live flowers and plants. In addition to those items, the delivery truck was bringing new Christmas pieces for her new shop. She could hardly wait.

Earlier, Sully had supervised a couple of workers who had done an excellent job of hanging a second sign right below Triple C Ranch-South. Cash had been there as well to see the new wooden sign installed, which read *Pretty Petals*. The signs above the arched entrance were a perfect match. Charley's heart sang.

Standing on the porch with Sully, they saw the moving truck approaching. Sully walked down the steps and waved the movers from the highway onto the ranch. The truck, carrying the furnishings and displays from Flemings Flowers, pulled in and stopped near the porch.

"Let's get the furniture here out first," Sully said to the two movers.

"Yes, sir," the mover who'd driven the truck agreed. "Show us what you've got, and we'll get it out of your way. Won't take us long."

"This way." Sully handed Wyatt over to Charley and teased her, "Who scheduled the movers and the delivery truck all in the same day, city slicker?"

"You did?"

"I don't think so," Sully replied and chuckled. "Cash arranged for the sign guys to hang your gift from all the Coopers, and I arranged for the movers. But you," he touched his index finger to her chest— "you scheduled your new deliveries on the same day."

"Oh yeah." Charley giggled and grabbed his finger. "Now I remember, that *was* me." Sully pulled his finger from her as Leon joined them on the porch. "But hey, it will all be somewhat in place by the end of the day."

"Yeah," Sully said with a pat to her fanny and disappeared into the cabin.

The sofa came out first, and then the chair. The movers

were efficient, and with Sully in charge of them, Charley and Leon stayed out of the way. When the two moving men hauled the mattress out of the cabin, Leon looked confused.

"Are you not living *and* working out of your shop? Sort of like you did on Colorado Avenue?" Leon asked. "I assumed that's why you kept the kitchen intact. I thought the movers were bringing more furniture here from your apartment, not clearing out the cabin."

"No," Charley replied in surprise. "Even though this cabin is a lot bigger than the Old Colorado City shop, there's no reason for me to be cramped here when I can live with Sully."

"Sully," Leon echoed under his breath.

Charley nodded at Leon and found Sully in the bedroom. Keeping Wyatt out of the way, she watched the movers tote the headboard and frame of the bed out of the cabin. She smiled at Sully, so thrilled at how well things were going. As he walked toward the footboard, Charley warned him not to pick it up. It was too heavy for one person. He gathered her and Wyatt up instead, set them aside, and plucked up the footboard. Chuckling as she fumed, he headed past her, strode out of the cabin, and set the footboard beside the moving truck. When the cabin was emptied of all items marked for Sully's house, the movers switched gears and brought in the items from her Old Colorado City shop. With everyone pitching in, they were soon done.

"I need to leave with the movers so that I can let them into my house and show them where we decided to put the cabin furniture," Sully told her, and as the moving truck departed, the delivery truck arrived. "And I need to check on the horses." With a guarded glance around outside and motioning to the delivery truck driver, he said, "But I don't like leaving you alone which is why I didn't want this to all happen on the same day."

"I'll be fine, and I'm not alone," Charley assured him.

"I'll stay until you get back," Leon said to Sully.

Sully reluctantly left to catch up with the moving truck

heading to his ranch. At the cabin, Charley and Leon stayed busy helping with the arrival of columbines, roses, daisies, tulips, orchids, carnations, irises, and lilies. She had also ordered a variety of her favorite plants such as the peacock, peace lily, and spider plants. She clasped her hands under her chin as three dozen of the most beautiful red, white, and pink poinsettias filled her new shop. When the truck was empty, Charley tipped and thanked the delivery man. Leon stayed busy arranging the new items with the ones already in place.

"I love the Christmas items filling the bay windows," Charley said, a broom in hand. "Things are taking shape."

"Yes," Leon said, arranging plants on a display. "I can see that now."

When Sully returned, they had the log cabin-turned-florist store in good order and were taking a coffee break in the kitchen/office area.

"Pretty Petals looks like a flower shop," came Sully's voice as he entered the front door.

"That's what Sully has always called this place and I love it," Charley told Leon as she and Wyatt hurried around the partition to greet him. Wyatt scampered ahead of her, and Sully picked him up. Leon followed her and she said, "I'll be open just in time for Black Friday shopping. I've got several ads running on social media, on the radio, and in the newspaper."

Leon asked, "Will you need my help?"

"I hope so," Charley said, praying she'd have customers. "Do you think you'd be available on Friday and Saturday?"

"Yeah," Leon replied.

"I've got things squared away at the house, and I'm starved," Sully said. "Whatever you put in the slow cooker in the kitchen smells great. Let's go home and eat."

"Leon, I made pulled pork barbecue and there is plenty," Charley said politely. "I'm going to add corn on the cob, and there's cheesecake for dessert. You're welcome to follow us to Sully's house and have dinner."

"I don't like pulled pork," Leon mumbled.

"Okay," Charley said and gave him a hug. She realized it was the first time she'd ever hugged Leon. Surely, he wouldn't get the wrong idea since Sully was standing three feet away. "Thank you for everything, Leon. You were so kind to help me after Rod Vaughn vandalized my old shop, and now you've helped me set up my new shop. I really appreciate it."

"Welcome," Leon said.

"Happy Thanksgiving," she said as Leon walked out of the cabin.

Charley looped her arm through Sully's as he held Wyatt and watched Leon walk to the old car in the parking area. Leon always seemed to shrink in Sully's presence. Not just physically, because he was a much smaller man, but emotionally as well. As Leon drove out of sight, Charley wondered if he would be alone on Thanksgiving.

LEON HAD BEEN SO HAPPY WHEN ROD VAUGHN WAS ARRESTED, he'd started taking his medication again. Despite the quack physician referring to Clozapine as a strong antipsychotic used to treat severe schizophrenia, it did ease his rage. The voices claimed he was no longer a danger to himself or society. The voices insisted he'd been *released* from that psych facility for people charged with a crime but found not guilty by reason of insanity. He'd had the Clozapine because he'd only pretended to take it during the final weeks of his unjust incarceration. The pills were gone now, and his anger had risen to an all-time high over Charley selling her Old Colorado City property. He'd assumed he could pursue Charley while working for her in the country and discourage her from being serious about that cowboy. That was until she said she would be living with Custis on his ranch. Talk about a stab to the heart! Leon repeatedly banged his forehead against the wall while shrieking at the top of his lungs.

CHAPTER THIRTY-THREE

"**S**omething's off about the guy," Sully said to Charley as they left his ranch for Thanksgiving dinner on Triple C Ranch-Central. Also accepting the Coopers' invitation, his dad had stopped by the house first and was following behind them now. "I wish you'd find somebody else to work with you in your shop."

"I don't disagree about Leon," Charley said, looking beautiful in a rust-colored sweater and snug pants the same shade as her glossy brown hair. He'd surprised her with a pair of brown cowboy boots from Cash's store, and she had them on with the hem of her pants tucked inside. She held a spectacular Tiffany glass Thanksgiving turkey floral arrangement that Jade had commissioned. She'd been honored to make it and wouldn't hear of Jade paying her for it, saying it was a gift for the dinner hosts. "But I feel so sorry for Leon, I can't imagine firing him."

Ponderosa pines swayed from the gusts of Chinook winds. Chinook meant snow eater. Native Americans had labeled these warm, northwesterly winds as Chinooks for their thawing power. Though the first snowfall of the season had yet to hit, Chinooks could vaporize a foot of snow within hours. Blasting you in the face, the Chinook winds felt icy. But their ability to melt snow off the sidewalks and streets was Mother Nature's gift to Colorado Springs.

"Have you noticed that Leon's expression rarely changes?" Sully asked.

"Sort of like people who have a lot of Botox in their face?" Charley replied.

"Sort of," Sully said and looked at the compassionate woman as they passed Triple C Ranch-South where Pretty Petals was all set for its grand opening. Moonlight kissed Charley's features as he'd done before leaving his ranch. "When he walks, his arms don't move."

"I've noticed that too," Charley said. As they passed Triple C Ranch-East, she seemed to be to picturing Leon's semi-humped over gait and commented, "The way he walks *is* peculiar."

When Triple C Ranch-Central came into view, Sully said, "You could use the excuse of saving Leon the expense of having to drive out to the country to let him go."

Charley nodded. "Despite Black Friday tomorrow, I doubt the shop will be too busy. I will keep my eyes and ears open for someone I might hire when I need help. How about you? Will your store be busy tomorrow?"

"Yes," Sully said and turned under the archway to Chase and Jade Cooper's ranch. "Whether bought for yourself or as a gift, guns are a big Christmas item."

"I feel safe having the gun you gave me," she said as they headed up the drive.

"And you've gotten good with it," he praised. Parking alongside vehicles he knew belonged to Cash and Derek, Owen pulled in on Charley's side of the truck. Sully placed his hand over her left one and said, "Vaughn's behind bars, but the Cave Killer is still out there. Don't let down your guard."

Charley smiled at him. "The Cave Killer will never find me out here in the country."

Owen opened Charley's door, and she carefully alighted, keeping the floral piece intact. Owen held a fancy carafe of wine as Sully rounded the truck. From the back seat, Sully removed the sweet potato casserole Charley had baked. Apparently, cousins Colton and Cooper were in charge of the arriving guests because the double doors of the house swung open wide.

"Happy Thanksgiving!" the cousins both called at once.

"Happy Thanksgiving!" the adults called back.

Sully couldn't remember a better Thanksgiving. Even when his mom was alive, their festivities had been small. Today the gathering was anything but small. Warm greetings echoed from all corners of the huge house as they entered the large, open living room.

Having Charley on one side of him and his dad on the other at the dining room table where the centerpiece was the elegant Tiffany glass turkey surrounded by roses matching the reds, oranges, and golds of the glass, made Sully happy and proud. With Chase at the head of the table, Jade and their children flanked him. Cooper Brevard sat next to his buddy, Colton Cooper. The opposite end of the table found patriarch, Grandfather Coop, with beloved girlfriend, Tammy Dalton, on his left. Seated across from Tammy was her granddaughter, Tracy Dalton Cooper. Sweet little Carly Cooper sat between parents, Cash and a very pregnant Tracy. Derek's mother had flown to Texas for the holiday season to visit her brothers, but the rest of the Brevard family, Chloe, Derek, Abilene, and Austin sat opposite Sully, Charley, and Owen.

With every head bowed, a prayer was offered by Coop and *amens* echoed from this close-knit gathering of family and friends. Sully wasn't sure how many turkeys had been cooked, but there was no end to the white meat, dark meat, and drumsticks. Great conversation, soft giggles of children, and mouthwatering food flourished around the long table. Cups of coffee and glasses of wine for the adults were offered along with a variety of desserts including pumpkin pie, pecan pie, and cranberry cheesecake. Milk, juice, and cupcakes decorated like turkeys thrilled the kids.

Sully's thankful heart was as full as his stomach as he helped carry empty dishes from the grand dining room through an archway into a kitchen half the size of a basketball court. Coop and Tammy had been lovingly shooed into the living room where a fire crackled in the hearth. After the children had helped with whatever had been asked of them, they eagerly followed their grandparents. The other adults had the kitchen and dining room back in shape in no time.

"Severely restricted facial expression is called a flat affect," Jade, who was a mental health therapist, was saying to Charley as the two of them stood at the granite island in the kitchen. Sully immediately knew they must be discussing Lerfeld. "It results from a decrease in the ability to express emotions in one's voice, face, and physical movements."

"What causes it?" Charley asked as Sully stopped beside her.

Jade replied, "Schizophrenia, autism spectrum disorders, and Parkinson's disease are often associated with a flat affect."

"You mentioned a decrease in physical movements, Jade," Sully said. "Would that include the way a person walks? Like the swinging or not swinging of arms?"

"Yes. It can definitely include ambulation," Jade said as Owen joined them. "Sometimes, but not always, people who walk without moving their arms are mentally ill."

"Right. Making note of people who walk without moving their arms is taught at Colorado police academies," Derek said after he and Chloe had entered the kitchen.

"Are schizophrenics dangerous?" Charley asked.

"They can become violent during acute onsets of psychosis due to hallucinations, delusions, or hearing voices," Jade explained as Chase joined them. "Or if they go off their neuroleptic drugs, which are antipsychotic medications, or if they mix in illegal drugs or alcohol, tendencies of aggression typically worsen."

Owen nodded and added, "Of all the mental health diagnoses, schizophrenia has the strongest correlation with homicide. Among patients who have murdered their relatives, for example, more than fifty percent were schizophrenic."

"Yes, I'd agree with those statistics," Jade said. "Within five years of a schizophrenia diagnosis, one in fifty people will commit suicide. One in ten men will commit some type of violent offense. For schizophrenics, the risk of dying prematurely is eight times greater than the general population."

His thoughts centering on Lerfeld, Sully felt his gut tighten.

"About one in seven prison inmates and one in four people in jail are seriously mentally ill," Owen said. "Up to four percent of incarcerated individuals are schizophrenic."

"Who are we talking about?" Chase asked with a frown of concern.

Sully glanced at Charley and replied, "Charley might not completely agree, but I think something is off with Leon Lerfeld, the guy who works in her flower shop part-time."

With a smile at Charley, Jade said, "Caregivers, family members, friends, and neighbors can benefit from education on symptoms of a schizophrenic patient in order to effectively communicate with the person when crisis management is crucial during a psychotic event."

"What can you do if a schizophrenic person is having a psychotic event?" Charley asked.

"Stay calm," Jade said.

"Call 9-1-1," Owen and Derek replied.

"Speaking of staying calm and calling 9-1-1," Cash began as he and Tracy entered the kitchen from the direction of the guest bathroom, "Tracy's water just broke."

"Are you okay?" Jade asked.

"Yes," Tracy said, both hands on her rounded belly. "We do not need to call 9-1-1."

"She's been having light contractions all day," Cash told them.

"How exciting," Chloe said. "What can we do to help?"

"The contractions are why we brought overnight bags in the car for Carly and me," Tracy said. Turning to Chase and Jade, "Does your offer to keep Carly still stand?"

"Yes, of course," Jade replied.

"For as long as you need," Chase added.

"Yes, and we can take Carly too," Chloe assured her. "Don't worry about her."

"I'd love to pitch in wherever I can help," Charley offered.

It was a hustle and bustle then as Cash and Tracy sought out Carly to let her know that Mommy was going to the hospital with Daddy. Carly and the other kids gave a whoop to find out Carly would be staying with her uncles, aunts, and cousins. When Daddy brought Mommy back home, it would be with Carly's new baby brother, Dalton Cooper. Another whoop came from the kids, along with well wishes from the family. Tammy Dalton and Coop escorted them to the door. Chase followed them out to the car and returned with Carly's overnight bag.

With a busy day ahead at Sully's store and Charley's grand opening, they said their thank yous and good nights. Owen did as well and followed them out of the house.

"Someday," Sully said, looking west in the direction Cash and Tracy had gone toward Memorial Hospital as they paused under the archway of Triple C Ranch-Central. He wondered if Charley would understand that he was referring to having children.

Charley followed his gaze down the highway and whispered, "At least a couple."

CHAPTER THIRTY-FOUR

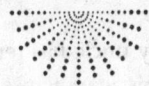

"Thank you and come again soon," Charley called to a lady and gentleman as they left her shop on Black Friday, one carrying a holiday floral arrangement and the other carting out a Christmas cactus full of cheery red blooms.

Charley loved the smell of the fresh pine garland she'd cut from the woods behind the shop as she placed a wreath on the front door. Between the Rocky Mountain Columbine on the stained glass and the pine trees to the back of the cabin, she felt she belonged here. The morning flew by, and it was almost noon when she saw Leon walking across the gravel parking lot. She'd actually hoped he wouldn't show up. What was she going to say to him? And how to begin?

Inside the middle pocket of her reindeer apron, which was tied around her neck and waist, her phone rang. "Hi, Chloe, do we have a bouncing baby boy yet?" Charley asked as Leon entered the shop. Wiggling her fingers in a wave at Leon, she listened to Chloe. Then Charley replied, "Ten fingers and ten toes. Wonderful. I can't wait to meet Dalton Cooper. Yes, I'll be sure to let Sully know." Chloe commented, and Charley laughed. "I'm next?" Smiling, she nodded and confided in her cousin, "I told Sully at least a couple someday." Thanking Chloe for the call, she hung up and faced Leon. "Hi Leon."

"A couple of rugrats?" Leon asked, not bothering to say hello.

Charley felt a stab of unease at his insensitive choice of words but answered, "Someday." She noticed a huge, bruised bump in the middle of his forehead and asked, "What happened?"

"I'm late because my uncle has temper tantrums and hit me," he said, making his way across the shop to the office area.

"I thought your uncle was deceased."

"I meant my aunt."

"You have an aunt?"

"Yes, totally demented. I had to settle her down before I could leave."

Maybe Leon had just given her a kind and caring opening. "Leon, I've been thinking that I can't expect you to make the drive from the Springs to the country for this job. Especially so if your aunt isn't well."

Ignoring that, Leon said, "Being Black Friday and your grand opening, I said I'd be here." He hung his jacket on a hall tree at the far end of the kitchen counter. "You don't have to pay me." He added, "Today or ever. I just enjoy the floral shop business and working with you."

"I would think the cost of gasoline to drive out here alone could be prohibitive," she said. He wasn't going to make this easy.

"I have the monthly income I mentioned."

"Did you have Thanksgiving dinner with your aunt?"

Leon looked around the shop made merry and bright with Christmas lights, festive red and green decorations, and scented with cinnamon.

"Opened a can of tuna fish," Leon mumbled.

"Oh." How different Leon's scenario was compared to the one Charley had enjoyed with Sully and a house full of family, friends, and a feast.

Again, feeling sorry for Leon, she noticed as he walked around the open shop area, his shoulders slumped and his arms didn't move. How badly would losing his job affect his mood? Before she could broach the topic of not working for her again, the tingling bell over the front door chimed and danced.

"It's about time we finally had ourselves a flower shop out here in the country," said a lovely blonde, perhaps sixty, wearing a tan suede jacket with fringe, a tan cowboy hat, and tan cowboy boots to match. A cold breeze blew in as she shut the door. "Welcome, Pretty Petals!"

"This shop is so beautiful!" the gray-haired lady with her, clad in denim, gushed with a smile as she gazed here and there around the shop full of delights and goodies.

"Yes, leave it to Triple C Ranch to do things up right," the first woman said and smiled at Charley. "My name is Henrietta Culpepper. I go by Henri."

"I'm Charlotte Cooper, and I go by Charley," she said, walking to them and extending her hand. They all shook hands, and the second woman introduced herself as Gloria Roberts.

Henri said, "Your signs read *Triple C Ranch-South* and *Pretty Petals*. Since your last name is Cooper, I take it you're family to Chase, Chloe, and Cash."

"Yes," Charley said. "Clarence Cooper was my father."

"Clarence was a good man," Henri said as Gloria nodded her agreement.

"All of the Coopers rank high with my husband and me," Gloria commented.

Charley belatedly noticed Leon lurking nearby and figured he felt out of place. Turning to include him, she said, "This is my friend, Leon, who stopped by to wish me well on my grand opening." She thought that might be a subtle hint to Leon that she was serious about not expecting him to work in her shop now that she was located out in the country.

"I worked for Charley in her Old Colorado City shop,"

Leon said, by way of introducing himself. "Now, I'll be getting some fresh country air."

"You let me know if the drive gets to be too much for Leon," Henri said. "Because I live down the road past the ranch owned by that handsome devil, Owen Custis, and I would enjoy helping out anytime, Charley."

"Thank you, Henri." Charley smiled. "Be sure to leave me your phone number."

Charley invited the ladies to browse just as Chase, Jade, their kids, and Carly entered the shop. The Coopers knew Henri and Gloria and chatting ensued. Henri and Gloria said they were planning on lunch at Coopers' Lodge and asked if Cash and Tracy's baby had been born.

Sully! Charley had forgotten to text Sully about baby boy Dalton Cooper. She pulled out her phone just as he walked in the door. He'd taken Wyatt to the gun store with him, and the puppy bounded into the flower shop beside him. Sully smiled across the shop at her and shook hands with Chase. Charley noticed a slight frown replacing the smile on Sully's handsome face upon seeing Leon. Colton, Courtney, and Carly were thrilled to meet the puppy, and Charley smiled at the sweet children. When her eyes met Sully's green ones again, he winked at her. She saw that he had a brown bag in his hand as he walked around the screens to the kitchen.

"I can't wait to see the new baby," Charley agreed with Jade, who had said they had heard from Cash.

"You can each pick out one thing," Chase said to the three children.

As the adults visited back and forth, the kids busily looked at the endless Christmas items on display. Leon, however, slunk into a corner. Colton soon found a ceramic Santa riding a horse, Courtney picked out a Christmas cactus in a flowerpot shaped like a cat wearing a Santa hat, and Carly knocked over a small, potted Christmas tree on the floor.

"Watch out, rugrat!" Leon shrilled, stomping out of the corner toward the child.

"Leon!" Charley snapped. She hurried to Carly, whose little chin quivered and assured her, "It's okay, sweetheart." Charley noticed Leon had stopped abruptly, most likely because both Chase and Sully were scowling at him as Jade made her way to the small tree lying on its side. Charley ignored the tree and scooped up Carly with a smile. "Carly, sweetheart, what is your favorite thing in the whole shop?" Charley asked as Jade easily returned the undamaged tree to its upright position.

"Reindeer," Carly said and pointed to the plush toy, with a red nose and a red bow to match, on the display table right above the tree she'd accidentally knocked over.

"Rudolph would love to go home with you," Charley said, and picking up the reindeer, handed the soft, furry toy to little Carly. Carly hugged Rudolph to her heart and smiled.

"Let's settle up with Charley and grab some lunch at the Lodge," Chase said.

Charley tried to wave them out of the store with their items bestowed as gifts. But Chase nor Jade would hear of it. Not charging them for Rudolph, Charley gave them the Cooper family discount for the other two items. Chase cocked a knowing brow over the discount, but peeled off several bills and handed her the payment. Charley thanked and hugged them. Sully opened the door for them, giving Colton a fist bump and Chase a clap on the back. When Sully shut the door and turned, Charley was behind the counter ringing up sales of red, pink, and white poinsettias to Henri and Gloria, but she didn't miss the glare he directed at Leon.

"Sully, please say hello to your father from Henri," Henrietta Culpepper said with two red poinsettias in hand as she stopped near the front door. Charley was right behind her, carrying two white poinsettias she had also purchased. "In fact, you tell that handsome devil to stop by my house and I'll make him a fancy cocoa hot toddy."

"Will do, Henri," Sully chuckled. "Let me help you ladies to your car," he offered and took the poinsettias from

Charley. He escorted Henri and Gloria, who was carrying two pink poinsettias, out to Henri's SUV. Wyatt followed Sully and stayed close to him as Sully helped the ladies carefully place the plants in the back of the vehicle. From the porch, Charley waved goodbye to the sweet ladies and then called Wyatt. When Sully came back into the shop, Charley closed the front door behind him and the puppy. "I brought us a hot lunch."

"I'm starved," Charley admitted.

As to why Sully hadn't brought something for Leon, he said, "I wasn't expecting to see you here, Lerfeld."

"That's the consensus," Leon mumbled, sulking in a corner of the shop.

Sully strode down the middle of the shop, turned back to Leon, and said, "Feel free to take off, I'm going to help Charley the rest of the afternoon."

"Oh." Leon was clearly shocked.

It occurred to Charley that's how little Carly must have felt when Leon had so harshly and unnecessarily shouted at her. *Touché, Leon.* Having had enough of Leon Lerfeld, Charley plucked his jacket off the hall tree and walked to him.

"Have a nice weekend, Leon," Charley said coolly.

Taking his jacket, Leon asked, "Are you still planning to stay closed on Sundays and Mondays?"

"Yes." Giving him an extra hint about her relationship with Sully, Charley said, "It's my tradition, and Sully's store is also closed on Sunday and Monday."

With a sideways glance at Sully, Leon said, "Guess I'll see you next Tuesday, Charley."

"Leon, I would never ask you to work for free," Charley said, and squaring her shoulders added, "As I said earlier, I can't expect you to drive from the Springs to the country for this job."

"Are you firing me?" Leon asked, straightening his stance.

"Please don't look at it like that, Leon," Charley said.

Letting her handle things, Sully was silent but remained squarely behind her, backing her up. "I'm just relieving you of an unnecessary burden."

"You were never a burden, but I can take a hint to get lost."

Charley splayed her hands and said, "You're welcome to stop by for a visit anytime."

With another glance at Sully, Leon said, "I doubt that."

Sully strode forward then and opened the front door. Taking a last look at Charley, Leon left the shop without another word. As Sully shut the door, the overhead bell tingled cheerily as if dispelling the tension.

"Whew, I'm glad that's over," Charley said, hoping it was.

CHAPTER THIRTY-FIVE

"*W*hen are they going to catch the guy?" Sully grumbled under his breath on Christmas Eve.

He and Charley were hosting a buffet-style dinner along with a gift exchange at his ranch this evening. Back on Thanksgiving, everyone at dinner had drawn a name from a cowboy hat. The kids had gone first, and even baby Dalton's name had been included. Then the adults had each picked out a name and no one knew who had drawn whose name.

Sully's cousins, Roy and Randy Custis, had standing traditions elsewhere. Thus, Sully had given them gifts at his store before they'd closed early.

Hands on his hips now, with Wyatt asleep in his brand-new, big dog bed, Sully stood in the den before the crackling fire in the hearth. With the flatscreen on, he was listening to the newscasters and watching the footage on the early evening news.

"*While Old Colorado Springs was teaming with happy folks out doing their last-minute Christmas shopping, the infamous Cave Killer has struck a seventh time,*" a female reporter confirmed from behind a studio desk. Sully frowned at the TV. The screen was split, with the studio newscaster on the left. A male reporter, on the right, stood near the scene of the crime and said, *"That's right, Sarah. With five dead in his wake and his sixth victim narrowly escaping, the infamous Cave Killer has struck a seventh time. And this time the killing seems personal."* The female newscaster replied, *"Yes, Dave, we're hearing from Detective Burt Groves this evening that the seventh attack, which appears to have happened within the last forty-eight hours, has resulted in the murder of victim six who avoided being strangled to death only weeks ago."*

"Oh, no," Charley said as she came up beside Sully and looped her arm through his.

Sully pulled his arm free and wrapped it around her. "I want this psycho stopped."

"Me too," Charley whispered.

Sully eased her back and let out a low wolf whistle. Her glossy, long brown hair reflected the Christmas lights on the towering live tree. Her thick black lashes batted playfully, and her ruby-red lips parted in a breathtaking smile. She was dressed in a soft ivory sweater boasting a scooped neck and decorated with shiny red and gold stars. She'd paired the sweater with snug red pants, and she wore them with the red cowboy boots he'd bought for her at Cash's store. She was the only gift he needed for Christmas.

"I love you, Charley," Sully said for the first time.

"What?" Charley asked softly, her royal-blue eyes taking on a glistening glitter.

Smiling down at her, Sully repeated with conviction, "I love you, city slicker."

"Sully, I—" Charley began, her voice breaking. With her hands folding over her heart, she looked him in the eye. "I love you, too, country boy. With all my heart."

Sully lowered his mouth to hers and wrapped both arms around her. Her slender arms twined around his neck, and she raised on her tiptoes as she kissed him. He buried his hands in her hair, and his tongue played with hers. Sliding his hands down her slender back, he cupped them to her rounded fanny and groaned.

"Do we have time to go to bed before the party?"

"No," Charley giggled.

"I'll make it quick."

"Don't tempt me."

"After the party?" Sully asked.

"It's a date."

With a grin, Sully turned the flatscreen from the news to a holiday music channel. He grabbed her hand, and they walked out of the den into the wide hallway. Every room in the house was decorated with professional touches made by the classy florist at his side.

Outdoors, Sully had strung lights across the porch for the first time and hung Fraser fir wreaths with red bows, which Charley had made in her shop, at the windows facing the main road. Two more huge Fraser fir wreaths, also decorated with red velvet bows, adorned the oversized front doors. In the foyer, mistletoe dangled from a chandelier. Charley pulled Sully under the mistletoe and kissed him just before the doorbell rang. Sully opened the door to his dad and a lady holding a huge white poinsettia from Charley's shop.

"Dad and Henri, we're so glad you could make it," Sully said.

"Yes, please come in," Charley said and hugged Owen, then Henri.

Right behind them came the Brevards, with their three children proudly carrying their gifts to be exchanged with their siblings or cousins. Derek had two more gifts in hand as Chloe held a covered dish. Arriving next, Chase and Jade had in tow not only Colton and Courtney but also Coop and Tammy. More covered dishes were carted into the house and placed in the dining room, while brightly wrapped gifts were stowed under the living room Christmas tree. Coats were placed on the king-size bed in the master suite.

"We're here," said little Carly, carrying her Rudolph reindeer and a gift, as she made her way into the living room ahead of Cash and Tracy. "We brought Dalton."

The adults laughed, and Charley said, "I can't believe Dalton is a month old already."

"Neither can I," Tracy said, coming to a stop beside her grandmother and Charley.

"May I hold him?" Charley asked politely. "Or does Tammy get to go first?"

"I had a turn earlier today," Tammy said with a smile. "It's your turn, Charley."

Cash took Carly and their covered dish to the dining room. Tracy handed the baby, with a headful of dark brown hair like Cash's, to Charley. Sully helped Tracy off with her coat and after hanging it up, his eyes lit on Charley. In her ivory sweater, amid the glow of the Christmas lights, she looked angelically radiant as she cuddled the baby boy. Sully walked to her and wrapped an arm around her. His heart brimmed with happiness as he smiled down at the love of his life and pictured her holding the baby he wanted to have with her. Charley smiled up at him and gently placed the baby boy in his arms.

"How right that looks," Charley said, taking the baby's tiny hand in hers.

"A couple of 'em," Sully said as the baby cooed.

Coop announced he was hungry, and Owen chimed in that he was too. The two older men, with their ladies beside them, were the first four in line at the dining room table, laden with prime rib and roasted asparagus, a spiral ham and scalloped potatoes, as well as sliced turkey and home-made gravy. Sides of mashed potatoes, broccoli casserole, green beans, buttery corn, and stuffing were overflowing. Covering a buffet sideboard along the dining room wall were desserts of cherry pie, apple pie, pumpkin pie, and a German chocolate cake. In line with Cooper tradition, no one would go home hungry or empty-handed.

Gifts followed dinner and dessert. The children squealed in delight as presents of video games, building blocks, dolls, boardgames, books, and clothes exchanged hands. Then the adults surprised one another by presenting gifts to the person whose name they had secretly drawn. Even Henrietta Culpepper received a gift from Charley and Sully in exchange for the beautiful poinsettia they had known she was bringing.

Charley, with help from Chloe and Jade, divvied up the leftovers and placed them into beautiful holiday to-go containers. By the time the kids started yawning, the dishes were washed, and the dining room was back to the way it had been before the Christmas Eve festivities. Gift bags holding food and presents were gathered up, and good nights were shared with heartfelt hugs and handshakes. The children from all three of the Cooper households had already talked about waking up early the next morning to see what Santa had left for them underneath the tree. Thus, the cars started pulling out of the driveway, and from the front porch, Sully and Charley waved good night. Before heading out, Owen shared a kiss with Henri under the mistletoe. Promising to touch base with his dad the next day, Sully closed and locked the front door.

"I think our first house party went well," Sully said. "What do you think?"

"Perfect, and I think we have a private party waiting for us in the bedroom."

"I'll race you there."

Charley took a step, but Sully caught her arm and pulled her behind him. She giggled his name as he jogged down the hallway ahead of her. Catching the back of his shirt, she slid her hand to his belt and curled her fingers over it. When she tried to slow him down, Sully turned to her. He tossed her over his shoulder and gave her sexy fanny a pat. Laughing wildly, Charley smacked his butt with both hands. Sully chuckled and carried her straight to bed.

LEON DROPPED INTO THE PIT OF THE DANK CAVE. EXPLORATION and practice in the tunnels were crucial. Most crawled with a cobweb of confusing turns and dead ends. The voices were still furious over the incident at the flower shop the previous month. How dare that cowboy throw him out of Charley's life. And she'd gone right along with it! He'd stormed back to Old Colorado City in a rage and searched for the street-walker who'd escaped him. It took so long to spot the noxious hooker that he'd almost decided she'd left town. But no, she had surfaced, and he'd made her pay for the sickening kick to his groin. Charley had delivered a mental kick just as crucifying. He'd dragged the corpse inside a cave and inched his way home through the maze of rats and mud. He was done wooing Charley. She would pay for her repeated rejections. He'd be waiting and watching. For as long as it took. Like the other whores, Charley would show up eventually.

CHAPTER THIRTY-SIX

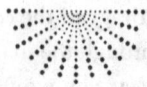

"$\mathcal{M}$erry Christmas," Charley whispered quietly so as not to disturb him.

She had awakened on Christmas morning, warm, naked, and cozy in Sully's arms. Her head was next to his on the pillow and her leg lay between his. She smiled at his handsome sleeping profile and eased out of bed. Plucking his long-sleeved, soft, flannel shirt off a chair, she put it on as she padded barefoot to the door. She heard the bed covers rustle and looking over her shoulder saw Sully roll onto his stomach. Charley sighed at the sexy picture this man made in the middle of the king-size bed. Wanting him and second-guessing her decision to turn on the Christmas tree lights and make breakfast, momentarily halted her in the doorway. But Wyatt hopped out of his doggy bed and trotted to her, so with a smile she continued to the living room. After lighting the tree, she let Wyatt outside, and when the puppy was back indoors, they went into the kitchen. She fed Wyatt and had just placed crisp bacon and French toast onto plates when muscular arms wrapped around her waist and a broad chest molded to her back.

"Merry Christmas morning," Sully said, moving her long braid to one side and nibbling her neck.

"It certainly is," Charley replied, turning in Sully's

embrace, and wrapping her arms around his naked torso. Standing between his bare feet, she flattened her hands to the skin along his spine and kissed his lips.

"I don't like waking up without you next to me in bed," he said, towering over her, clad only in a pair of low-riding pajama pants.

"I was just about to come wake you up with breakfast in bed," she said and plucked the tray holding their breakfast off the kitchen countertop.

"Lead the way," he said with a grin.

Charley did so, and when they reached the bedroom, Sully turned on the crackling gas fireplace, giving the room extra heat and a flickering ambiance. Flipping aside the sheet and comforter, he sat with his back to the headboard and patted the mattress. Charley handed him the breakfast tray and joined him. As they ate, she could not imagine being happier or more content than she was at this very moment. So much had changed in her life, all for the better and all because of Sully.

"I've made more money since my grand opening here in the country a month ago than I ever made at Christmas time in my Old Colorado City shop," she said between bites of bacon.

Sully smiled. "A good sign you made the right choice in moving your business. I had a great month too. Maybe we should work a few more weeks and take a break. Go somewhere."

"Like go on a vacation together?" Charley asked. When he nodded, she realized aloud, "I have never actually been on a real vacation."

"Then you're way overdue," he suggested and took a bite of bacon.

"I'll pay my half."

"No, you won't," he said with a chuckle and a shake of his head. "It'll be my gift."

"Speaking of gifts," she began as they finished eating. "I might have something for you under the tree."

"Yeehaw. I might have something for you too."

Charley smiled at him and then at Wyatt, who was in one of his new dog beds, the other ones being in the den and in the living room. "We might have something for you, too, Wyatt."

Wyatt barked as Sully set the breakfast tray on the bedside table. He crawled out of bed and Charley scooted out after him. He tugged a long-sleeved tee shirt over his head, and she pulled on a pair of leggings to wear with his flannel shirt. In the living room, Sully stopped and smiled at the tree sparkling with white lights, gold balls, and red bows. Wyatt joined them as Sully pulled Charley close.

"You can go first," Sully said, and picking up a present, sauntered to the leather sofa.

"Wyatt gets to go first," Charley said, picking up gifts. Once they'd settled onto the sofa, she opened the first gift which was a plush dog toy and gave it to the puppy. Wyatt scampered away with it to his dog bed.

"Come back for your second gift, Wyatt," Sully said. Wyatt came bounding back to them, and Sully unwrapped a safe chew toy for him. When the puppy was back in his bed with his plush toy and chew toy, Sully said, "Now it's your turn, Charley."

"Yeehaw." Charley accepted the pretty box he gave her. "Give me a hint," she said and rattled the gift close to her right ear.

"I already did."

"Hmm..." Charley raised a brow and tore the wrapping off the box. Opening his gift and finding what was inside, her jaw dropped. Stunned, she looked at Sully and could only stare at him for a moment. "Two tickets to Hawaii from February tenth through the twenty-fourth?" So thrilled and unable to resist teasing him, she asked, "Who in the world would I take with me for two weeks?"

"You'll figure it out." Sully cocked a black brow, and Charley giggled as he yanked her onto his lap. She wrapped her arms around his neck and planted her lips on his. He smoothed a loose lock of hair away from her cheek and said, "I want to go someplace warm to swim in the ocean and lie on a beach with you."

"Yes," Charley whispered seriously. "Sully, I would absolutely love that. I've never been to Hawaii, and I've always wanted to go."

"Same here."

"There's a famous and beautiful hotel there known as the Pink Palace."

"Officially, the name of the Pink Palace is the Royal Hawaiian and it's on—"

"Waikiki Beach," they both said at the same time.

"Look in the box again," Sully said.

"Sully," Charley gasped softly as she pulled out the confirmation of their reservation at the luxury resort. "The Pink Palace. This is too much."

"It's not nearly enough."

"Thank you." With tears in her eyes and voice, she hugged him and said, "I can't wait to fly to Hawaii with you. We'll have the time of our lives." She eased back, wiped away a stray tear, and handed Sully a gift. "Your turn."

Sully unwrapped his gift and opened a black box. Inside was a smartwatch. It had cost Charley a thousand dollars, and Sully was worth every single penny. He looked at her with a smile and carefully took it out of the box.

"Did you know my previous watch was broken in the car crash?" he asked.

"Yes, your dad mentioned it in passing at the hospital."

"This is the perfect gift, Charley. But it's too much."

"It's not nearly enough," she echoed with love. "It is the outdoorsman sports model," she said as he put it on. "It's a minicomputer. It's durable enough to wear scuba diving, skydiving, and running marathons. You can use apps, you can track your health and fitness, it can find your phone, and the battery life is better than that of a cell phone."

Sully chuckled at her enthusiasm. "I love it, but not as much as I love you."

Charley snuggled into his arms again and rested her head against his. "I love you too."

The remainder of their morning was quiet and just the two of them, along with Wyatt and his new toys. Henri had invited them, as well as Owen, to her house for Christmas dinner at six. They met up with Owen there and enjoyed a veritable banquet, as Henri loved to cook and bake. Charley nudged Sully after dinner and grinned when they caught Owen and Henri kissing under mistletoe from Pretty Petals. Sully winked at her, leaned her back over his arm, and kissed her. Owen and Henri saw them and clapped.

In Henri's comfortable living room, the four of them shared delicious cocoa hot toddies and homemade cheese-cake drizzled with chocolate sauce. Sully and Charley gave Owen two thick flannel shirts for Christmas from Cash's store. They all laughed when he gave each of them a flannel shirt from Cash's store as well. Sully and Charley gave Henri a basket brimming with chocolates, fruits, and nuts. In turn, she gave them a cutting board stacked with cheeses, meats, and crackers. Charley sighed with happiness as she sat on a comfortable couch with Sully's arm around her. What a stark difference a few months had made in her life.

"Ready to go home?" Sully whispered a half hour later.

"Yes, I want you all to myself."

"Yeehaw," Sully said in a husky voice with a cocky grin and quick squeeze that sent tingles to every part of Charley's body.

CHAPTER THIRTY-SEVEN

"*I* think it's a good offer," Sully said a few days later, looking at the page the realtor had faxed to Charley regarding her Old Colorado City property.

"I do too." Charley nodded, standing next to him. With a cold rain threatening to ice the roads and plans to go to dinner at the Lodge, Sully had driven her to Pretty Petals. He was back now as she closed for the day. "I consider myself lucky to have any offer considering the body of the woman who initially escaped the Cave Killer was found in a cave near my property."

"I say accept this offer and be done, Charley."

"Yes, I agree. It's not the full asking price but close enough."

"Right, and the buyers are paying cash. That's a plus."

"I told my realtor I'd meet her tomorrow afternoon if the offer was acceptable. So, I'll do that and sign whatever paperwork is needed to make this a quick, done deal."

"Sounds good." Sully smiled in relief. He'd be glad to have Charley's ties cut to the property where she'd been attacked, and her mother murdered. "Both of our stores will be closed tomorrow, so I'll go with you."

He grabbed her hand, and they were off in his four-wheel drive Jeep to have dinner at Coopers' Lodge. To their delight, they ran into Cash, Tracy, Carly, and Dalton there. The Coopers had just arrived and waved them to a big, round, cushioned booth. As the baby slept, Carly, sitting in a booster seat between Tracy and Charley, told them exactly how much he weighed and how many inches he'd grown since birth.

"Dalton will talk soon," Carly assured them.

"Since Dalton can't hold up his own head yet, it may be a while before he's talking, Sis," Cash said to his daughter as he and Sully sat at outside ends of the booth facing each other.

Carly wasn't too sure about that. Charley hugged her, and everyone laughed. Charley told them about the potential sale of her shop and duplex. Cash and Tracy agreed it was a good offer. Sully added that they planned to meet with the realtor the next day to make it official.

After a delicious dinner, they bid the Coopers good night. From the Lodge, Sully drove straight home to his ranch. As usual, the remainder of the evening flew by. Sully could hardly recall, nor did he want to remember how the days and nights had often dragged before Charley burst onto the scene and changed his whole world. He was one lucky man.

They went to bed, made love, and when he'd awakened, she was in his arms just where he wanted her. From bed, on that lazy Sunday morning of December thirtieth, Sully saw snow lightly falling as Charley soundly slept. It was his opportunity to surprise her with breakfast. He slipped out of bed without waking her. Wyatt followed him through the house, and Sully let him out the side door. The snow covering the mountain tops in the distance was beautiful. Winter had arrived, and with the temperature dropping, Wyatt soon scampered back into the warm house. He ate breakfast and with a dog biscuit, took off to his bed in the master bedroom.

"Well, lookie there, Wyatt," Charley said twenty minutes later, as she and the puppy walked into the kitchen. "Your dad is making us breakfast."

"His dad?" Sully laughed, turning to face them. "You know that makes you his mom."

"I know," Charley giggled and scooped up the puppy.

"Don't let Wyatt fool you about breakfast. He's already been fed, gone outside, and had a dog biscuit. This breakfast is just for you and me."

"Mmm, what are we having?"

"Pancakes and scrambled eggs."

"Yum!"

They ate at the quartz island and cleaned up the kitchen together. Then it was a race to the master bath, and Sully let her beat him into the shower. Charley turned on the water and pulled him into the hot spray with her. The shower took longer than usual. Damn, it was a pleasure to wash Charley's sensational body from head to toe and have her wash his. Her hands found his hard length, and Sully closed his eyes in sweet ecstasy before turning off the water.

"Ready to go?" Sully called in the foyer. Charley's appointment with her realtor was more than an hour and a half away. But he was allowing extra time to get there due to the worsening weather conditions. Snow now blanketed the ranch.

"Coming," Charley replied, and from the master bedroom came hopping into the hallway on one foot. Stopping to tug on her other red boot she then jogged to him. She pulled on red gloves that matched her red toboggan-style hat decorated with snowmen and a white pompom on top. The set had been a Christmas gift to her from Sully, and he thought she looked adorable. On the same page, as usual, she'd given him black leather gloves and a wool scarf to match his black cowboy hat and black leather jacket. "Ready to go."

Grinning at the gorgeous girl whose trademark long, loose brain hung down her back, Sully stood with his hand on the doorknob as his cell rang. He answered the call and frowned. "No, problem, Dad. I'll be right there."

"What's wrong?" Charley asked when he'd put his phone in his pocket.

"Dad slipped on a patch of ice and thinks he may have broken his right ankle." Sully rubbed his forehead. "He can't put weight on it to get to his car and needs to go to the ER."

"Sully, go see about him," Charley urged as Sully glanced at his new smart watch. "I can drive myself to Old Colorado City and sign the paperwork."

"I don't want you alone in Old Colorado City."

"I won't be alone. I'll be with Margo, my realtor."

"Yes, but the realtor's office is right up the street from your property." Sully knew that's why Charley had chosen the woman, as the realtor had often purchased flowers or plants as thank you gifts for her buyers and sellers from Charley's shop before it had closed. "Tell you what, let's go get Dad. We'll drop you off at the realtor's office, and I will take him to the ER. You call me the second you're done, and I'll come back for you. By that time, Dad might be done too. If not, it won't matter because you'll be safely back with me, and we can pick Dad up from the hospital together."

"Sounds like a plan." Charley gave him a sharp nod of her head. "Let's go."

CHAPTER THIRTY-EIGHT

"*H*i, Margo," Charley said to the woman who greeted her in the lobby of the real estate office.

"Hi, Charley," Margo said, shortly after four o'clock. About a decade older than Charley, Margo had short hair and a trim figure. She wore black glasses over her smiling brown eyes.

"I'm so sorry I'm late." Standing on a wide doormat just inside the office, Charley tugged off her gloves and toboggan. She gave her head a shake and brushed snowflakes off her shoulders. "Like I texted to you, my friend, Sully, and I had to stop by his father's place and pick him up. His dad slipped on a patch of ice and thinks he may have broken his ankle."

"I hope his ankle's not broken," Margo replied, with a frown of concern. "No problem as to being late. I've lived in Colorado Springs all my life and I'm used to dealing with the occasional blizzard. The Chinook winds won't be able to melt the ice until the snow stops."

"Blizzard is the right word," Charley agreed. "The snow steadily increased as we made our way into town. Sully dropped me off here and is on his way to the ER with his dad. I'll call Sully to pick me up when we're done."

"Great." Margo waved Charley into her private office. With cups of coffee, they settled into comfortable chairs on either side of Margo's desk and the realtor said, "My car slid a couple of times on my way into the office."

"I can imagine," Charley acknowledged with a nod. "Sully is an excellent driver, but because of the weather, we came into town in his four-wheel-drive Jeep. After picking up his dad, it took almost a half hour longer than usual to reach Old Colorado City."

They sipped their coffee, and while enjoying a few minutes of catching up with each other, Margo printed out the paperwork regarding the offer on Charley's shop and duplex. She explained it all line-by-line, ending with, "This is a good offer, Charley, and as you know, they're paying cash. So, it will be a fairly fast transaction if you do in fact accept their offer."

Charley nodded her agreement. "Yes, it is a good offer, and I am accepting it."

"Great." Margo handed her a pen, and Charley signed in all the appropriate seller spots. "I will let the buyers know they have purchased the property for their tattoo shop and duplex."

"Thank you for everything, Margo," Charley said with a smile and glanced out of the window. It was five thirty p.m., and being the last week in December, it was already dark.

"It's been my pleasure," Margo replied with a tilt of her head. "My only regret is not having you as my Old Colorado City neighbor anymore. I will miss you."

"I will miss you too," Charley said. "I hope you'll come see Pretty Petals soon."

"Oh, absolutely. I promise I will. I'll still order all my flowers from you too."

"Wonderful," Charley said. "If we're done, I'll text Sully and he'll come pick me up."

"Yes, go ahead and text him. You're my last client of the day, so I'll wait with you and lock up." Margo had just spoken those words when she received a text from her daughter saying she needed a ride home from the nearby skating rink. It was closing early due to the worsening snowstorm. "I'll be there as soon as I can, sweetheart."

"If you need to go, I can make sure your door is locked when I leave," Charley offered.

"If you don't mind, that works for me. Thank you, Charley."

Charley and Margo put on their coats and walked into the front office. As Charley pulled out her phone to text Sully, through the snowy window she glimpsed his stormtrooper Jeep. A perfect ride for this stormy night.

"Oh! He's already here," Charley said and shoved her phone back into her purse.

"Great timing!" Margo opened the door to the blustery snow and wind. "I'll keep you posted on the progress of the sale, Charley."

"Yes, please," Charley said as they walked out of the office into the snow and icicles. "Thank you, Margo," she added as the realtor locked the door.

"You're welcome," Margo replied and gave her a hug. "Take care," she called as they parted, going their separate ways.

Shielding her eyes the best she could against the blowing snow, Charley carefully made her way across the slippery sidewalk toward the street and Jeep. Margo gave her a farewell honk from her car, and Charley waved goodbye. Margo vanished into the darkening street as Charley placed her hand on the door to the Jeep. When it didn't open, she looked inside. The older man driving the black and white Jeep was a total stranger and looked as surprised to see her as she was him. Charley removed her hand from his vehicle and gave him a small, apologetic wave. The traffic light changed, and the stranger in the Jeep was gone.

Finding herself alone in the blizzard, Charley started walking in the direction of her shop. Doing her best not to slip and fall, she reached into her purse for her cell phone. She couldn't find it, and her heart thumped as she feared she'd left it inside Margo's office. Pressing forward through the snow, she yanked off her glove and breathed a sigh of relief as her fingers curled around her phone. Charley was nearly to the door to her shop by the time she punched Sully's name on her cell. He answered immediately.

"Sully, Margo and I are done," she said as the wind blew. "She's gone because she had to pick up her daughter and I told her by mistake that I saw your Jeep. I'm almost to my shop where I can wait for you out of the snowstorm."

"Okay. I left my dad at Memorial Hospital getting his sprained, not broken, ankle treated," Sully said. "I'm heading up Colorado Avenue now. I'm five minutes from you."

"Wonderful on both counts," Charley said happily. "I've just reached my shop but I'm having a little trouble getting my key to work. I think the lock is frozen."

"Stand under the lamppost and stay on the phone with me," Sully said. "I'm only a few stoplights away."

"I will," Charley said. Then, seeing the man walking toward her, she gasped, "Leon!"

"Charley!" came Sully's alarmed voice over the phone. "Charley!"

"Sul—"

CHAPTER THIRTY-NINE

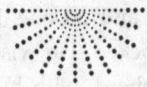

"*D*ammit!" Sully barked as Charley's cell phone went dead.

Stomping his foot on the gas pedal, he slid sideways on the snow and ice before the tires regained traction. Tightening his grip on the steering wheel, Sully dodged around one slow-moving car and then sped in between two others. His eyes were peeled for Charley, but the relentless storm was blinding. His windshield wipers were on high, but visibility remained frustratingly low. Glancing both ways, he raced through an intersection as the light was turning red. Nearing the next stoplight, it was already red, but he ran it. Running the third stoplight almost got him T-boned as the driver of a pickup truck blared his horn long and loud.

"Where are you, Charley?" Sully whispered.

He focused on the left side of the street, where her now-empty shop was, as he closed in on the location. With Christmas shopping over and the blizzard raging, no one was on the sidewalk, and only a few drivers were braving the icy roads. Turning left, the Jeep's tires fishtailed some, but he managed to come to a stop on the corner of Charley's former shop. She was nowhere in sight. Hopping out of the Jeep, he hurried onto the sidewalk.

Under the glow of the lamppost, he recognized Charley's

red glove lying on the ground at the entrance to her shop. He picked it up and shoved it in his coat pocket. Cursing under his breath, he glanced in all four directions. Besides his own, there were two other sets of footprints in the snow. There appeared to have been a scuffle near her doorway. From there, the footprints disappeared across the sidewalk and into the street. To a car? Had Lerfeld forced her into his car? Sully saw nothing and no one. He jiggled the door to the shop. It was still locked. He wished he had Spike, the Brevards' German shepherd, with him. But with the snow, he figured the dog wouldn't be able to pick up Charley's scent anyway. Standing in the snow near the spot where he'd found her red glove, Sully called Burt Groves who answered on the first ring.

"Detective Groves, this is Sullivan Custis, and I need your help," Sully said. He briefly explained Charley's disappearance, where he was, and asked, "Do you know anything about a man in his mid-forties named Leon Lerfeld? Like where he lives?"

"No, I don't know him, Sully. But I can find out. I'll call you right back."

On his way to the Jeep, Sully texted his dad the circumstances and then jammed his cell phone into his jacket pocket. Reaching the Jeep, he got in, and even with four-wheel-drive reaching Charley's duplex at the top of the hill was no easy task. The Jeep's tires spun, and the vehicle fishtailed back and forth, but he made it up the hill. The headlights didn't show any tire tracks or footprints. Nevertheless, he jumped out and jogged across the parking pads to her front door. The apartments were dark, and both doors were locked. He glanced around feeling helpless and returned to the Jeep. He knew his dad was also making some calls as his phone rang.

"Detective Groves," Sully said. "What did you find out?"

"A Lerfeld couple lives on a dead-end side street about three blocks north of where you are now." There was a pause, and then Groves said, "But Leon Lerfeld is a man in his mid-eighties. Are you sure that's the correct name?"

"That's the only name I have for him."

"Copy that. Lerfeld lives on Bleak Road. I'm headed there now."

"Then so am I."

"No, I will have backup. You wait where you are, Sully."

"No chance. I'll see you on Bleak Road, Detective."

Sully hung up and headed back down the steep hill. He turned left onto Colorado Avenue and drove three blocks northwest. Windshield wipers swiping, he saw a street sign for Bleak Road and made another left. Fresh tire tracks showed in the snow. Had to be from Leon's car. There were no homes and only a shadowy wooded area for at least two blocks. Bleak described this road perfectly. Uneven pavement turned to gravel under the snow and then a small wooden house and Lerfeld's old car appeared at the end of the Jeep's headlights. Sully drove a little closer and stopped. Earlier, he'd locked his revolver in the glove compartment when he'd escorted his dad into the ER. He'd found Charley's SIG Sauer there and remembered her placing it in the glove box the evening they'd taken the Jeep to have dinner at the Lodge..

Leaving the Jeep's headlights on, Sully cautiously emerged from the vehicle. Standing behind the open door of the Jeep, he observed the shabby dwelling. The place appeared dark and dead, but he knew differently. There were footprints in the snow. Once again, two sets. He grabbed a flashlight from the console, shut the Jeep door, and followed the prints. They headed straight into the house. Stepping onto a worn-out porch, he stood to one side of the entrance, as he'd learned from his dad, and banged his fist against the door.

"Charley?" Sully called. Nothing. Complete silence. Snow was falling heavily all around him. "Lerfeld!" he yelled. Nothing. He kicked the front door open a split second before headlights shone in the distance, and then an

SUV pulled up next to his Jeep. Sully glanced over his shoulder to see Detective Groves getting out of his vehicle. "I'm going in."

"Wait. I don't have a search warrant," the detective said, also shining a flashlight.

"Door's open," Sully said, shining his flashlight on the door.

"Did you hear a cry for help?" Groves asked. "Which would give us probable cause for entering this house?"

"Yes," Sully said. Though he'd heard it on his phone when Charley cried out half of his name, he knew his answer gave them a legal way to enter the residence. With that, Sully stepped into the dwelling and found a switch just inside the door, but when he flipped it, no lights came on. "Hell," he muttered as Groves entered right behind him.

"Colorado Springs Police!" Groves announced. "Is anybody here?" No answer.

Sully and the detective shone their flashlights around a tiny living room. With trash lining all four walls it could only be described as a pigsty. Walking forward, wind howled through cracked windows. On a broken-down futon was a filthy cushion. A dingy lamp with a crooked shade sat on a small end table. Groves tried the lamp, but it didn't work.

The place smelled. Bad. It was also freezing cold. Peeling wallpaper and buckets of water on the floor further attested to the fact the place was not only unkempt but exposed to the elements. Beyond the living room was a kitchen barely big enough to turn around in. An apartment-size stove and refrigerator framed either end of a chipped and stained countertop.

"Look," Sully said, shining his flashlight on a pile of toadflax on a rickety kitchen table.

"I'll be damned," Grove replied. "Toadflax, the Cave Killer's calling card."

"Charley said once that toadflax was found in degraded areas. How right she was."

Groves led the way down a short hallway past a disgusting bathroom. It stunk, and a rat scurried across a floor marred by patches of missing linoleum. In the bedroom across the hall was a bed. Lying on it were two people. And a small dog.

"Police!" Groves announced and shined his flashlight on the bed.

A closer look showed the corpse of an aged, decaying man with dried blood on his torso. The decomposing body of the elderly woman beside him had a knife stuck in her chest. The dog's head lay twisted at a fatal angle from its body.

"Think that man is Leon Lerfeld?" Sully asked under his breath.

"And his wife," Groves said, pulling out his cell phone. "Explains some of the stench."

As Groves called in a report on the bodies, Sully wondered if the couple had been killed in their sleep as they were clad in pajamas. Sully backed out of the room and opened a door in the hallway. What he saw stopped him in his tracks.

"Detective," Sully called. "Come look at this."

"Crime scene investigation, forensics, and the coroner are on their way," Groves said, coming up alongside him. "Is that a hole in the floor?"

"Yeah, big enough for a person to fit through," Sully said, shining his light into the hole. "And escape into the tunnels." He looked at Groves and said, "Leon Lerfeld or whatever his name is, is definitely the Cave Killer."

"Sure as hell looks like it," Groves said, staring into the pit equipped with a wooden ladder. "If this hole leads to a tunnel or the maze of tunnels under this area, that would explain how he's been killing women and getting away without being seen."

"He has Charley. I'm going after them," Sully said and took a step.

"No, I can't let you do that," Groves said and caught his arm.

"You can't stop me," Sully replied and jerked his arm free. Before the detective could grab him again, Sully shimmied down the ladder into the pit. He slowly aimed his flashlight in a full circle. Darkness, muddy ground, and more rats. He pulled his Ruger Redhawk .44 Magnum out of his holster. Sure enough, a tunnel opened to his right. Holding the flashlight in his left hand, he veered in that direction. Hearing a noise at his back, he made a half-turn in time to see Groves drop off the bottom rung of the ladder and into the pit.

"I let my team know we're possibly on the Cave Killer's trail," the detective said.

Sully nodded, and this time it was he who led the way. Except for the scuttling and occasional hiss of a rat, it was silent. Sully and Groves were both tall and neither could traverse the tunnel standing up straight. Charley and her captor could do so. Picturing Charley being dragged through this nightmarish dungeon at the hands of a psychotic serial killer was almost more than Sully could deal with and keep his cool. He and Groves had gone several yards when the tunnel split in two.

"Damn," Sully grumbled, wishing he knew which one would take him to Charley. "I'll keep to the right."

"Okay, I'll go left," Groves said. "Be careful, Sully."

"If he's got Charley, he's a dead man."

"I'll pretend I didn't hear that."

CHAPTER FORTY

"*Y*ou're hurting me, Leon," Charley snapped and jerked her arm. "Let go!"

He held on tight. It had never occurred to Charley to take her gun with her to pick up Owen or to meet with Margo at her office. But oh, how she wished she had that weapon now. Not that she could actually shoot someone, but she was certain she could have used it as a means to threaten and escape Leon Lerfeld.

"Keep moving!" Leon sneered, shining a flashlight in her face.

The tunnel was cold, damp, and grim. Pitch black, except in whatever direction Leon shined a small flashlight, Charley mostly just felt the rats at her feet. She'd cringed as she had stepped on at least two. After Leon had grabbed her in front of her shop, he'd been the one to brandish a weapon. He'd forced her into the old car with a knife, driven her to a dilapidated house, and dragged her inside.

"Whose house was that back there?" Charley asked, stumbling along behind him.

"My uncle's. He was hateful and violent, instead of appreciative. I had to siphon off his social security checks because I deserved to be paid for my care." Over his shoulder, Leon bared his teeth and gritted out, "When I bought my scooter with his money, he had a moment of lucidity and threatened to tell them where I was. I silenced him." Snickering to himself, he said, "Did the same to his crazy wife and that stupid dog."

"Tell who?" Charley asked as calmly as possible. "Who's looking for you, Leon?"

"Stop calling me Leon! That old geezer in the house was Leon Lerfeld. My name is Dorian Fester! Those jerks at the psych facility, where I was held against my will for twelve long years, are probably looking for me. I had to pretend I was catatonic when I first got there." Halting suddenly, he turned to her, rolled his eyes up in his head, opened his mouth, and stuck out his tongue as if he were in a stupor before saying, "I deserved to be released. I shouldn't have had to escape." Then, with the familiar deadness returning to his face and dulling his eyes, he said in a chilling monotone, "I *was* released. I *am* no longer a threat to myself or society."

Charley winced in pain as he suddenly yanked her forward again. "Why were you there?"

"Evaluation for competency to stand trial."

"For what crime?"

"Murder," he snickered.

"Who did you murder, Le—Dorian?"

"I was found not guilty by reason of insanity in the state of Colorado's criminal court."

"Who did you murder?" Charley repeated.

"My streetwalking whore of a mother. She was always telling me to leave, but I had nowhere to go," he said as though Charley would understand. In the next breath, he spat, "She was as useless as all the females who have rejected me. You're just like the others, you know that, Charley?" He turned to glare at her. "I gave you a chance, but you rejected me too. Over and over and over and—"

"Let me go!" Charley's brain had been whispering that Leon, or Dorian Fester, was the Cave Killer. Now, she was convinced he had brutally murdered six women. When he didn't comply with releasing her, she was forced to follow along behind him. "Where are we going?"

"Shut up. I need to think."

Although there were no holes in the floors leading to tunnels beneath the property which she'd just sold, Charley and Sully, along with a lot of people, had since learned of the numerous hidden passageways crisscrossing under Old Colorado City. If the pioneers could escape danger using the tunnels, why couldn't she? Charley formed a plan as she was dragged behind Dorian Fester a few more yards. The dim view illuminated by his flashlight soon indicated a wider, open section in the cave with tunnels branching off in three different directions. When rats hissed again, Charley purposely pretended to trip over them.

"Oww!" she cried. Falling to the ground broke Fester's hold on her. Pulling her left foot close to her chest, Charley wrapped her left hand around her uninjured ankle and rubbed it.

"Get up!" Fester ordered.

"No! Let me go!"

The second Fester reached down to grab her again, Charley used her right hand to yank the flashlight from him. With all her strength, she slammed him in the head with the flashlight. Then, instantly shining the harsh glare in his eyes, she scrambled to her feet in relative obscurity.

"You bitch! After I strangle you, I'm gonna cut you into tiny pieces and let the rats feast on your dead body."

Staring at him in horror, Charley watched Fester swipe at the blood running into his left eye. She backed away, hoping, praying she was retreating in the direction from which they'd come. If so, maybe she could make it back to the shack ahead of him and escape up the ladder and through that hole in the closet. Dear God, how had it come to this? Without another thought, she turned and ran as fast as she could. The glow from the flashlight jumped here and there along the narrow tunnel walls. Rats ahead of her scattered as the one behind her clutched the back of her coat. Hauled up short, Charley screamed.

"Stop!" Fester shrieked manically.

Grabbing her left arm, he gave her a hard half-turn and retrieved the flashlight. Charley swiveled and with her bare right hand, raked her fingernails down his face. She instantly recalled the raw scratches she'd seen on his face in the past and instinctively knew one of his victims had also clawed him. He'd asked her to visit him when he supposedly had a virus. Why? So he could strangle and stab her? Well, she would not become his next dead body. Charley fought furiously, punching him repeatedly with both fists as he forced her back to the section of the cave open to the other tunnels. There, Fester hit her hard across the side of her head. The blow jolted her, and this time when she fell, it was for real.

"I thought you were my friend," Charley spat as he loomed over her.

"I wanted to be more than your friend, but you *rejected* me." He leaned down and jerked her to her feet. Madness lit up his eyes. She'd seen this hint of his insanity the day he'd shouted at little Carly Cooper. With Fester's face close to hers, he sneered, "Your repeated rejections are the reason I had to kill those six women! Strangling them was the only way to achieve numbness from the pain you caused me." Pulling a knife out of his jacket with his right hand, he dropped the flashlight and gripped her throat with his left hand. "Their blood is on your hands, and now it's your heart, instead of mine, that will bleed!"

"Let her go," ordered a calm voice.

Light shone at the mouth of the tunnel from which they'd emerged. Fester pressed the knife to Charley's throat. Twisting around, he imprisoned her against his chest as a shield.

"Sully," Charley breathed, feeling the sharp blade against her throat.

"I said let her go," Sully growled, aiming his flashlight and a gun at Fester.

"She's mine!" Fester shrilled. "You tried to steal her from me. Get out of here, Custis."

"I'll be glad to get out of here," Sully said, walking a few steps closer. "But I'm not leaving without Charley."

"Stop! Or I'll slice her up."

Sully stopped. "Throw the knife down. The cops are on their way, and you've got nowhere to run."

"That's what you think. I know these tunnels like the back of my hand," Fester replied. "You throw your gun down or I swear I'll cut her head off."

"I'll throw my gun down if you promise to let her go."

Charley felt the knife move slightly away from her neck as Fester seemed to consider the offer. Sully waited.

"Okay," Fester said. "I promise. Now throw your gun down."

"Don't do it, Sully," Charley pleaded. She was stunned when Sully dropped his gun into the glow of the flashlight on the tunnel floor.

"Yes!" Fester, like the madman he was, whooped feverishly in her ear. He hollered, "You're an idiot, Custis!"

Instantly taking the knife away from Charley's neck, Fester shoved her aside with a victorious grunt. Swinging his arm up in the air, he lunged at Sully. The two gunshot blasts that followed were deafening. On wobbly legs, Charley watched Dorian Fester fall.

"Sully!" Charley cried and ran. Sully's arms closed around her, holding her protectively against his rigid body. She clung to him and whispered, "Thank God. Thank you, Sully."

Sully gently eased Charley out of his arms and shoved her SIG Sauer P365 9mm, which he'd shot Fester with, into the back of his jeans. Then he picked his .44 Magnum off the ground.

"I own a gun store," Sully growled and kicked the knife out of Fester's hand. "You were the idiot."

"A dead one," Detective Groves said as he emerged from

a tunnel to the left of Sully. "I heard him scream his confession to murdering those six women."

"So did I," Sully said.

"Both our bullets were headshots," Detective Groves noted as he joined them, aiming his flashlight on Fester. "Your bullet drilled the middle of his forehead. Looks like my shot entered his skull just above his right ear."

"Yeah," Sully said. "Charley, did he hurt you?"

CHAPTER FORTY-ONE

"*J*'m fine," Charley said, her blue eyes glistening as she looked up at him. "Are you okay?"

As he and Groves stood with Charley in the dank cave, illuminated only by their flashlights and with a dead body at their feet, Sully took a moment to study Charley to convince himself she was alive and safe. He'd noted the bloody claw mark on the corpse's face.

"Yeah, I'm good now," Sully whispered.

"His name wasn't Leon Lerfeld," Charley said to him and Groves while shaking her head in confusion and certainly with a good deal of shock. "He said it was Dorian Fester."

"Dorian Fester?" Grove repeated immediately as though he recognized the name.

"Yes," Charley said.

"You heard of him?" Sully asked Groves. Seeing the maniac with a knife pressed to Charley's throat had been the single most terrifying thing Sully had ever witnessed in his entire life. He wrapped an arm around her and hugged her tightly.

Holding on to him as well, Charley asked, "How on earth did you find me, Sully?"

"I called Detective Groves and told him what was going

on," he said, giving the cop a nod of appreciation. "He gave me the address of Leon Lerfeld."

"Custis, here, took off like a bat out of hell after you," Groves said. Staring down at the bloody corpse, he told them, "There's an APB out on Dorian Fester."

"For what?" Sully asked.

"An all-points bulletin went out after he escaped from the mental institution about forty miles from here, down in Pueblo," Grove said. "He murdered his mother and two sisters years ago by strangling and stabbing them. Obviously, we've kept an eye out for Fester, but using Lerfeld's identity and that shack in the woods he stayed hidden."

"I think he murdered his uncle and aunt too," Charley said.

"Fester had no living relatives. The Lerfeld address was never on our radar. The Lerfelds were just in the wrong place at the wrong time. I'm sure my team checked out the Bleak Road house," Groves said. "But if one or both of the Lerfelds had dementia, along with age and seclusion out in the sticks, they were easy prey for Fester."

"Fester said he was held in the institution after being found not guilty by reason of insanity. He pretended to be catatonic after murdering his mother," Charley said. "He never mentioned killing two sisters too."

"Officially, they had him for three murders and who knows how many more," Groves reported.

"Let's get out of this rathole," Sully said.

"Yeah, let's go." The detective nodded. "CSPD should be here by now with a couple of our best K-9s."

Sully pulled Charley's glove out of his pocket and gave it to her. Having dropped her glove had allowed her to strike a defensive blow against Fester. Charley's eyes glittered in silent confirmation as she stuck the glove in her pocket. Grasping her hand and trailing her behind him, Sully shooed rats out of their way and entered the same tunnel he'd traveled to get here.

"The rats will have a go at Fester by the time I get back

here with my team," Groves said, following close behind Charley. "That's karma for you."

"People can feel safe again in Old Colorado City," Charley said quietly. "That makes me happy for the couple who bought my property and for everyone else in Colorado Springs."

Sully agreed, keeping a grip on Charley's hand. He never wanted to let go. He couldn't imagine his life without her. Had Fester murdered her...with every step through the tunnel, Sully thanked God for keeping Charley alive. Nearing the ladder they had descended, he heard voices before he saw the flashing lights.

"Police!" somebody up in the house yelled into the pit.

Detective Groves stepped in front of Sully and Charley, and called, "Detective Burt Groves." A light flashed into the hole, and Groves shielded his eyes. "The Cave Killer has been killed in his cave. I'm coming up with the two people who helped us catch him." Turning to Sully, he said, "I'll climb out first, and you send Charley up after me. Together, we'll make sure she escapes this cave in one piece."

"Yes, sir," Sully agreed.

When Groves was out of the pit and in the house, he turned and looked down at them. "Okay, Charley, come on up."

"Okay," Charley said and took hold of the ladder.

"Careful," Sully said with a pat to her fanny before placing his hands to her waist. He watched her climb and saw Groves assist her to safety. Sully followed her out of the pit.

Police and other first responders filled the old shack. Sully wrapped an arm around Charley as they paused beside Detective Groves. Advising them he would take their statements the following day, the detective escorted them out of the house. Outside, Sully took a welcome breath of fresh air. He felt Charley do the same as he took her hand and gently squeezed.

Narrowly cheating death, they had achieved freedom from stark raving madness.

As the snow continued to fall, red and blue lights flashed from the police cars, ambulances, and fire trucks parked around the wooded area surrounding the rundown residence. While one officer used yellow tape to identify the house as a crime scene, another policeman moved his patrol car to allow Sully and Charley access to his Jeep. Walking her to the Jeep, Sully opened Charley's door and pulled her into his arms. Amid the blizzard and chaos, he kissed her for the first time since finding her, loving her with all his heart. Then he helped Charley into the Jeep and hurried around to the driver's side. Charley was buckling her seat belt as he turned on the windshield wipers and heat. Sully buckled up, too, and turned to her with a smile.

"I love you, Sullivan Custis," Charley whispered.

"Are you gonna marry me or what, Charley Cooper?"

In spite of everything, Charley giggled her one-of-a-kind laugh, making him grin. "Is that your idea of a proposal?"

"Yeah," Sully said. "I don't have a ring, but we'll get one if you say yes."

"Yes," Charley replied without hesitation. Unbuckling her seat belt, she leaned over the console and hugged him. He hugged her back and they kissed. She wiped a tear from her eye as she leaned back and said, "I'll marry you whenever and wherever."

"Hawaii?"

"Valentine's Day?" she suggested.

"Yeah." Sully's cell phone rang, and he looked at the caller before answering. "Hey Dad." He listened for a moment and said, "Yes, Charley is okay, I'm okay, and we're gonna get married." Sully held the phone away from his ear as his dad howled with relief and happiness. "We're on our way to pick you up." Sully clicked off the call, and to Charley, he said, "Let's get out of here and leave this nightmare behind."

～

"Morning, fiancée," Sully said as Charley rolled over in his king-size bed and, with her blue eyes still closed, she hugged him.

"Morning," she murmured and tilted her head so that he could kiss her lips. "Let's flirt, fiancé."

"Let's."

Sully pulled her closer and slipped his hand to her soft breast. They'd showered the previous night and fallen into the big bed naked. He'd made love to Charley passionately and urgently. She had responded to him as though her life had depended on it. Charley had whispered her love and gratitude. If he'd saved her life, he knew she'd saved his too. He'd told her so, and their happiness and love had spiraled into sex, wild beyond all imagination.

This morning was no different as Sully rolled on top of her. Charley spread her silky thighs and wrapped her legs around him. Gently opening her velvety feminine folds, he entered the unique tightness that was Charley. Enjoying her warm, wet clasp around him, he buried himself to the hilt.

"Mmm, Sully, yes," Charley purred near his ear. "I love this."

"Me too," he groaned.

Sully moved slowly and then faster, with Charley meeting every plunge and thrust. When he sat up, he took her with him. Impaled, she moved up and down, driving him to near madness. Lying on his back again, he placed Charley in the cowgirl position atop him. She ran her hands under her long brown hair, letting it fall around her body in silky waves. He stacked his hands behind his head to watch her in action. She flung her head backward and stretched. Then, leaning forward, she rested her hands on his shoulders, bowed her head and let her glossy tresses caress his bare chest. Pulling her to him, he rolled Charley onto her back. Between her legs, he moved hard and fast. His release built, and when her orgasm burst, rippling and gripping the length of him, it triggered his own ecstasy, spilling his hot seed deep inside her. When heartbeats slowed, she whispered to him.

"I love you, Sully."

"I love you, too. Let's get you a ring today."

"Let's."

CHAPTER FORTY-TWO

"Thank you for coming into the station," Detective Groves said in his office at 705 South Nevada Avenue, located in the southern part of the Colorado Springs downtown area. "I appreciate your statements regarding Dorian Fester." Meeting the gaze of each, he said, "Sully and Charley, I'm glad we stopped his killing spree once and for all."

"Me too," Charley replied with gratitude and relief.

"So am I," Sully agreed and took Charley's hand. Sully's hand was large, warm, and comforting to Charley, and she gave him a squeeze as they sat next to each other on the opposite side of a large oak desk from the detective. As a senior member of the police force, Groves had earned his private office and the respect from other law enforcement and the public that went with it. Sully added, "We were happy to come in and help."

Charley nodded her agreement. "Detective Groves, I also want to thank you again for catching my mother's killer."

"You helped with that, Charley, by securing Vaughn's gun so I could run the ballistics test." He smiled and said, "Maybe the two of you missed your calling by not becoming police."

Sully chuckled and replied, "Thanks, but I'll stick with my gun club and ranch."

"I'll stick with my flower shop on Triple C-South," Charley said and smiled.

"Fair enough," Groves said with a laugh. "Well, Fester's dead and with no one to claim his body, El Paso County will cremate him." Groves splayed his hands and told them, "Vaughn's plea agreement from first-degree murder to second-degree murder will keep him behind bars for at least the next fifteen years in the Colorado State Penitentiary in Canon City."

"Not long enough, but okay," Sully said and looked at Charley.

"Yes." Charley nodded at the love of her life who had been by her side in the aftermath of Rod Vaughn's crimes and throughout the reign of horror dealt by Dorian Fester's. To Detective Groves, she echoed Sully's sentiment. "Not long enough, but okay."

"You'll be notified whenever the day comes that Vaughn is eligible for parole, Charley," Groves informed her. "Should you choose to do so, you can make a statement to the judge as to your agreement or disagreement regarding his release."

"Good to know," Charley said quietly. "Thank you."

"You're welcome," the detective replied. "Sully, please tell Owen I said hello and that I hope he's up and around again soon."

"I sure will," Sully said. "Dad's at home today watching football with his sprained ankle propped up on a pillow."

"Sounds good," Groves said. "Especially the day after a record snowfall." When the detective stood up, Sully and Charley stood as well. "Last but not least, congratulations on your engagement. Just so you know, the County Clerk and Recorder's Office is open today and there's no waiting period to get married in the state of Colorado."

"Did you hear that, city slicker?" Sully teased.

"I did." Charley smiled at him and then said to Groves,

"But this country boy promised me a February wedding in Hawaii."

"Hold him to it," Groves said as he came around the desk and shook hands with Sully. With Charley, he gave her a fatherly hug. Charley hugged him back and then took Sully's hand. They thanked the detective who had been so kind to them, and he offered to escort them out of the police station. He got them only a few feet from his office door before two different police department employees called his name.

"We can find our way out," Sully said to Groves.

Groves gave them a thumbs up and stopped to talk to a uniformed officer and a detective Charley recognized from the Fester crime scene. Holding tight to Sully, Charley felt tremendous gratitude for the excellent work of the Colorado Springs Police Department.

Stepping outside, the sun was bright against the snow. Charley let go of Sully long enough to pull on her red toboggan and gloves. Sully tugged on his leather gloves and tucked his wool scarf into his coat. The Chinooks gently blew, which would help melt the effects of the blizzard. Taking Sully's hand again, Charley walked beside him as they made their way down East Rio Grande Street to the public parking lot.

At his Jeep, on the passenger's side, she stopped and said, "I don't know how I can ever—" Her voice broke with emotion, and a tear escaped her eye.

"How you can what?" Sully asked and tilted his head.

"Thank you," she whispered. "I could not have made it through all of this without you."

"Sure you could have."

"No, Sully." Charley shook her head and hugged herself to him. "No, I couldn't."

"How about you thank me by going to the jewelry store with me?" he suggested. "Then I'll take you to a New Year's Eve lunch."

Charley nodded and pulled Sully to her for a kiss. "Let's pick out a wedding band for you while we're at it."

"And one for you."

"Matching?" she asked.

"Matching."

An hour later found them sitting next to each other again, but this time in front of a jeweler instead of a detective. As they'd driven from the police department a few blocks away to the downtown shopping area, Sully had told Charley that, according to Cash, this was the same jewelry store which had supplied the engagement rings and wedding bands for all the Coopers.

Looking into Sully's forest-green eyes, she had asked, "How did you know that?"

"I asked about a jewelry store recommendation after getting permission from Cash, Chase, Chloe, and Coop to propose to you." When her eyes widened, he added, "By the way, they're all on board for flying to Hawaii in February. Coop said he and Tammy wouldn't miss it for the world." Sully splayed his hands. "Apparently, Coop's always wanted to go to a luau."

Charley's eyes had teared then, and they threatened to do so now.

"Really," she began and looked from the jeweler, who had just handed her a spectacular diamond solitaire engagement ring, back to Sully. "A one-carat diamond is more than enough."

Sully grinned, and then gently taking the ring from her, he handed it back to the jeweler and said, "I like this two-carat diamond for the *two* of us."

"The two of us," Charley whispered as Sully lifted her left hand and slid the ring on her fourth finger. The brilliant diamond was set in six prongs with three additional diamonds decorating each side of the narrow platinum band. "It sparkles as brightly as the snow outside."

"That's gotta be a sign it's *the* ring," Sully whispered.

When Charley swiped away a tear and nodded at him, Sully said to the jeweler. "We'll take this two-carat diamond."

Charley hugged him and choked out, "The fact this ring fits perfectly is a sign too."

Sully chuckled and with a quick hug, said, "Yeah, it is."

Charley, still looking at her engagement ring, said to the jeweler, "I'll pay for both wedding bands."

"You can pay for mine, I guess," Sully said with another chuckle. "But I'll buy yours."

They picked out matching platinum wedding bands. When they emerged from the jewelry store, Charley was staring at her left hand as Sully carried the bag containing the bands.

"Never in my wildest dreams did I ever think I could be so in love and so happy," Charley said as they reached his Jeep.

"Me neither," Sully said and kissed her. "Hungry?"

"Yes, let's go eat because you're going to need your strength."

"Is that right?"

"Yes, I've got plans for you."

Sully's grin was wicked. "Like what?"

"This city slicker is going to keep a certain country boy in bed until New Year's Day."

"I can't think of a better way to welcome the New Year."

EPILOGUE

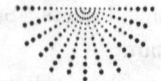

THE FOLLOWING YEAR

"*J* can't believe it's been a year since we got married," Sully said on Valentine's Day as Charley lit the tall red candles on either side of the long-stemmed red roses in the center of their dining room table.

"It's flown by." Charley smiled. She looked from the table, about to be lavishly laden with a catered dinner for family and friends coming to celebrate their anniversary, to her handsome husband. "Because we're so happy."

The previous year, they had been tempted to run over to the county courthouse and let a judge marry them. But knowing Owen Custis, the Coopers, and the Brevards would be disappointed to miss the nuptials, they restrained themselves from taking the early opportunity to become husband and wife.

A year ago in January, Chloe, Jade, and Tracy had helped Charley pick out the perfect white wedding gown and veil in their favorite boutique near Denver. Airline tickets and hotel reservations had been made by the family. During the first part of February, the ladies had celebrated with a bachelorette party. Cash had thrown Sully a bachelor party with the other Cooper men and Custis men in attendance. Though Valentine's Day was a big event for florists, her wedding day far outweighed that, and Pretty Petals closed for two weeks. Roy and Randy had volunteered to keep Sully's gun store open and take care of the horses. Pets had been boarded or were being watched by staff on the ranches. Charley had asked Chloe to be her matron of honor, and Sully's dad had agreed to be his best man. Owen was thrilled to have Henrietta Culpepper fly with them to Hawaii.

After landing on the big island of Oahu on February tenth, sightseeing, boat rides, swimming, sunbathing, and hiking were on the agenda, with families enjoying activities together and separately. When the late afternoon wedding rolled around on Valentine's Day, a sunset of yellow, purple, and red painted the tropical sky, melting into the blue waters of the Northern Pacific Ocean. A wooden archway laced with white tulle and red roses had decorated a private, sandy shore owned by the hotel on Waikiki Beach. Cooper and Colton had served as ushers, escorting folks to white folding chairs divided by a white runner. Austin was the ring bearer, while Abilene, Courtney, and Carly had been flower girls. Thus, with everyone barefoot and wearing leis, the bride carried a bouquet of Rocky Mountain Columbines as Coop walked her down the aisle to the groom, clad in black slacks and a white shirt adorned with a lavender columbine pinned over his heart.

Amid smiles and sniffles, Sully and Charley became husband and wife.

At the beginning of a fabulous luau, Coop made the congratulatory toast. There wasn't a dry eye to be seen after Coop had spoken of the Triple C Ranches legacy dating from the 1800s to the present moment and how blessed he was as the patriarch to officially welcome Sully and Charley Custis into the Cooper fold.

A party of Polynesian food, drinks, and entertainment ensued. With tiki torches blazing and live music filling the air, Sully and Charley were the first to dance. During the second dance, when Owen asked to cut in on Sully and Charley, Sully danced with Henri. Then everyone joined them. The children took turns dancing with each other and the adults. Even Dalton was on the sandy dance floor as Tracy held him while dancing with Cash.

Those memories would forever be lodged in grateful hearts.

Since returning from Hawaii, Sully and Charley had combined his thirty-thousand-acre ranch with her ten, putting their combined ranch at forty thousand acres, the same size as Triple C Ranches-East, Central, and West. With the last name of Custis fitting right into the mix, they'd kept the name Triple C Ranch-South.

Sully's gun club continued to prosper. Perhaps even more so as countless customers from far and wide visited, wanting to hear about his part in stopping the infamous mass murderer known as the Cave Killer. Not only the local, but national news had reported on and praised Sully, along with Burt Groves, for saving a courageous Charley and stopping Dorian Fester.

Charley's flower shop had flourished. Packed with flowers and plants, she'd hired Henri, who was now happily married to Owen, to help her. She'd also hired Mindy, the wife of Sully's cousin, Roy, to make deliveries. Together, the three of them managed to keep up with the customers flowing into Pretty Petals and the orders pouring out of the shop's front door.

For their first anniversary, on the front doors of Sully and Charley's house, huge wreaths of ponderosa pine branches worked into the shape of two hearts were made festive with columbines, red ribbon, bows, and LED lights. Inside, in addition to more columbines and roses, their house was decorated with tulips, peace lilies, and orchids. It was all Charley's doing, and Sully had said he couldn't imagine his life or home without her. Charley had echoed the sentiment back to him.

Owen and Henri were already present for the anniversary celebration. While Sully was bringing in firewood for the hearth in the den, Owen stood behind the wet bar ready to play bartender. Henri had helped Charley set the table and prepare appetizers.

Leaving the den, Sully found Charley in the dining room. He'd made her blush with a compliment about her hourglass figure and how he couldn't wait to strip off the red velvet dress she was wearing. Sully's eyes dipped to the hint of her ivory cleavage exposed in the scooped neckline, and Charley gave him the onceover. Clad in a black, Western-style jacket, and a white button-down shirt, along with dark jeans and black boots, he was magnificent.

"I couldn't be happier, Mrs. Custis," Sully said with a grin and pulled her into his arms.

Charley tilted her head, and the light from the chandelier over the dining room table danced in his eyes. "Are you sure about that, Mr. Custis?"

"Yeah, why?"

"Because I have a secret I've saved to tell you on our first anniversary."

"I may have already seen the new black cowboy hat hidden in the closet."

"Sully!" she gasped. "You're so ornery. You peeked?"

"I didn't mean to," he said and splayed a hand over his heart. "I was getting something out of the hall closet when a box fell off the shelf and the lid opened." With a chuckle, he said, "But for what it's worth, it fits perfectly."

"Sully." Charley laughed. "You're forgiven. I may have accidentally seen a bracelet box from the jewelry store where we bought our rings."

"Charley, you bad girl!" Sully said, sweeping the sides of his jacket back and placing his hands on his hips.

"I'm sorry! I was looking for a pen in the kitchen and the jewelry box was in that drawer. I promise I didn't peek."

Sully cocked a brow and then chuckled. "You came into the kitchen right after I got home from the jewelry store, and

I slipped the box into a drawer. I forgot about it until an hour or so later." He pulled the box from his jacket pocket and offered it to her. "Wanna peek now?"

"You know I do." Charley took the box and carefully opened it to see a diamond and ruby bracelet sparkling on red velvet. "Oh, Sully, it's beautiful," she said, smiling up at him. "I love it." She took the bracelet out of the box, and he fastened it around her wrist. "Thank you."

"Happy Valentine's Day and anniversary, wife. Now tell me your secret."

"I'm pregnant, husband."

"Charley." Sully whispered. Ever so tenderly, he placed his left hand on Charley's flat stomach. "You're right. That makes me even happier than ever."

"Me too," she said, her left hand flattening over his. "I feel so lucky to be married to my best friend and my protector. I love you with my whole heart, and I will take care of you for the rest of my life," she whispered and swallowed the lump in her throat as he pulled her into his arms again. "Happy Valentine's Day and first anniversary, Mr. Custis."

"Thank you, Mrs. Custis. I love you, and I will take care of both of you for the rest of my life." Holding her and their unborn child to his heart, he asked, "When is our baby due?"

"I haven't been to the doctor yet," Charley said, looking up at him. "But by my calculations, September seventeenth."

No sooner had Sully kissed her than they heard a vehicle arriving. With an ear-to-ear smile, he grabbed Charley's hand, and they made their way out of the dining room. Owen and Henri caught up with them in the foyer as a knock sounded on the front. The caterers bustled into the house and were steered toward the dining room and kitchen as appropriate.

Stainless serving trays lit with candles kept filet mignons, sauteed vegetables, and loaded baked potatoes warm. Another tray offered chicken parmesan and noodles covered in tomato sauce and mozzarella. For any of the children who wanted a less grown-up meal, there were trays filled with macaroni and cheese, burgers, hotdogs, and fries.

More vehicles arrived as the caterers departed. Right on cue, members of the Custis crew, along with Coopers and Brevards, arrived for the Valentine's Day anniversary party with salads and desserts. Coats and wraps were collected, and hugs distributed. The den was lively as Owen tended bar. The kitchen was bustling as last-minute items were taken to the dining room.

Sitting at the head of the long table, with Charley on his right and his father at the other end of the table, Sully smiled at her. How close had she come to losing this one-of-a-kind man? Too perilously close. She pushed that thought out of her mind and smiled back, loving him so much she felt her heart might burst.

"Sully!" Owen called from the opposite end of the room. "You've been grinning all through dinner. Want to let the rest of us in on your secret?"

Sully looked at Charley who nodded. "It's our secret," he said and picked up his wineglass. As Charley picked up a glass of sparkling water, he said, "You tell 'em."

"Come September, Sully and I are going to add to the Triple C Ranches and Cooper-Custis clan."

Whoops and hollers, clinking glasses, and clapping erupted around the room as people left their seats and came to congratulate them.

Charley glanced around the room filled with Chase, Jade, Colton, and Courtney Cooper, all smiles and offering congratulations. Derek and Chloe Brevard with Cooper, Austin, and Abilene were grinning and toasting the good news. Cash, probably the Cooper to whom Sully was closest, gave him a bear hug as Tracy embraced Charley. Their children, Carly and Dalton Cooper, would be nearest in age to the new baby. How blessed she was to have had the opportunity to add the Cooper, Brevard, and Custis clans to her life.

The Custis crew also congratulated them, mingling with

the Coopers and Brevards as they celebrated the baby that would tie their families together. Then Sully and Charley made their way to Coop, the beloved patriarch of the Coopers who had cheered as loudly as anyone, and to Tammy as she sat beside him, wiping a tear of joy from her eye.

Amid the celebration, Sully tugged Charley aside and said, "Charley Cooper Custis, you're the one who brought our families together."

"You were all friends years before I came along," Charley said modestly.

"We were friends. But my dad and I were two bachelors living alone on separate ranches," Sully pointed out. "Because of you, I'm no longer alone. Because of your shop, Dad reconnected with Henri. Because you hired Mindy, Randy met Mindy's best friend at Pretty Petals. Now, he's engaged and happier than I've ever seen him. The people in this house tonight are here because of you."

"And Wyatt?" Charley smiled as the big black Labrador padded up to them.

"And Wyatt." Sully chuckled.

"It's you, Sully. Wyatt, the baby, and I are here because of you."

"Yeehaw, city slicker."

"Yeehaw, country boy."

A LOOK AT: KINDRED SPIRITS

A PARANORMAL GHOST ROMANCE

A captivating paranormal romance that embarks on a journey of newfound love...and the everlasting effects of grief.

After a devastating accident, young billionaire Jack Malone is left wanting for the family and life he lost. Closing his heart off to the world in fear of feeling the same heartache, he has become a notorious recluse and landlord to several houses in St. Augustine. But despite his best efforts to keep people at arm's length, his carefully constructed world is about to crumble.

When teacher Sydney Crane blows into town, she doesn't expect her first encounter with her landlord to involve property vandalization—and unexpected nudeness. Off to a rocky start, she is determined to change Jack's opinion of her. But after the unexplainable shakes her world and she finds herself in his protective embrace...she worries she may have ventured too far.

As Jack and Sydney's connection deepens, so do their supernatural encounters. Navigating past heartache and an increasingly haunted house, their pursuit of love becomes a race against time that even they fear they won't survive.

Will Jack and Sydney be able to unravel an ancient murder before their chance at love evaporates faster than a fleeting apparition?

Get swept away by this heart wrenching paranormal romance that showcases the strength of one couple's resolve and their key to happily ever after.

AVAILABLE NOW

www.ingramcontent.com/pod-product-compliance
Lightning Source LLC
Chambersburg PA
CBHW011432240626
47153CB00011B/2946